This 50th anniversary edition of *Mumbo Jumbo* is dedicated to the great editor Anne Freedgood, who ignored the sales department and let me do my thing.

The Road to *Mumbo Jumbo*

A New Introduction by Ishmael Reed

My road to *Mumbo Jumbo* began with a family legend about a HooDoo curse that originated in the 1930s, when a woman rented a bedroom occupied by my mother and grandmother. It was a room they maintained for their days off from working as a live-in cook and housekeeper in wealthy homes located in the Chattanooga mountains. One was a plantation-style estate that was owned by a German family. I remember it as having elevators that connected the mansion's floors. Mrs. Clifford Grote, the matriarch, helped my mother and grandmother through tragedies that happened to them in the 1930s.

My mother, Thelma V. Reed, wrote about one in her book *Black Girl Tannery Flats*:

> One day when we came home on our day off, we discovered that this couple had rented out our bedroom to friends of theirs, another couple, without Mother's permission. And we didn't have any place to sleep. They said we could sleep in the living room. So my mother questioned the woman about renting out our bedroom. She and that woman got into a heated argument. During the argument about renting out our bedroom, she told my mother she could have her barking like a dog or crawling like a snake. I never heard anything that mean and low in my life. Never.
>
> So my mother easily forgives people, and she made up with the woman. And the woman made my mother a dinner of turnip greens

and cornbread. She poisoned the turnip greens. After that, my mother was taken ill in bed. Her eyes turned red, and her hair fell out. She walked from room to room, aimlessly. She started losing weight and was drawing money out of her bank account.

So my father, Mack Hopkins [who was stabbed by a white man and allowed to bleed to death at Chattanooga's Erlanger's Hospital after the attending physician told the nurse, "Let that nigger die"], *appeared to me in a dream at the foot of my bed while I was sleeping. In a loud voice, he said, "If I were living, I would get that spell off of Emma." I didn't know what a spell was. But now I think the roomer woman put a spell on my mother to get her out of the way so she could get the insurance money.* [Her mother had named the poisoner as beneficiary.]

So I told one of my mother's girlfriends. She started talking about witchcraft and what African people did and the Seven Sisters in New Orleans. And that people of the dead practice spells and witchcraft like people in Haiti, and Hoodoo, things which my family had never discussed before me.

The roomers were still staying at our house. So I wrote to my father's people, my father's brother and his sister, whose names were Pleasant Hopson and Aunt Louella Foster. We didn't have a telephone, so I had to write to them, and they answered, instructing me to bring my mother to Anniston, Alabama. Before I took her to Anniston, Alabama, the Grotes and the Spencers for whom she worked took her to ten doctors who gave her a complete physical. They said that they had never seen anything like it. A black doctor said she needed a witch doctor.

So I took her to Anniston, on the train, to my father's brother and sister. And she walked the whole time, up and down the aisle on the train. All of the passengers on this train were black. They all felt sorry for my mother and were sympathetic to me too. And the conductor was very kind to my mother. He felt sorry for her. And they all seemed to have been Christian people.

My mother stayed in Anniston, Alabama, and Uncle Pleas and his wife Rita took her to a lady named Mrs. Sarah, who described our house in Chattanooga, with the two mattresses. And she charged a price to remove the spell. So we stayed there two months, and the lady gave my mother herb medicine because she was poisoned by the turnip greens.

My mother began to get better. Mrs. Sarah told my mother that when we returned home, we should examine the furniture and open up the pillows. We would find the roomer had put hair wrapped in red flannel and differently shaped objects made out of wood inside, and we would find where she put that Hoodoo stuff in the pillows and in the chairs and such. And it was really frightening for me to be so young to hear all of this. Before we left, Mrs. Sarah addressed a letter for us to send to the roomers who were still living at our place. And she said the woman would have to answer back. She did answer back in a letter she wrote to my mother in Anniston, apologizing that she did put a spell on her and that she wanted her to forgive her for what she did.

And when we got to Chattanooga after two months, when we returned to our flat upper apartment, we did what the lady said. We looked in our chairs, and in our pillows and stuff. And that woman had my mother's hair, and she had red flannel wrapped in it with a match and cloth, and it was really frightening. And the mattress, we found it split at the ends like the lady in Anniston told us, and she had wooden objects in there, stuff sewed in there and the pillows, and we flushed it with running water.

And instead of my mother forgiving her for what she did, she hit the woman upside the head with an iron poker. The woman called the police, and they put my mother in jail, where she stayed overnight. They sent her to a hospital for treatment. She was there for a few days. Then some strange looking lady came into the room and dropped something around my mother's bed that looked like snuff. She rubbed it around the bed. My mother went "Berserk" that night. My mother lost her mind and was taken to Silver Dale State Hospital for recovery. She stayed there for two years.

When I first heard this HooDoo story, I didn't take it seriously. I was an "educated" person and considered it to be based on superstition. I didn't take the hint that my mother and grandmother held beliefs that weren't compatible with their version of Christianity. When my grandmother once instructed me on how to dispose of the debris left after I trimmed my fingernails and toenails, I was baffled.

But later, in the late 1960s, I took another look at the source of this story. It was only then that HooDoo culture opened the door to a revelation that ultimately influenced *Mumbo Jumbo*. That despite brutal suppression, African religion—or at least a form of it, no matter how degraded—had survived the slave trade, something of which neither our families nor our Western education informed us.

The African religion is as close to a universal religion as we have. It extends beyond any malicious form that can be found in the American South (like the psychic attack aimed at my grandmother) or in Haiti (the Sect Rouge). That's because, like Greek religion, it can absorb the deities of other faiths, just as hip-hop absorbs, mixes, and samples from worldwide cultures and a multiplicity of musical forms, and just as in an Afrika Bambaataa global musical mash-up you might find Kraftwerk, Fela Anikulapo-Kuti, the *Pink Panther* theme, the Rolling Stones, and the Magic Disco Machine, according to Jeff Chang and Dave "Davey D" Cook in their book, *Can't Stop Won't Stop*. (I've been using this mash-up technique since the 1960s, which is why when George Clinton of Funkadelic and Bootsy Collins invited me to Los Angeles to MC a show, they introduced me as the man who was doing what they were doing before they were doing it. Clinton later bought two film options for the rights to *Mumbo Jumbo*.)

Likewise, elements of African religion can slip seamlessly into the practice of other religions. To escape persecution by Christian colonists, African entities have at times been disguised as Catholic saints. And some saints have an African equivalent; for example, since St. Patrick is connected to snakes, his African equivalent is Damballah, a white python who is "strongly associated with the ancestors, and he and his companion Ayida-Wedo are the oldest and wisest of the loa."[1] I have heard it said that Haitians are 90 percent Catholic and 100 percent African religion.

In New York, such was the demand among worshippers that their Catholicism be mixed up with West African Yoruba religion that the Catholic Church found it necessary to accommodate the figures of Cuban Santeria in a form that combines Yoruba and Catholic beliefs. And of course, this flexibility extends beyond the limitations of Christianity: there is even a debate about whether Jews can become converts due to Jewish stockbrokers making tributes to African entities.[2]

For Christianity, acknowledging this growing influence is a retreat from the position that African religion involves "Devil worship." During my research, I discovered that Puritans (the actual founding fathers) accused the Native Americans, who helped them survive, of "Devil worship" as a way to maintain distance between their own religious beliefs and that of "the other." The "Devil worship" stigma was applied to Islam, as well, in a kind of religious megalomania that has led to the deaths of millions. (Megalomania and persecution of African religion not being unique to Christianity; some followers of Islam label nonbelievers as "infidels," which has caused conflict between followers of Muhammad and those of indigenous religions of Africa. While popular culture emphasizes the transatlantic slave trade, there was a trans-Sahara slave trade as well.) Yet African religion was able to accommodate Allah in its pantheon after Islam was nearly exterminated in Brazil. There is a theory that the orisha Obatala harbors Allah.

DN·FL·CL·IVLIANVS·P·F·AVG·

And so the influence of African religion is to make things more, and not less, open and adaptable. Though some have dismissed *Mumbo Jumbo* as anti-white, one of the book's heroes is Julian, the "Last Pagan Emperor," who tried to restore the Greek religion when Christianity began to dominate Rome. His writings, titled "Against the Galileans," condemned the Christians, who, using hammers, had destroyed art depicting Greek and Roman gods and goddesses.[3]

Even the HooDoo of the American South has a side other than hexing people; there is a healing side as well. In my work as a publisher, I published a book by the botanist Faith Mitchell called *HooDoo Medicine*, about plants that Blacks, deprived of medical services, used for healing. This book is an excellent resource for anyone interested in this practice. I also published Dr. Louis Mars, a Haitian psychiatrist who applied the notion of possession as it is defined in African religion to his field. Dr. Mars's book, *The Crisis of Possession in VooDoo*, was translated from the French by Kathleen Collins, who later made a film, *Losing Ground*, which drew upon Mars's theories. (None of the critics who praised her film noticed this influence.)

Am I anti-Christian? I depicted Jesus as the orisha of the poor, one of hundreds of orishas, in my Gospera, *Gethsemane Park*, about a park inhabited by homeless people. The Gospera was originally commissioned by the San Francisco Opera Company in 1995. I was instructed to write the book for a famous composer, who would write the music. They told me that the story should be about the arrest of Jesus in the garden of Gethsemane. The book I wrote was based upon Haitian religion. Instead of a physical Jesus, the poor people are possessed by Jesus, the orisha, and so when the Romans ask Judas to kiss Jesus, he kisses all of the poor people on stage. After the composer rejected the book, and the book rights reverted to me, I hired the leading New York composer Carman Moore to write the music. This Gospera (so named because the singers were drawn from Gospel singers and those trained in opera) baffled the theologians, ministers, and laypeople who saw it. A Hampton, Virginia, minister, who showed a film of the Gospera on Good Friday, was fired the following Monday.

Christianity inspired Aretha Franklin, Bach, Handel, Duke Ellington, Mahalia Jackson, Michelangelo, and even Salvador Dalí. Christianity has influenced architecture and literature. African religion, too, has influenced architecture, art, the great Haitian painters, and the choreographers Katherine Dunham and Alvin Ailey. It is the foundation of Black classical music, whose roots are in the ritual drumming that one finds in Cuba, Brazil, and Puerto Rico.

It took me years of research and travel to evolve from HooDoo, a variation and mutation of African religion, to its source. It was a process that began with a family legend, through traveling to Nigeria in 1999, and continued when, upon my return, my partner Carla Blank and I published two books by Nigerian authors, *Twenty New Nigerian Poets* and *Sixteen Short Stories by Nigerian Women*, edited by Toyin Adewale-Gabriel. I'd traveled a long way from the family curse to the source of Yoruba religion, which has millions of followers in our hemisphere. (My connection to Nigeria did not end there. Ancestry.com recently revealed that the majority of my genetic history could be traced to Nigeria. Maybe that's the reason when I visited Nigeria, I was told that I had a "pan-Nigerian face.")

I began to incorporate HooDoo first as comic relief in my first novel, *The Free-Lance Pallbearers* (1967), but more seriously in my second novel, a Western called *Yellow Back Radio Broke-Down*. ("Yellow Backs" was the name given to picaresque fiction that exaggerated the antics of cowboys. "Radio" because tales like those of the Lone Ranger came to us via radio. The character Loop Garoo is a combination of a Haitian and New Orleans entity and a movie cowboy from the 1940s and 1950s, Lash LaRue, who used a whip as a weapon. And "Broke-Down" because the book was based on the elements associated with Westerns, which I listened to on Buffalo radio.) Later, I discussed it specifically in a manifesto called "Neo-HooDooism."

Before I left my hometown of Buffalo, New York, in September 1962, I'd written two short stories, and a play about clashes between Muslims and Christians on a southern campus. I worked for a newspaper published by A. J. Smitherman, hero of the 1921 Tulsa Rebellion. First as a teenaged printer's devil and then returning at the age of twenty or so to help Joe Walke, who became editor after Smitherman died. Back in Tulsa, Smitherman had been accused by racist officials on the local and state levels of riling up Black people with anti-lynching editorials in his newspaper *The Tulsa Star*. He didn't just write about anti-lynching; he had on at least two occasions interrupted lynchings by vigilantes and government officials. He was eventually forced to flee Tulsa for Buffalo after he led an uprising of Black men against a planned lynching. Though depicted in popular culture as a white assault on passive Black neighborhoods, Blacks fought back and were defeated because the full power of the state of Oklahoma was employed against the uprising. Around this time, I also wrote some "experimental" work based upon a nonlinear short story by Nathaniel West, "The Dream Life of Balso Snell." James Joyce's work was also an influence. The story was called "Something Pure," and based on this short story, the University of Buffalo, an expensive private school at that time, offered me a full scholarship.

Nathaniel West came to me from Reader's Subscription, a book club. I found West's satire *A Cool Million*, written in a literary comic book style that appealed to me. I was acquainted with the use of the collage, having had access to art books at the Grosvenor Library, where I worked, but I'd never seen its employment on the page until "Balso Snell." I think of my Terrible series, Two, Three, and Four—and Five's in progress—as the books that West would have written had he not been killed.

Other influences introduced to me at the university were Ezra Pound's samplings from different cultures: his writings in Kanji, and his nod to Nigerian mythology. The Celtic Revival, an aesthetic revolt against the British Occupation, was another significant influence, which felt revolutionary in part because I hadn't yet read Alain Locke's *The New Negro*, in which he encourages folklore as a source for Black writers. The Celtic Revival would eventually inspire my idea of Neo-HooDooism, based upon the HooDoo stories of Black folklore—magical realism before there was a name for it. Stories in which the natural and the supernatural intersected, an element one finds in Native American and Latinx folklore of the Southwest. (When I was a child, staring out at the Tennessee River at sunset, I wasn't aware that the Cherokee believed that cities existed beneath the river.)

Before I left Buffalo, I wrote a short story called "Glasses with False Bottoms," based on a character named Shorty who frequented a real bar called Seibert's located on Jefferson Avenue and Northland in Buffalo. There was the poet Lucille Clifton and a group of Black nerds, intellectuals, artists, actors, and musicians, that I hung out with, mixed with a Black working-class clientele.

An Irish American poet named Dave Sharpe suggested that I had the talent to become a successful writer in New York City. During a weekend in New York, I showed my play *Ethan Booker* to a screenwriter while drinking at Chumley's on Bedford Street. His approval convinced me I should follow Sharpe's direction and move to New York. I moved there in the fall of 1962. A Buffalo friend, union organizer John Black, got me a job at 1199 Hospital Workers' Union.

Mumbo Jumbo would never have been written if I hadn't relocated to New York. At that time, it was a home for talented Black and white artists who were advancing our ideas of art. The rent and food were cheap. I paid eight dollars a week for a room in a run-down rooming house located on Saint Mark's Place between First Avenue and Avenue

A. (Years later, in 1969, during the last summer of Carla's and my residence in New York, I lived again on St. Mark's Place, on the second floor of a brownstone between First and Second. There was a garden in the backyard, and my next-door neighbor was W. H. Auden. He lived in a building where Trotsky had once lived. New York was a radical international city, which, like my early experience living in Paris, provided me with intellectual growth.)

Having met African students during a trip to Paris as a member of a YMCA delegation in 1955 and realizing they were different from the Africans who appeared in our textbooks and popular culture, I began early to doubt what I was being taught about Africa in school. Typical was the outburst from a teacher who said she couldn't understand why Emperor Haile Selassie was classified as Caucasian because he was "as black as the ace of spades."

When I returned from Paris, I dropped out of high school and went to work in Grosvenor Library, where I read work by James Baldwin. But it took years for me to discard the myths imposed upon me by an Anglocentric education and popular culture.

As late as 1966, in an introduction to an anthology about Adam

Clayton Powell's struggles with Congress, I honored Napoleon, who I now know reinstituted slavery in the Caribbean and kidnapped Toussaint Louverture. Around the same time, inspired by the movies, I cited my film hero Jesse James. I was to learn later that he was a Confederate guerrilla fighter who murdered Abolitionists. I submitted the Powell introduction to Larry Neal, who at the time was coediting the anthology titled *Black Fire*. Saying that the piece "wasn't together," he rejected it. He saved me from embarrassment by dismissing it. Larry Neal was the genius of the Black Aesthetic. He and the contributors to the anthology vowed to depart from the previous generations' dependence upon white masters, critiqued Ellison's reliance upon Hemingway and Faulkner and James Baldwin's use of Henry James as a writing guide. Neal dismisses Baldwin as "an entertainer." "The New Breed" desired to throw off the shackles of the "white aesthetic." *Mumbo Jumbo* fulfilled this mission. It has no Western antecedent. (Critics may object, and suggest that it's written in English. It is not. It's written in Indo-European, which chauvinists—wishing to deny that dark-skinned people had a hand in its origin—called English, meaning a language spoken by Anglo-Saxons. I know better because I've studied Hindi. The root language of English is Sanskrit.)

Still, even though I was led to a Black bibliography through my contact with New York's Black cultural nationalists and had seen a different Africa in Paris from the one depicted in my education and the movies, I had a long way to go before discovering new histories and techniques. This is why Lin-Manuel Miranda is a sympathetic figure in my play *The Haunting of Lin-Manuel Miranda*, in which historical figures awaken him to the real history of the United States. We've been brainwashed by lies our teachers told us, and propaganda distributed by film and television.

Being a member of the Umbra Workshop of writers, which I joined in 1963, helped. I began to explore Black history and culture. Askia Touré's poem "Dawnsong!," the manifesto of the Black Arts Movement, defined our poetic obsessions during the early '60s. We wanted to include African images in our work instead of European, having accepted the narrow meaning of "Europeanness" that we learned from our professors. Like them, we saw Europe as a monolith, a view I discarded after a number of trips to Europe. In our poetry, we invoked Egypt, an African civilization, which grew out of Nubia. Egyptian mythology was an alternative to the European models embraced by our predecessors. Keats could have been writing about our approach with the line "When sages look'd to Egypt for their lore."

I began writing poems about Queen Hatshepsut and invoked figures from Egyptian mythology: Thoth, Ra, and Anubis. The poetic height of my interest in Egyptian mythology came with the poem "I Am a Cowboy in the Boat of Ra," which combines Egyptian and cowboy culture derived from Westerns I'd seen growing up. Recalling the Celtic Revival's model to plumb folk roots and mythologies, I turned my attention to sources closer to home. The search began with a tourist excursion into New Orleans Voo-Doo, where I was introduced to Marie Laveau, a sort of nineteenth-century queen of HooDoo. In the front-page photo of the *New York Times Book Review*, August 6, 1972, an image of one of the Maries (sometimes the mother is confused for the daughter) appears on the mantel behind me.

A visit to the painter Joe Overstreet's studio changed my direction further. I asked him to identify the geometric designs on his canvas. He called them Ver Vers, which one writer has called "landing strips for the gods." I was later to learn when studying with Adebisi T'Olu Aromolaran that they were not gods, but "entities." In Haitian religion, these entities are called loas—of which there are hundreds. They show up at ceremonies and overtake the bodies of participants.

Zora Neale Hurston says that there is an X factor that gives rise to a loa, which was similar to James Weldon Johnson's observation that certain Black songs "Jes Grew." Jes Grew became my loa—not a personality, or seductress, or warrior, but a force. A force arising from Black culture that has caused mass hysteria since the citizens of Salem imagined a Black Man, the Devil, who inhabited the woods. His mission was to corrupt the citizens of the town. This entity takes the form, in my novel *Mumbo Jumbo*, of the rhythms of jazz and dance that caused the dance epidemics about which I read in high school in the '50s and in the mid-'60s in *The Putnam's Dark and Middle Ages Reader*, by Harry E. Wedeck, published in 1964.

In *Mumbo Jumbo*, "Jes Grew," this loa or orisha, causes the establish-ment conniptions. The establishment, as represented by the Wallflower Order, tries to stamp it out. (A contemporary loa, which won a Virginia governorship, would be Critical Race Theory, which is as invisible in Virginia schools as Salem's Black Man was in the woods of Salem. Or the hip-hop performers who provided the half-time entertainment at the 2022 Super Bowl, who caused a panic in some circles.)

Mumbo Jumbo suggests that there is something about Black cul-ture, whether it be rock and roll, or hip-hop, or "wokeness," the current Bogey Thing, that causes unrest.

I've often exclaimed that if I'd remained in New York, I would have "died from an overdose of affection," and never been pushed to write *Mumbo Jumbo*. New York in the 1960s still had the European style of pampering its artists. Seen as the next token, I was overindulged. This led to bad habits. It went to my head. I was young and dumb.

In 1967, Carla and I left for Los Angeles. A humbling experience, away from the adulation. Life in Los Angeles was lonely for me. Carla was away most of the time, working, teaching drama to the children of the wealthy in the San Fernando Mountains at Eddie Rickenbacker's camp, which had been used as a set for cowboy movies. I was holed up in our one-bedroom apartment in Echo Park. Since we didn't have a car, it was a sort of comfortable minimum-security prison. In this solitary situation, I wrote the "Neo-HooDoo Manifesto," a summary of what I had learned by that time. Written in a trancelike state in 1967, the manifesto was published in the *Los Angeles Free Press*, September 18–24, 1970.

In 2008, Franklin Sirmans organized a show based on the manifesto. It opened at the Menil Collection in Houston, Texas, then traveled to the P.S.1 Contemporary Art Center in New York and, later, the Miami Art Museum. Writing about the show in the October 28, 2008, *New York Times*, Holland Carter wrote:

> *Somewhere between Pollock and Pop, new art developed an allergy to the word spiritual unless it was attached to ethnicity. It was O.K. to make altars in galleries if you were Mexican-American—in fact, you were sort of required to—but if you were plain old American, no. Yet on the fringes, where the most together thinking tends to take place, there was resistance to this bias. In the late 1960s the American poet Ishmael Reed coined the term Neo-HooDoo to describe an aesthetic that was devotional without being dogmatically religious, ritual-related without having prescribed forms, and rooted both outside and inside the Western mainstream.*

John Cage's Zen painting was included alongside works inspired by Santeria, again an example of African religion's ability to accommodate different religions and aesthetics. In the Yale University book that accompanied the show, called *Neo HooDoo: Art for a Forgotten Faith*, there is a photo of me standing at the New Orleans tomb of Marie Laveau. In one of my recent novels, *Conjugating Hindi*, a loa of Irish origins, Mamam Bridget, a redhead, is a successor to Saint Bridget, who is based upon the pagan goddess Brigid. She is married to Baron Samedi, Lord of the Cemetery in Haiti.

Should I be called the prophet of Fifty-third Street? It took years to get here.

Carla and I moved to Berkeley in the fall of 1967. We moved through some ticky-tacks until landing a place on Edith Street. Eventually, we moved to Bret Harte Way in the Berkeley Hills, where we rented an apartment in an estate called Pinebrook, which was built in 1913 and hosted world-famous symphony conductors in the 1920s and '30s, including Arturo Toscanini. It featured a Japanese tea garden. Once again, like in Los Angeles, I was in solitary, Carla having decided to pursue a master's degree at Mills College. I knew that I was on to something when the great editor Anne Freedgood visited me in Pinebrook. When I described the plot of *Mumbo Jumbo*, she said it would be the book of the year. Anne knew my rhythms and my style. She was a great book editor who, like many in the seventies, would eventually be forced to obey the rules of bottom-line commercialism. She was my editor for *The Last Days of Louisiana Red*, *Flight to Canada*, and *Mumbo Jumbo*.

Research on *Yellow Back Radio* and friendships with Black innovators of music, painting, and the other arts led to *Mumbo Jumbo*. I threw all the knowledge that I had accumulated up to that point—the kitchen sink—into the book: Egyptology, jazz, the Harlem Renaissance; the work of visual artists and collagists like Art Bevacqua, Joe Overstreet, and Walter Bowart; pulp novels, a noir detective PaPa LaBas, based on the orisha Legba, a crossroads figure. (Another proof that African religion survived the slave trade is that stories about Legba still exist in the South.)

But there were other influences. I included an excerpt from Frank Chin's novel *A Chinese Lady Dies* in my anthology *19 Necromancers from Now*. I'd read the excerpt in an underground newspaper called *The Great Speckled Bird*, and Frank and I had become friends. We still publish Frank in *Konch*, a magazine that I began in 1991. The writer Shawn Wong, whose novel *Homebase* I published, charts the beginning of the Asian American Renaissance in writing back to a collaboration between Japanese and Chinese American writers that began when they met at the Oakland book party for *19 Necromancers from Now*. Frank Chin educated me about the oppression of Chinese

Americans in California. That's why illustrations of the Yellow Peril and anti-Chinese persecution appear in *Mumbo Jumbo.*

Meeting Native American, Asian American, and Hispanic writers on the West Coast was a crossroads event for me. The blues musician Robert Johnson was supposed to have met the Devil at the crossroads. In fact, it was not the Devil, but Legba. He didn't sell his soul, but went there for wisdom. "Papa Legba is such an interesting character as he exists on the border between the physical and the spiritual, providing an interface for people to speak with their gods. While Papa Legba, and the Esu Elegbara derivatives of Exú in Brazil, Echu in Cuba, and Papa La Bas in Louisiana, are tricksters in their nature, they differ from the traditional tale of the Devil or Satan figure at the crossroads in that they are not malicious. For these gods, the crossroads is a place for decisions of both good and evil essence. People go to the crossroads to make a spiritual connection with their gods and ask for help."[4] A collaboration with writers and artists from different ethnic backgrounds wised me up to the idea that American culture was not merely mainstream, but an ocean.

Doubleday had taken a chance on three of my novels considered "experimental," of which *Mumbo Jumbo* was one. Word had it that Doubleday was not prepared for the critical acclaim. Nor was I. The book was supposed to have been published in 1971, but the schedule was interrupted because my editor, Anne Freedgood, had moved to Random House. Before she left, Anne had given me complete control of *Mumbo Jumbo*. I designed the cover, which showed Josephine Baker as Erzulie, the Haitian Venus, and had the book laid out like a film. I selected the illustrations, which were changed in a subsequent edition because some of the artwork had been misplaced. And instead of using the standard blurbs that praise the author, I chose the negative comments on my work. In the end, not only did Doubleday publish the first three novels, but I also got them to publish N. H. Pritchard's *The Matrix.* The late Pritchard is now acknowledged as one of the leading innovators of the twentieth century. I also persuaded them to reissue an edition of William Melvin Kelley's *A Different Drummer* and to publish *Where Is Vietnam?*, a poetry anthology edited by Walter Lowenfels.

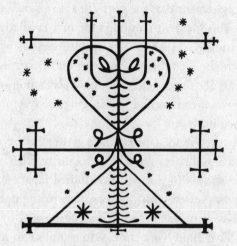

I was lucky to have my books published during a period when literary editors like Lynn Deming and Anne Freedgood had the power to determine which books would be published. Now it's the sales department. A young Black editor recently tried to get his publisher to publish my books only to be told by the sales department that they would receive only critical praise and prizes (code for an unwise financial investment).

Following the backlash against me after I wrote *Reckless Eyeballing*, a novel that satirized some of the more extreme positions of the feminist movement, I was left as literary roadkill in this country. For example, white feminists at the University of Louisiana at Baton Rouge organized a boycott of my appearance there. They were critical of my comments regarding the film *The Color Purple*, made during an appearance on the *Today* show. Had they read my books (which they confessed they had not), they would have discovered that the only character in the book with integrity was a Black feminist and that the guys were pretty awful, including a psychopath who goes around cutting the hair of feminists, which was how the French treated women who collaborated with the Nazis. (I guess they also missed Alice Walker's statement that the film *The Color Purple* was not based on her book.) This incident reminded me of a prediction that Amiri Baraka made in 1983. That the bourgeoise version of the feminist movement—which, according to Harriet Fraad, writing in *Tikkun*, February 20, 2013, co-opted the working-class faction—would be led by racists who weren't interested in changing the system. Who, in the end, just wanted in.

In order to survive as a Black male writer in the mid-1980s, I decided to reach audiences outside the country. The beginning was *Japanese by Spring* (1996), for which I studied Japanese. When I visited Japan, I was pleased with the reception to the book. I read my song "Azabu Kissaten De" before it was performed by the Conjure Band at the Tokyo Blue Note club. While subject to mostly bad reviews in the United States, in China, *Japanese by Spring* and my other work became a national project from 2012 to 2016, which meant that the government provided research funds for its study. This was brought about by the late Yunging Lin, a scholar who died recently at the age of forty. Carla and I were invited to universities in Hunan and Beijing where we discovered the widespread interest in an African American literature, which some demagogues in the United States seek to banish. Carla directed an all-Chinese cast in a production of my play *Mother Hubbard*, which received a rave review in the *Hunan Daily*, circulation two million. I've composed and recorded songs in both Japanese and Yoruba. When I read my poem "Mo Ju Lani, Mo Jinde Loni" to Nigerian intellectuals and writers, the audience was astonished and pleased. In 1996, I read from *Japanese by Spring* before a global audience at the Sorbonne. And my global strategy continues to work. In 2012, the Conjure Band and I performed at the Sardinia Jazz festival in Paris.

In March 2015, a group of experts from four continents and a wide range of disciplines met with me in Mulhouse, France, and Basel, Switzerland. Guided by the Swiss cultural and literary theorist Sämi

Ludwig, this group discussed my work and looked more widely at the different meanings assigned to multiculturalism in North America, Europe, and other parts of the world. In 2016, I received the Alberto Dubito Award for poetry in Venice.

Though my op-eds are regularly rejected by mainstream publications, over the last two years they've been welcomed by *Haaretz* in Israel, *Liberation* in Paris, and *El Pais* in Spain. My books are still reviewed internationally. On January 31, 2022, there was a three-page review of *Mumbo Jumbo* in *Tygodnik Powszechny*, one of Poland's leading newspapers. Some readers still tell me that *Mumbo Jumbo* changed their lives.

The musician David Murray and the singer Taj Mahal recorded a tune based on a passage from the novel. The book has drawn fans from all American classes and entertained prominent individuals. The actor David Duchovny of *The X-Files* says he wanted to write his dissertation on the novel when a student at Yale.[5]

The *New York Times* critic John Leland called *Mumbo Jumbo* the best novel of the 1970s. An Aspen rock band is called Jes Grew. Jemeel Moondoc, a saxophonist, led the Jes Grew Orchestra. Jean-Luc Godard wanted to make a film. He thought I was a woman. A feminist dance collective was called the Wallflower Order. Maria van Daalen, who read the novel, went to Haiti and became a priestess. She now has a following in the Netherlands. At least two individuals suffered nervous breakdowns after reading the novel. The late Andrew Hope, a traditional Head Man of the Tlingit, used the novel's theme of returning art that Western museums looted to make demands that Tlingit art be returned. The scenes about a multicultural gang returning art from Western museums to countries from where they were looted were inspired by visiting museums in the United States and Europe. Since then, Western museums have begun returning art to Africa. The French are returning sculptures with no conditions. Britain stipulates that the art is on loan. On March 1, 2022, the Smithsonian Institution announced its plans to return its collection of Benin bronzes to Nigeria.

W. H. Auden said that for him poetry arrived on High Holy Days of the Spirit. I've written novels that have been celebrated since their publication, and because of the Trump years, the first one, *The Free-Lance Pallbearers* (1967), is receiving renewed interest as a harbinger.

But when writing *Mumbo Jumbo*, I was touched by the spirit. What have I distilled from African religion? The most important orisha is your mind, and just as orishas welcome offerings, rum, fowl, perfume, rice, etc., one feeds the mind with knowledge because the greatest curse is ignorance. I call it Orism.

Ishmael Reed
Oakland, California
September 22, 2022

1. Santookoorisha, Tumblr post. "Damballah-Wedo is depicted as a serpent or snake . . ." Oct. 24, 2015, santookoorisha.tumblr.com/post/131856389597/damballah.

2. Migene González-Wippler. *Santeria the Religion: A Legacy of Faith, Rites, and Magic*. New York: Harmony Books, 1989.

3. Catherine Nixey. *The Darkening Age*. London: Pan Books, 2018.

4. Miles Fertel. "Robert Johnson and the Crossroads in African and African American Folklore." *Medium*, Dec. 8, 2018, medium.com/@miles fertel/robert-johnson-and-the-crossroads-in-african-and-african -american-folklore-b3ae5927d73e.

5. Cindy Lys. "90% Catholic 100% Vodou: Haitian Immigrant Religious and Spiritual Identity." Master's thesis, Smith College, 2013.

Mumbo Jumbo

1 A True Sport, the Mayor of New Orleans, spiffy in his patent-leather brown and white shoes, his plaid suit, the Rudolph Valentino parted-down-the-middle hair style, sits in his office. Sprawled upon his knees is Zuzu, local doo-wack-a-doo and voo-do-dee-odo fizgig. A slatternly floozy, her green, sequined dress quivers.

Work has kept Your Honor late.

The Mayor passes the flask of bootlegged gin to Zuzu. She takes a sip and continues to spread sprawl and behave skittishly. Loose. She is inhaling from a Chesterfield cigarette in a shameless brazen fashion.

The telephone rings.

The Mayor removes his hand and picks up the receiver; he recognizes at once the voice of his poker pardner on the phone.

Harry, you'd better get down here quick. What was once dormant is now a Creeping Thing.

The Mayor stands up and Zuzu lands on the floor. Her posture reveals a small flask stuck in her garter as well as some healthily endowed gams.

What's wrong, Harry?

I gots to git down to the infirmary, Zuzu, something awful is happening, the Thing has stirred in its moorings. The Thing that my Grandfather Harry and his generation of Harrys had thought was nothing but a false alarm.

The Mayor, dragging the woman by the fox skins hanging from her neck, leaves city hall and jumps into his Stutz Bearcat parked at the curb. They drive until they reach St. Louis Cathedral where 19th-Century HooDoo Queen Marie Laveau was a frequent worshiper; its location was about 10 blocks from Place Congo. They walk up the steps and the door's Judas Eye swings open.

Joe Sent Me.

What's going on, hon? Is this a speakeasy? Zuzu inquires in her cutesy-poo drawl.

The door opens to a main room of the church which has been converted into an infirmary. About 22 people lie on carts. Doctors are rushing back and forth; they wear surgeon's masks and white coats. Doors open and shut.

1 man approaches the Mayor who is walking from bed to bed examining the sleeping occupants, including the priest of the parish.

What's the situation report, doc? the Mayor asks.

We have 22 of them. The only thing that seems to anesthetize them is sleep.

When did it start?

This morning. We got reports from down here that people were doing "stupid sensual things," were in a state of "uncontrollable frenzy," were wriggling like fish, doing something called the "Eagle Rock" and the "Sassy Bump"; were cutting a mean "Mooche," and "lusting after relevance." We decoded this coon mumbo jumbo. We knew that something was Jes Grewing just like the 1890s flair-up. We thought that the local infestation area was Place Congo so we put our antipathetic substances to work on it, to try to drive it out; but it started to play hide and seek with us, a case occurring in 1 neighborhood and picking up in another. It began to leapfrog all about us.

But can't you put it under 1 of them microscopes? Lock it in? Can't you protective-reaction the dad-blamed thing? Look I got an election coming up —

To blazes with your election, man! Don't you understand, if this Jes Grew becomes pandemic it will mean the end of Civilization As We Know It?

That serious?

Yes. You see, it's not 1 of those germs that break bleed suck gnaw or devour. It's nothing we can bring into focus or categorize; once we call it 1 thing it forms into something else.

No man. This is a *psychic epidemic,* not a lesser germ like typhoid yellow fever or syphilis. We can handle those. This belongs under some ancient Demonic Theory of Disease.

Well, what about the priest?

We tried him but it seized him too. He was shouting and carrying on like any old coon wench with a bass drum.

What about the patients, did you ask any of them about how they knew it?

Yes, 1, Harry. When we thought it was physical we examined his output, and drinking water to determine if we could find some normal germ. We asked him questions, like what he had seen.

What *did* he see?

He said he saw Nkulu Kulu of the Zulu, a locomotive with a red green and black python entwined in its face, Johnny Canoeing up the tracks.

Well Clem, how about his feelings? How did he feel?

He said he felt like the gut heart and lungs of Africa's interior. He said he felt like the Kongo: "Land of the Panther." He said he felt like "deserting his master," as the Kongo is "prone to do." He said he felt he could dance on a dime.

Well, his hearing, Clem. His hearing.

He said he was hearing shank bones, jew's harps, bagpipes, flutes, conch horns, drums, banjos, kazoos.

Go on go on and then what did he say?

He started to speak in tongues. There are no isolated cases in this thing. It knows no class no race no consciousness. It is self-propagating and you can never tell when it will hit.

Well doc, did you get other opinions?

Who do you think some of those other cases are? 6 of them are some of the most distinguished bacteriologists epidemologists and chemists from the University.

There is a commotion outside. The Mayor rushes out to see
Zuzu rejoicing. Slapping the attendants who are attempting to
placate her. The people on carts suddenly leap up and do their
individual numbers. The Mayor feels that uncomfortable
sensation at the nape and soon he is doing something resembling
the symptoms of Jes Grew, and the Doctor who rushes to his
aid starts slipping dipping gliding on out of doors and into the
streets. Shades of windows fly up. Lights flick on in buildings.
And before you know it the whole quarter is in convulsions
from Jes Grew's entrance into the Govi of New Orleans; the
charming city, the amalgam of Spanish French and African
culture, is out-of-its-head. By morning there are 10,000 cases
of Jes Grew.

*The foolish Wallflower Order hadn't learned a damned thing.
They thought that by fumigating the Place Congo in the 1890s
when people were doing the Bamboula the Chacta the Babouille
the Counjaille the Juba the Congo and the VooDoo that this
would put an end to it. That it was merely a fad. But they
did not understand that the Jes Grew epidemic was unlike
physical plagues. Actually Jes Grew was an anti-plague. Some
plagues caused the body to waste away; Jes Grew enlivened
the host. Other plagues were accompanied by bad air (malaria).
Jes Grew victims said that the air was as clear as they had
ever seen it and that there was the aroma of roses and
perfumes which had never before enticed their nostrils. Some
plagues arise from decomposing animals, but Jes Grew is
electric as life and is characterized by ebullience and ecstasy.
Terrible plagues were due to the wrath of God; but Jes Grew
is the delight of the gods.
So Jes Grew is seeking its words. Its text. For what good is a
liturgy without a text? In the 1890s the text was not available
and Jes Grew was out there all alone. Perhaps the 1920s will
also be a false alarm and Jes Grew will evaporate as quickly
as it appeared again broken-hearted and double-crossed (++)*

Once the band starts, everybody starts swaying from one side of the street to the other, especially those who drop in and follow the ones who have been to the funeral. These people are known as "the second line" and they may be anyone passing along the street who wants to hear the music. *The spirit hits them and they follow*

(My italics)

Louis Armstrong

Mumbo Jumbo

[Mandingo *mā-mā-gyo-mbō*, "magician who makes the troubled spirits of ancestors go away": *mā-mā*, grandmother+*gyo*, trouble+*mbō*, to leave.]

The American Heritage Dictionary of the English Language

BY ISHMAEL REED

Ishmael Reed

SCRIBNER

New York   London   Toronto   Sydney   New Delhi

Scribner
An Imprint of Simon & Schuster
1230 Avenue of the Americas
New York, NY 10020

This Scribner trade paperback edition 2022

SCRIBNER and design are registered trademarks of The Gale Group, Inc.,
used under license by Simon & Schuster, Inc., the publisher of this work.

For information about special discounts for bulk purchases, please contact Simon &
Schuster Special Sales at 1-866-506-1949 or business@simonandschuster.com.

The Simon & Schuster Speakers Bureau can bring authors to your live event.
For more information or to book an event, contact the Simon & Schuster Speakers Bureau
at 1-866-248-3049 or visit our website at www.simonspeakers.com.

Manufactured in the United States of America

33 35 37 39 40 38 36 34 32

Library of Congress Cataloging-in-Publication Data
Reed, Ishmael, date.
Mumbo jumbo.
I. Title.
PS3568.E365M84 1988
813'.54 88-16628

ISBN 978-0-684-82477-2

A Coming Attraction for This Work Entitled "Cab Calloway Stands In for the Moon" was
published in *Amistad* 1 and *19 Necromancers from Now* copyright © 1970 by Ishmael Reed.

Grateful acknowledgment is made to the following for the use of illustrations appearing within
the text Page 7: © 1971 by The New York Times Company. Reprinted by permission; 14: Jose
Fuentes; 61: Bonnie Kanu'n; 65: Fred McDarrah; 66: Underwood & Underwood; 77: Gerald
Duane Coleman; 84: Courtesy, The Bancroft Library, 88: Copyright of Radio Times Hulton
Picture Library; 118: Lincoln Center Library; 123: National Museum of Anthropology, Mexico
City, 145: Mark Citret; 145 top and bottom: Courtesy of Sengstacke Newspapers; i4*:Courtesy
Ohio Historical Society Library; 155: Copyright of Radio Times Hulton Picture Library; 161:
Xavier Zeara; 163: © 1971 by The New York Times Company. Reprinted by permission; 169:
Basil Rakoczi; 181: Deutsches Archaeologiscb.es Institut, Rome Italy, 184 top: International
Publishers; 184 bottom: Gundar Strads; 210 both: From *The American West* by Lucius Beebe and
Charles Clegg. Copyright © 19S5 by E. P. Dutton & Co., Inc., and reproduced by permission;
215: Manchete Revista Semanal, Bloch Editores S.A., Brazil

Some *unknown natural phenomenon* occurs
which cannot be explained,
and a new local demigod is named.

Zora Neale Hurston on the origin of a new loa

The earliest Ragtime songs, like Topsy, "jes' grew."

...we appropriated about the last one of the "jes' grew" songs.
It was a song which had been sung for years
all through the South. The words were unprintable, but
the tune was irresistible, and belonged to nobody.

James Weldon Johnson
The Book of American Negro Poetry

To my grandmother
      Emma Coleman Lewis.
And to
      Clarence Hill, proprietor of
      Libra's on East 6th Street
      between A & B
and also for
      George Herriman, Afro-American,
      who created Krazy Kat.

Mumbo Jumbo

2 With the astonishing rapidity of Booker T. Washington's Grapevine Telegraph Jes Grew spreads through America following a strange course. Pine Bluff and Magnolia Arkansas are hit; Natchez, Meridian and Greenwood Mississippi report cases. Sporadic outbreaks occur in Nashville and Knoxville Tennessee as well as St. Louis where the bumping and grinding cause the Gov to call up the Guard. A mighty influence, Jes Grew infects all that it touches.

3 *Europe has once more attempted to recover the Holy Grail and the Teutonic Knights, Gibbon's "troops of careless temper," have again fumbled the Cup. Instead of raiding the Temples of Heathens they enact their blood; in the pagan myth of the Valkyrie they fight continually; are mortally wounded, but revived only to fight again, taking time out to gorge themselves on swine and mead. But the Wallflower Order had no choice. The only other Knight order had been disgraced years before. Sometimes the Wallflower Order was urged to summon them. Only they could defend the cherished traditions of the West against Jes Grew. They would be able to man the Jes Grew Observation Stations. But the trial which banished their order from the West's service and the Atonist Path had been conclusive. They were condemned as "devouring wolves and polluters of the mind."*

The Jes Grew crisis was becoming acute. Compounding it, Black Yellow and Red *Mu'tafikah** were looting the museums shipping the plunder back to where it came from. America, Europe's last hope, the protector of the archives of "mankind's" achievements had come down with a bad case of Jes Grew and *Mu'tafikah* too. Europe can no longer guard the "fetishes" of civilizations which were placed in the various Centers of Art Detention, located in New York City. Bootlegging Houses financed by Robber Barons, Copper Kings, Oil Magnets, Tycoons and Gentlemen Planters. Dungeons for the treasures from Africa, South America and Asia.

The army devoted to guarding this booty is larger than those of most countries. Justifiably so, because if these treasures got into the "wrong hands" (the countries from which they were stolen) there would be renewed enthusiasms for the Ikons of the aesthetically victimized civilizations.

* *Mu'tafikah*—According to *The Koran*, inhabitants of the Ruined Cities where Lot's people had lived. I call the "art-nappers" *Mu'tafikah* because just as the inhabitants of Sodom and Gomorrah were the bohemians of their day, Berbelang and his gang are the bohemians of the 1920s Manhattan.

4   1920. Charlie Parker, the houngan (a word derived from
n'gana gana) for whom there was no master adept enough to award
him the Asson, is born. 1920–1930. That 1 decade which doesn't
seem so much a part of American history as the hidden After-
Hours of America struggling to jam. To get through.

Jes Grew carriers came to America because of cotton. Why
cotton? American Indians often supplied all of their needs from
one animal: the buffalo. Food, shelter, clothing, even fuel. Eskimos,
the whale. Ancient Egyptians were able to nourish themselves
from the olive tree and use it as a source of light; but Americans
wanted to grow cotton. They could have raised soybeans, cattle,
hogs or the feed for these animals. There was no excuse. Cotton.
Was it some unusual thrill at seeing the black hands come in
contact with the white crop?

According to the astrologer Evangeline Adams, America is born
at 3:03 on the 4th of July, Gemini Rising. It is to be mercurial,
restless, violent. It looks to the Philippines and calls gluttony the
New Frontier. It looks to South America and intervenes in the
internal affairs of its nations; piracy is termed "bringing about
stability." If the British prose style is Churchillian, America is
the tobacco auctioneer, the barker; Runyon, Lardner, W.W., the
traveling salesman who can sell the world the Brooklyn Bridge
every day, can put anything over on you and convince you that
tomatoes grow at the South Pole. If in the 1920s the British say
"The Sun Never Sets on the British Empire," the American motto
is "There's a Sucker Born Every Minute." America is the smart-
aleck adolescent who's "been around" and has his own hot rod.
They attend, these upstarts, a disarmament conference in Washington and play diplomatic chicken with the British, advising them
to scrap 4 hoods including the pride of the British Navy: H.M.S.
King George the 5th. Bulldog-faced British Admiral Beatty leaves
the room in a huff.

5 The Wallflower order attempts to meet the psychic plague by installing an anti-Jes Grew President, Warren Harding. He wins on the platform "Let's be done with Wiggle and Wobble,"* indicating that he will not tolerate this spreading infection. All sympathizers will be dealt with; all carriers isolated and disinfected, Immumo-Therapy will begin once he takes office.

Unbeknown to him he is being watched by a spy from the Wallflower Order. A man who is to become his Attorney General. (He is also surrounded by the curious circle known by historians as "The Ohio Gang.")

The 2nd Stage of the plan is to groom a Talking Android who will work within the Negro, who seems to be its classical host; to drive it out, categorize it analyze it expell it slay it, blot Jes Grew. A speaking scull they can use any way they want, a rapping antibiotic who will abort it from the American womb to which it clings like a stubborn fetus.

In other words this Talking Android will be engaged to cut-it-up, break down this Germ, keep it from behind the counter. To begin the campaign, No DANCING posters are ordered by the 100s.

All agree something must be done.

"Jes Grew is the boll weevil eating away at the fabric of our forms our technique our aesthetic integrity," says a Southern congressman. "1 must ponder the effect of Jew Grew upon 2,000 years of civilization," Calvinist editorial writers wonder aloud.

6 New Orleans is a mess. People sweep the clutter from the streets. The city's head is once more calm. Normal. It sleeps after the night of howling, speaking-in-tongues, dancing to drums; watching strange lights streak across the sky. The streets are littered with bodies where its victims lie until the next burgeoning. 1 doesn't know when it will hit again. The next 5 minutes? 3 days from now? 20 years? But if the Jes Grew which shot up a trial balloon in the 1890s was then endemic, it is now epidemic, crossing state lines and heading for Chicago.

* *The Harding Era*—Robert K. Murray.

●   ○

Men who resemble the shadows sleuths threw against the walls of 1930s detective films have somehow managed to slip into the Mayor's private hospital room. They have set up a table before his bed. A man wearing a mask that reveals only his eyes and mouth calls the meeting to order.

This is an inquiry, it seems, and the man officiating wants to get to the bottom of why the Mayor, a Mason, allowed his Vital Resistance to wear down before Jes Grew's Communicability. This augurs badly, for if Jes Grew is immune to the old remedies, the saving Virus in the blood of Europe, mankind is lost. No word of this must get out. The Mayor even volunteers to accept the short bronze dagger and "get it over with." All for the Atonist Path. The visitors await his final groan, and when the limp hand falls to the side of the bed and begins to swing, they leave as quickly as they came.

This was no ordinary commission. When an extraordinary antipathy challenges the Wallflower Order, their usual front men, politicians, scholars and businessmen, step aside. Someone once said that beneath or behind all political and cultural warfare lies a struggle between secret societies. Another author suggested that the Nursery Rhyme and the book of Science Fiction might be more revolutionary than any number of tracts, pamphlets, manifestoes of the political realm.

7 New York is accustomed to gang warfare. White gangs: the Plug Uglies, the Blood Tubs of Baltimore, the Schuylkill Rangers from Philadelphia, the Dead Rabbits from the Bowery, the Roaches Guard and the Cow Bay Gangs terrorize the city, loot, raid and regularly fight the bulls to a standoff.

A gang war has broken out over Buddy Jackson, noted for his snappy florid-designed multicolored shoes and his grand way of living. There are legends about him. He went into the police station and knocked the captain cold when he didn't come forward with policy protection. Later, while orators and those affected with "tongues and lungs" were rapping as usual, he sent a convoy into Peekskill and rescued "Paul from the Crackers."

Schlitz, "the Sarge of Yorktown," a Beer Baron, has a lucrative numbers and Speak operation in Harlem. His stores are identified by the box of Dutch Masters in the window.

1 day, collection day, 3 Packards roll up to a store, 1 of the fronts belonging to the Sarge. The street, located in Harlem, is unusually quiet. The only sounds heard are the Sarge's patent-leather shoes coming in contact with the pavement. Where are the salesmen, the New Negroes, the "ham heavers," "pot rasslers" and "kitchen mechanics" on their way to work? Where are the sugar daddies and their hookers, the peddlers, the traffic cops, the reefer salesmen who usually stand on the corners openly peddling their merchandise? (Legal then.) There are no revelers and no chippies. The streets are deserted . . .

Schlitz looks into the window of his 1st store. What? No Rembrandt Dutch Masters but the picture of Prince Hall founder of African Lodge ⚹1 of the Black Masons stares out at Schlitz, "the Sarge of Yorktown."

The mobster moves on, the 3 Packards following his course. The next store, the same story. The portrait of Prince Hall dressed in the formal Colonial outfit of his day, the frilled white blouse and collar showing beneath the frock coat and vest. The short white wig.

The painting is so realistic that you can see his auras. In his right hand he holds the charter the Black Freemasons have received from England. Schlitz shrugs his shoulders, puts a cigar in his mouth and walks over to the curb to speak to the driver of 1 of the Packards. He feels something cold at the back of his neck. He turns to see Buddy Jackson standing behind him, aiming a Thompson Automatic at him. The gun which has acquired the name of "The Bootlegger's Special."

Packing their heat, the hoods begin to open the car doors to assist their Boss. But they are pinned in. Up on the roofs, firing, are Buddy Jackson's Garders. Exaggerated lapels. Bell-bottoms. Hats at rakish angles. The Sarge's men sit tight. The bullet pellets zing across the front of the automobiles and graze the top and trunk. Buddy Jacksons exhorts the Sarge to leave Harlem and "Never darken the portals of our abode again." He marches the Sarge down to the subway, followed by many people coming from the hallways and apartments and alleys, bars, professional offices, beauty parlors, from where they've watched the whole scene. Most people read the newspaper to tell them what're the coming attractions. In the 1920s folks in Harlem used the Grapevine Telegraph. Booker T. Washington observed its technology. Booker T. Washington the man who "bewitched" 1000s at the Cotton States Exposition, Atlanta, September 18, 1895.

8   Picture the 1920s as a drag race whose entries are ages vying for the Champion *gros-ben-age* of the times, that aura that remains after the flesh of the age has dropped away. The shimmering Etheric Double of the 1920s. The thing that gives it its summary. Candidates line up like chimeras.

The Age of Harding pulls up, the strict upper-lip chrome. The somber, swallow-tailed body, the formal top-hatted hood, the overall stay-put exterior but inside the tell-tale poker cards, the expensive bootlegged bottle of liquor, and in the back seat the whiff of scandal. The Age of Prohibition: Speaks, cabarets, a hearse with the rear-window curtains drawn over its illegal contents destined perhaps for a funeral at sea.

Now imagine this Age Race occurring before a crowd of society idlers you would find at 1 of those blue-ribbon dog shows. The owners inspecting their pekinese, collies, bulldogs, german shepherds, and then observe these indignant spectators as a hound mongrel of a struggle-buggy pulls up and with no prior warning outdistances its opponents with its blare of the trumpet, its crooning saxophone, its wild inelegant Grizzly Bear steps.

For if the Jazz Age is year for year the Essences and Symptoms of the times, then Jes Grew is the germ making it rise yeast-like across the American plain.

An entry in the table of contents of a △205 book tells the story.

THE UNITED STATES, WHEN HARDING BECAME PRESIDENT

A Period of Frazzled Nerves, Caused by the End of War-time Strain; of Disunity Caused by the End of the More or Less Artificially Built-up Unity of the War Period; of Strikes Caused by Continuation of War-time's High Cost of Living; of Business Depression Which Came when War-time Prices Began to Fall; and of Other Disturbances Due in Part to Economic Dislocations Brought by the War and Its Aftermath. From All of Which Arose Emotions of In-security and Fear, Which Expressed Themselves in Turbul-ence and Strife. The Boston Police Strike, the Steel Strike, the "Buyers' Strike" and the "Rent Strike." The "Red Scare." The Bomb Plots. A Dynamite Explosion in the New York Financial District. Deportation of Radicals. Demand for Reduction of Immigration. The I. W. W. and the "One Big Union." Sacco and Vanzetti. Race Riots Between Whites and Negroes. The Whole Reflecting an Unhappy Country when Harding Became Its President.

* *Our Times*, vol. 6, *The Twenties*—Mark Sullivan.

9 Wall Street is tense. An incident has occurred which threat-ens to flapperize those yet uncommitted youngsters who adamantly refuse to eschew Jes Grew, last heard flying toward Chicago with 18,000 cases in Arkansas, 60,000 in Tennessee, 98,000 in Mississippi and cases showing up even in Wyoming. It would take a few months before a woman would be arrested for walking down a New Jersey street singing "Everybody's Doing It Now."† A week before, 16 people have been fired from their jobs for manifesting a symptom of Jes Grew. Performing the Turkey Trot on their lunch hour. Girls in peekaboo hats and straw-hat-wearing young men have threatened reprisals against the broker who dismissed them.

The kids want to dance belly to belly and cheek to cheek while their elders are supporting legislation that would prohibit them from dancing closer than 9 inches. The kids want to Funky Butt

† *Castles in the Air*—Irene Castle.

and Black Bottom while their elders prefer the Waltz as a suitable vaccine for what is now merely a rash. Limbering is the way the youngsters recreate themselves while their elders declaim they cease and desist from this lascivious "sinful" Bunny-Hugging, this suggestive bumping and grinding, this wild abandoned spooning.

VooDoo General Surrounds Marines
At Port-au-Prince

. . . only adds to the crisis. A corpulent, silkily mustached Robber Baron for whom a seal has been sacrificed to provide his hunk of toxic wastes with a covering notices this headline in the New York *Sun* and avers gruffly: The only thing they have in Haiti are mangoes and coffee. With prohibition there's no need for coffee, and mangoes appeal only to a few people. A glamour item. Haiti is mere repast after a heavy meal of meat and potatoes. It doesn't have any culture either. I didn't see a single cannon or cathedral while I was there. Look at this!

The Robber Baron removes a wood sculpture from his pocket. Look at this ugly carving my wife gave me. She bought it from 1 of those leathernecks in the black market . . . Have you ever seen such an ugly thing. The obtuse snout; the sausage lips? It was really clever of Wilson to send Southern Marines down there. Those doughboys will really be able to end this thing and quick! VooDoo generals. Absurd.

Why do you think he sent them there in the 1st place? says his companion, who carries a black umbrella and wears a bowler hat, grey suit and black shoes, a copy of a Wall Street newspaper under his arm.

I have figured it out. Word has it that the old man was feeble and his wife was running the government. Maybe it was an expedition for some new fashions for the old girl. Can't you see her walking across the White House lawn with a basket on her head above a torniquet? Wouldn't that be rich?

As the 2 men approach the intersection of Broad and Market a Black man opens the door for Buddy Jackson who struts alongside a high-yellow girl. They head toward the entrance of the bank where they plan to deposit the take from the previous night's cabaret business. Jackson is carrying a large sack. The broker is about to comment about Jarkson's date, a "hotsy totsy," when a loud pop occurs. The picket line of young flappers disperses. People fly about the streets until they land dazed and bloodied. 3 Packards reach the intersection far from the scene and turn the corner on 2 wheels.

Flappers, ginnys, swell-eggs, brokers, stenographers, carriages, automobiles, bicycles are scattered about the streets. The broker and his friend, a few moments before engaged in a penetrating analysis of the economic implications of the Haitian occupation, lie dead, bubbles forming on the broker's lips. ½ his companion's torso lies next to him.

10 Some say his ancestor is the long Ju Ju of Arno in eastern Nigeria, the man who would oracle, sitting in the mouth of a cave, as his clients stood below in shallow water.

Another story is that he is the reincarnation of the famed Moor of Summerland himself, the Black gypsy who according to Sufi Lit. sicked the Witches on Europe. Whoever his progenitor, whatever his lineage, his grandfather it is known was brought to America on a slave ship mixed in with other workers who were responsible for bringing African religion to the Americas where it survives to this day.

A cruel young planter purchased his grandfather and was found hanging shortly afterward. A succession of slavemasters met a similar fate: insanity, drunkenness, disease and retarded children. A drunken White man called him a foul name and did not live much longer afterward to give utterance to his squalid mind.

His father ran a successful mail-order Root business in New Orleans. Then it is no surprise that PaPa LaBas carries Jes Grew in him like most other folk carry genes.

A little boy kicked his Newfoundland HooDoo 3 Cents and spent a night squirming and gnashing his teeth. A warehouse burned after it refused to deliver a special variety of herbs to his brownstone headquarters and mind haberdashery where he sized up his clients to fit their souls. His headquarters are derisively called Mumbo Jumbo Kathedral by his critics. Many are healed and helped in this factory which deals in jewelry, Black astrology charts, herbs, potions, candles, talismans.

People trust his powers. They've seen him knock a glass from a table by staring in its direction; and fill a room with the sound of forest animals: the panther's *ki-ki-ki*, the elephant's trumpet. He moves about town in his Locomobile, the name of which amused many of his critics including Hank Rollings, an Oxford-educated Guianese art critic who referred to him as an "evangelist" and said he looked forward to the day when PaPa LaBas "got well." To some if you owned your own mind you were indeed sick but when you possessed an Atonist mind you were healthy. A mind which sought to interpret the world by using a single loa. Somewhat like filling a milk bottle with an ocean.

He is a familiar sight in Harlem, wearing his frock coat, opera hat, smoked glasses and carrying a cane. Right now he is making a delivery of garlic, sage, thyme, geranium water, dry basil, parsley, saltpeter, bay rum, verbena essence and jack honeysuckle to the 2nd floor of Mumbo Jumbo Kathedral. They are for an old sister who has annoying nightly visitations.

The sign on the door reads

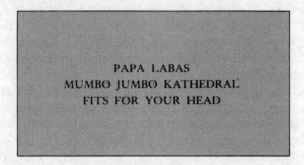

PAPA LABAS
MUMBO JUMBO KATHEDRAL
FITS FOR YOUR HEAD

When he climbs to the 2nd floor of Mumbo Jumbo Kathedral. The office is about to close for the day. Earline, his assistant Therapist, is putting her desk in order. She is attired in a white blouse and short skirt. Her feet are bare. Her hair is let down. PaPa LaBas places The Work on her desk.

Please give these to Mother Brown. She must bathe in this and it will place the vaporous evil Ka hovering above her sleep under arrest and cause it to disperse.

Earline nods her head. She sits down at her desk and begins to munch on some fig cookies which lie in an open box.

PaPa LaBas glances up at the oil portrait hanging on the wall. It is a picture of the original Mumbo Jumbo Kathedral taken a few weeks ago: Berbelang, his enigmatic smile, the thick black mustache, the derby and snappy bowtie, his mysterious ring bearing the initials E.F., his eyes of black rock, 2 mysterious bodies emitting radio energy from deep in space, set in the narrow face; Earline in the characteristic black skirt, the white blouse with the ruffled shoulders, the violet stone around her neck; Charlotte, a French trainee he has hired to fill in for Berbelang, wears a similar costume to Earline's and smokes a cigarette. In the painting, completed 2 weeks before Berbelang left the group, she stands next to Earline.

Earline, now sitting at her desk, is smoking. 1 hand supports her head as she checks an order for new herbs and incense.

Daughter?

She looks up, distantly.

Jes Grew which began in New Orleans has reached Chicago. They are calling it a plague when in fact it is an anti-plague. I know what it's after; it has no definite route yet but the configuration it is forming indicates it will settle in New York. It won't stop until it cohabits with what it's after. Then it will be a pandemic and you will really see something. And then *they* will be finished.

Earline slams the papers down on her desk.

What's wrong, daughter?

There you go jabbering again. That's why Berbelang left. Your conspiratorial hypothesis about some secret society molding the consciousness of the West. You know you don't have any empirical evidence for it that; you can't prove . . .

Evidence? Woman, I dream about it, I feel it, I use my 2 heads. My Knockings.* Don't you children have your Knockings, or have you New Negroes lost your other senses, the senses we came

* B. Fuller terms this phenomenon "ultra ultra high frequency electromagnetic wave propagation."

over here with? Why your Knockings are so accurate they can chart the course of a hammerhead shark in an ocean 1000s of miles away. Daughter, standing here, I can open the basket of a cobra in an Indian marketplace and charm the animal to sleep. What's wrong with you, have you forgotten your Knockings? Why, when the seasons change on Mars, I sympathize with them.

O pop, that's ridiculous. Xenophobic. Why must you mix poetry with concrete events? This is a new day, pop. We need scientists and engineers, we need lawyers.

All that's all right, what you speak of, but that ain't all. There's more. And I'll bet that before this century is out men will turn once more to mystery, to wonderment; they will explore the vast reaches of space within instead of more measuring more "progress" more of this and more of that. More Increase, Growth Inflation, and they don't know what to do when Jes Grew comes along like the Dow Jones snake and rises quicker than the G.N.P.; these scientists, there's a lot they don't know. And as for secret societies? The Communist party originated among some German workers in Paris. They called themselves the Workers Outlaw League. Marx came along and removed what was called the ritualistic paraphernalia so that the masses could participate instead of the few. Daughter, the man down on 125th St. and Lenox Ave. on the stand speaking might be mouthing ideas which arose at a cocktail party or from a transcontinental telephone call or —

Earline puts her head on the desk and begins to sob. PaPa LaBas comforts her.

O there I go, getting you upset . . .

She confesses to him. O it isn't you, pop, it isn't you, it's . . . Berbelang?

O pop, he thinks you're a failure, he felt that you were limiting your techniques. He thought you should have added Inca, Taoism and other systems. He felt that you were becoming all wrapped up in Jes Grew and that it's a passing fad. He isn't the old Berbelang, pop; his eyes are red. He seems to have a missionary zeal about whatever he's mixed up in. I get so lonely, I would like to go out; tonight for instance. I'm invited to a Chitterling Switch.

A Chitterling Switch? What's that, Earline?

She shows him the card.

FOOD!   GAMES!   DRINK!

A CHITTERLING SWITCH

sponsored by

Madame Lewaro

for

anti-lynching campaign

108 West 136th Street

THURSDAY, OCT. 22, FROM 9 TILL ?

let's get our brothers off the limb

by chipping in a barrel of fins

(surprise appearance by Mystery Blood!)

We're attempting to raise money for anti-lynching legislation; James Weldon Johnson is supposed to speak . . . It's like a Rent Party, you know?

You and T use so much slang these days I can hardly communicate with you, but your Chitterling Switch sounds interesting. Do you mind if an old man comes along?

O pop, 50 is not old these days.

You flatter me; just wait until I lock the office.

,And I must change, pop. I'll be right with you.

PaPa LaBas glances into another office toward the main room of Mumbo Jumbo Kathedral.

Where's Charlotte?

Earline has entered the ladies room.

You know pop, she's been acting strangely these days. She's listless and cross. She had an argument with a client this morning and began to swear at him in French; isn't that a sign?

He pauses for a moment.

I must speak to her. Perhaps she's upset about Berbelang leaving as he did. You know, they were fond of each other. My activist side really charms the women; I suppose this is how he was able to woo such a beautiful thing as yourself.

O cut it out, pop!

Earline looks at her features in the mirror. Something has come over her. She finds it necessary to go through the most elaborate toilet ritual these days, using some very expensive imported soaps, embroidered towels, and she has taken a fancy to buying cakes even though she never before possessed a sweet tooth. She glances at the sign above the marble sink.

REMEMBER TO FEED THE LOAS

O, that reminds her. She hasn't replenished the loa's tray #21. On a long table in the Mango Room are 22 trays which were built as a tribute to the Haitian loas that LaBas claimed was an influence on his version of The Work. This was 1 of LaBas' quirks. He still clung to some of the ways of the old school. Berbelang had laughed at him 1 night for feeding a loa. This had been 1 of the reasons for their break. Of course she didn't comprehend their esoteric discussions. PaPa LaBas hadn't required that the technicians learn The Work. The drummers, too, were clinical; their job was that of sidemen to PaPa LaBas' majordomo. They didn't know PaPa LaBas' techniques and therapy. Didn't have to know it. As long as they knew the score LaBas wasn't interested in proselytizing. But feeding, she thought, was merely 1 of his minor precautions. It seemed such a small thing. She would attend to it tomorrow or the next day.

I'll be with you in a moment, she shouts through the door to LaBas.

We have plenty of time, no rush, PaPa LaBas answers her. He is inspecting the trays. He stops at the 12th tray, then returns to join Earline who is ready to go.

The pair moves down the steps. Outside T Malice is talking to a young woman who has her hands clasped behind her back and is swaying coquettishly. When he sees PaPa and Earline he pulls down the brim of his chauffeur's cap and looks straight ahead. They tease him and of course being a good sport he can take it.

11 Every time Woodrow Wilson Jefferson chases the dogs, chickens, hogs and sheep, the animals recoup and follow him. W.W. turns on his pursuers.

Go on now. Heah. Go on before I chucks you good with a stick. I told you to go on back to the farm before daddy comes back from the deacons' council and finds you gone, Woodrow Wilson Jefferson threatens his 4-footed friends. His head resembles that of a crocodile wearing granny glasses.

Woodrow Wilson Jefferson has decided to quit the farm and hit the Big City. He is ready. His grandfather had accompanied his slavemaster to New York in the 1850s and had returned with articles and editorials written by 2 gentlemen: Karl Marx and Friedrich Engels. The old issues of the *New-York Tribune* edited by Horace Greeley had been in the attic all these years. He liked the style. Objective, scientific, the use of the collective We, Our. Therefore there were no illusions and unforeseen events like these country folks in Rē′-mōte Mississippi, believing in haints and things; and spirits and 2-headed men; mermaids and witches. He would abandon this darkness for the clearing. Make something out of himself. The local people had said that he would be a doctor or even a preacher, but what did they know, backward, lagging behind.

He feels some feathery object brush against his heel and turns again.

Now get out of here, damnit. Where's my stick?

Jefferson goes over to a bush to make a switch. He commences to cut off a branch and whittles the stick so it would leave welts and draw blood. The animals get the message and begin to scamper toward the farmhouse, on the hill, in the background.

He continues on down the road apiece until he reaches the train depot. His bag is stuffed with the newspaper articles (487 to be exact. Wilson didn't always understand the issues but he certainly appreciated the style). When he reaches the train depot, he comes upon 2 men sitting on the station's porch, playing checkers. Behind them were ads for Doctor Pepper, hex signs, Chesterfield Cigarettes and Bull Durham tobacco.

Well if it ain't Rev. Jefferson's boy. Where you going with your hair all spruced down with butter? Where you on your way to?

Jefferson stands there at the Rē'-mōte train depot. He would ignore these men, lazy, shiftless, not ready. He would do something with his life. Not become just another hayseed whose only recreation is catching junebugs and chirping along with the crickets.

I'm gon on way from this damned town.

Well ex-cuuuuuuuuuuuuuu..s..e me! the man answers, mimicking. His companion spits some tobacco against the station house wall.

The train is in sight. The train that would take him to Jackson Mississippi. Then on to New York.

12   The party is held at a Townhouse in Harlem. It was lent to the revelers by a wealthy patron. It isn't an authentic Chitterling Switch but an imitation 1. It is what some of the New Negroes would imagine to be a Rent Party given, to meet the 1st of the month, by newly arrived immigrants from the South. In fact there is nowhere in evidence a delegate from the "brother-on-the-street." A man is' pounding out some blues on the piano. Once in a while he sips from a cup of King Kong Korn that someone has placed on its top. People are moving from room to room; some of them are passing drinks. Ladies are wearing richly colored dresses, earrings, bracelets, brooches and beads and are well-plumed in a style that neuter-living Protestants would call "garish." 1 woman dressed in an exotic high-gypsy is taking in cash at the door, cash used to supply funds to anti-lynching campaigns.

61 lynchings occurred in 1920 alone. In 1921, 62, some of the victims, soldiers returning from the Great War who after fighting and winning significant victories—just as they had fought in the Revolutionary and Civil wars and the wars against the Indians—thought that America would repay them for the generosity of putting their lives on the line, for aiding in salvaging their hides from the Kaiser who had been tagged "enemy" this time. Instead, a Protestant country ignorant even of Western mysteries executes soldiers after a manner of punishments dealt to witches in the "Middle Ages." Europe and the Catholic Church are horrified but not surprised at this "tough guy" across the waters whose hor-

rendous murders in Salem led Europe to reform its "witch laws."

Until Marcus Garvey came along to rescue the American Negro he was basking in his lethargy like a crocodile sleeping in the sun.

The man the Guianese art critic is directing his comments to mutters something about "ringtail" or "monkey chaser"; LaBas and Earline move on to avoid the ensuing conflict this exchange usually brings.

They see Berbelang and a well-dressed young blond White man whom they recognize from the society pages as Thor Wintergreen, the son of a famous tycoon.

O hello . . . Berbelang greets PaPa LaBas and Earline.

Berbelang, what are you doing here?

No time to explain. We're leaving. I'll be home later on.

Berbelang and his friend move toward the door.

But . . . but what *time* are you going to be home?

I'll call you, Berbelang says, edging toward the exit.

Come up to the Kathedral sometime, Berbelang; I'd like to talk to you, LaBas calls after Berbelang.

He and his companion are putting on their coats which have been handed to them by the Hostess.

Yes I will . . . maybe 1 day next week. I'd like to talk to you too.

You see, pop? He doesn't seem to have any time for me at all.

This unhappy plea from Earline is a contrast to the gay laughter, the couples dancing, and the sound of glasses touching in the many rooms.

I think I'm going to leave, PaPa.

But we just got here, Earline. It looks interesting.

You stay. I'm going to go home to wait for him. Maybe we can have a talk.

PaPa LaBas helps Earline with her coat. No sooner does she have it on than she rushes from the house, almost tearfully.

Shaking his head, LaBas turns around. *Nothing like an affair of the heart*, LaBas thinks, remembering the bittersweet days of his youth. *They'll work it out. They're beautiful young people*, LaBas thinks to himself as he moves through the halls and among the guests and into 1 of the back rooms inhabited only by 2 men and a Kathedral radio resting on a table, where 1 of them is playing cards. PaPa LaBas recognizes him immediately as Black Herman the noted occultist who after a triumphant engagement in Chicago is visiting New York. He sits at the table: the famous batwinged eyebrows, goatee, and narrow mustache which travels from the bridge of his nose to the top of his upper lip. He wears a tuxedo over a white vest and about his neck he is wearing an amulet made in the shape of a triangle. He looks like his picture on his book jacket in which he sits on a globe, 1 booted foot atop a stack of 3 books, the top 1 entitled *The Missing Key* and subtitled *Key to Success.* In the photo his body is framed by designs of an arabesque nature.

A ribbon of black and red travels from his left shoulder to his waist. He sits quietly at a table, sipping from a cup and playing cards. Solitaire. Against the wall Abdul Hamid, the noted magazine editor, stands, his arms folded. He stares in the direction of the merrymakers in the other room. There seems to be a permanently fixed scowl on his face. They are listening to the Situation Report which comes from the 8-tubed Radio.

S.R.: JÈS GREW ONFLYING GIVING AMERICA A RISE IN THE TOWN OF MUNCIE INDIANA WHERE IT IS ENGENDERING MORE EXCITEMENT THAN THE LAST DENTAL INSPECTION. 800 CASES REPORTED SINCE LAST NIGHT WHICH WERE IMMEDIATELY ISOLATED IN HASTILY BUILT Y.M.C.A. BARRACKS. A HEAVY TOLL OF STRUT GALS AND O YOU KIDS . . . SIMILAR OUTBREAKS REPORTED IN ST. PAUL MINNESOTA AND WHEELERSBURG PENNSYLVANIA . . . POTENTIAL VICTIMS GATHER ABOUT THE ALREADY INFECTED REJOICING CHANTING GIVE ME FEVER GIVE ME FEVER . . .

As the news report dies down the radio begins to blare the song "When The Pussy Willow Whispers To The Catnip."

Turn off that ofay music, Abdul almost snarls. He walks over to the radio and turns it off himself and then returns to the wall where he has been standing watching the other people dance. He wears a bright red fez and a black pinstriped suit and a black tie emblazoned with the crescent moon symbol.

Black Herman raises his head from the cards and sees LaBas standing in the doorway.

Why PaPa LaBas, you old jug-blower you! I haven't seen you since the last Black Numerology convention. How have you been?

PaPa LaBas walks into the room; Abdul stares sneeringly at his shoes. Then his face.

I didn't want to interrupt you, how have *you* been? I hear you're packing them in at Liberty Hall.

That's right. 4000 per night; as big as Garvey.

The man stood, a rare and elegantly limbed tree springing from the soil in time-capsule film.

That's a beautiful medal you're wearing.

Yes, Black Herman answers, shaking hands with LaBas. It was awarded to me by a foreign Potentate for my ability to perform the trick of the Human Seed. Lying buried underground for 8 days. Looks as if the prophecy you made at the Black Numerology convention is all around us, LaBas. This Jes Grew thing. How did you predict that? Mundane astrology?

No. Knockings.

Knockings, huh? You're quite good at that. What do you think that this Jes Grew is up to?

It's up to its Text. For some, it's a disease, a plague, but in fact it is an anti-plague. You will recall, Black Herman, that in the past there were germs that avoided words.

$$
\begin{array}{ccccc}
S & A & T & A & N \\
A & D & A & M & A \\
T & A & B & A & T \\
A & M & A & D & A \\
N & A & T & A & S^*
\end{array}
$$

was used to charm a germ in the old days. Being an anti-plague I figure that it's yearning for The Work of its Word or else it will

* The Conquest of Epidemic Disease—Charles Edward Amory.

peter out as in the 1890s, when it wasn't ready and had no idea where to search. It must find its Speaking or strangle upon its own ineloquence.

Interesting theory.

I don't quite agree with it, in fact I think it's a whole lot of Bull.

Black Herman and PaPa LaBas direct their attention to the man standing against the wall. Gradually, Abdul came from the wall.

You both are filling people's heads with a lot of Bull. Do you think that Harlem will always be as it is now? Poorer people are traveling north and the signs are already showing of its deterioration. The people will have to shape up or they won't survive. Cut out this dancing and carrying on, fulfilling base carnal appetites. We need factories, schools, guns. We need dollars.

But surely, Abdul my friend, you don't believe that the Epidemic is a hoax. It is taking the country by storm; affecting everything in its path, PaPa LaBas challenges.

O that's just a lot of people twisting they butts and getting happy. Old, primitive, superstitious jungle ways. Allah is the way. Allah be praised.

The door is filling with others who've been attracted to the discussion. Abdul, seeing them, begins to turn up the decibels.

It's you 2 and these other niggers imbibing spirits and doing the Slow Drag who's holding back our progress.

We've been dancing for 1000s of years, Abdul, LaBas answers. It's part of our heritage.

Why would you want to prohibit something so deep in the race soul? Herman asks.

That's right, LaBas joins Black Herman. When you reviewed my last work in your *Journal of Black Case Histories*—that magazine whose contents resemble the scrawls the patients compose with their excreta on the walls of those Atonist "hospitals"—you accused me of having a French woman on my staff. I guess your teachings haven't made you realize your bad manners. The people who support your magazine are no longer available since some of your vitriolic remarks about them, and now you have turned against us. A new phenomenon is occurring. The Black Liberal; a new mark extorted in the manner of your former victims who became fed up with it and have withdrawn funds for your support. You are no different from the Christians you imitate. Atonists

Christians and Muslims don't tolerate those who refuse to accept their modes.

Some of the people who were listening have decided that it's 1 of those discussions and have drifted away.

Christianity? What has that to do with me?

They are very similar, 1 having derived from the other. Muhammed seems to have wanted to impress Christian critics with his knowledge of the Bible, LaBas continues. They agree on the ultimate wickedness of woman, even using feminine genders to describe disasters that beset mankind. Terming women cattle, unclean. The Koran was revealed to Muhammed by Gabriel the angel of the Christian apocalypse. Prophets in the Koran: Abraham Isaac and Moses were Christian prophets; each condemns the Jewish people for abandoning the faith; realizing that there has always been a pantheistic contingent among the "chosen people" not reluctant to revere other gods. The Virgin Mary figures in the Koran as well as in the Bible. In fact, 1 night you were reading a poem to the Black woman. It occurred to me that though your imagery was with the sister, the heart of your work was with the Virgin.

You'd better be careful with your critique PaPa LaBas, Abdul replies. Remember "He that worships other gods besides Allah shall be forbidden to Paradise and shall be cast into the fires of Hell."

Precisely, Black Herman replies. Intolerant just as the Christians are.

Yes, LaBas joins in, where does that leave the ancient Vodun aesthetic: pantheistic, becoming, 1 which bountifully permits 1000s of spirits, as many as the imagination can hold. Infinite Spirits and Gods. So many that it would take a book larger than the Koran and the Bible, the Tibetan Book of the Dead and all of the holy books in the world to list, and still room would have to be made for more.

And I resent you accusing us of taking advantage of the people, Black Herman joins in. Why have you established yourself as an arbiter for the people's tastes? Granted that there are as many charlatans in our fields as in yours. Some sell snake oils, others propose the establishment of separate states and countries while at the same time accepting all of the benefits of this 1. I think that what bothers me most is your review of my dreambook in which you call me "crazy."

Abdul smiles. The smile of sheer mockery that makes you want to pulverize.

Strange, Herman says, for isn't the Koran accused of lacking chronological order, and hasn't your prophet Muhammed been accused of being prolix contradictory and unclear by critics? Accused of inaccuracy because he confuses Miriam, Moses' sister, with Mary.

Besides, "crazy" is a strange description for a man to be using who cane-whipped those flappers outside the Cotton Club just because they wore their dresses short, LaBas accuses.

I didn't do it, but they had it coming. This time a cunning smile sweeps Abdul's face.

The girls pointed you out at the lineup, why do you deny it, Abdul?

Because I didn't do it, but they still deserved what they got, wearing their dresses like that. Tricks. Sluts. Swinging their asses nasty.

Maybe they felt that they should decide themselves what was best for them to wear, Abdul. It wasn't any of your business. And if you weren't the person who meted out those beatings of the high-yellow chorus girls, why were you suspiciously loitering about the Cotton Club?

None of your business, gris-gris man, Abdul utters with contempt.

Sounds as if you've picked up the old Plymouth Rock bug and are calling it Mecca. In the ancient Egyptian religions the emblems used in ritual were so bold that foreign countries burned their temples of worship and accused the participants of "obscenity" and "pornography."

Abdul sees that the doorway is empty. Deprived of an audience, he changes his demeanor. He suddenly becomes polite affable patient reasonable.

O.K. LaBas, Herman. You got me. Johnny James Chicago South Side. Are you satisfied? I wasn't born with a caul on my face, PaPa LaBas. Nor was my coming predicted by a soothsayer as yours was, Black Herman, the old woman who predicted that you

would be "the marvel of your age." I haven't developed a Hoo
Doo psychiatry as you have, PaPa LaBas, nor can I talk to animals
or spend 1 dollar twice as you've done, Herman. You see, while you
are cloistered protected by your followers and patrons and clients
I'm out here on the street watching what was once a beautiful
community become a slave hole. People are beginning to trickle
in here from down home and I'll bet that sooner or later there
will be an exodus rivaling the 1 of the Good Book. Who is going
to help them? Happy Dust is here now. What strange enslaving
drugs will be here later? Where are these people going to work
and who is going to feed them? Are they going to eat incense,
candles? Maybe what you say is true about the nature of religions
which occurred 1000s of years ago, but how are we going to
survive if they have no discipline? Look. I spent 9 long years in
prison for stabbing a man who wanted to evict my mother because
she wouldn't fuck him. I walked into the house 1 day and
there he was, her clothes nearly off and his grubby fat fingers
plying her flesh. 9 years I was in the clink and 2 of them in
solitary confinement. It was then that I began to read omnivorously.
I always wondered why the teachers just threw the knowledge at
us when we were in school, why they didn't care whether we
learned or not. I found that the knowledge which they had made
into a cabala, stripped of its terms and the private codes, its slang,
you could learn in a few weeks. It didn't take 4 years, and the
4 years of university were set up so that they could have a process
by which they would remove the rebels and the dissidents. By
their studies and the ritual of academics the Man has made sure
that they are people who will serve him. Not 1 of them has
equaled the monumental work of J. A. Rogers, a 1-time Pullman
porter. Some of these people with degrees going around here
shouting that they are New Negroes are really serving the Man
who awarded them their degrees, who has initiated them into his
slang and found them "qualified," which means loyal. I applied
myself. I went through biochemistry philosophy math, I learned
languages, I even learned the transliteration and translation of
hieroglyphics, a skill which has come in handy recently. I had no
systematic way of learning but proceeded like a quilt maker, a
patch of knowledge here a patch there but lovingly knitted. I
would hungrily devour the intellectual scraps and leftovers of the

learned. Every day I would learn a new character and learn how to mark it. It occurred to me that I was borrowing from all of these systems: Religion, Philosophy, Music, Science and even Painting, and building 1 of my own composed of their elements. It was like a Griffin. I had patched something together out of my own procedure and the way I taught myself became my style, my art, my process. Look, LaBas, Herman. I believe that you 2 have something. Something that is basic, something that has been tested and something that all of our people have, it lies submerged in their talk and in their music and you are trying to bring it back but you will fail. It's the 1920s, not 8000 B.C. These are modern times. These are the last days of your roots and your conjure and your gris-gris and your healing potions and love powder. I am building something that people will understand. This country is eclectic. The architecture the people the music the writing. The thing that works here will have a little bit of jive talk and a little bit of North Africa, a fez-wearing mulatto in a pinstriped suit. A man who can say give me some skin as well as Asalamilakum. Haven't you heard? This is the country where something is successful in direct proportion to how it's put over; how it's gamed. Look at the Mormons. Did they recruit 1000s of whites to their cause by conjuring the Druids? No, they used material the people were familiar with and added their own. The most fundamental book of the Mormon Church, the Book of Mormon, is a fraud. If we Blacks came up with something as corny as the Angel of Moroni, something as trite and phony as their story that the book is the record of ancient Americans who came here in 600 B.C. and perished by A.D. 400, they would deride us with pejorative adjectival phrases like "so-called" and "would-be." They would refuse to exempt our priests from the draft, a privilege extended to every White hayseed's fruit stand which calls itself a Church. But regardless of the put-on, the hype, the Mormons got Utah, didn't they? Perhaps I will come up with something that will have a building shaped like a mosque, the interior furnishings Victorian, the priests dressed in Catholic garb, and soul food as offerings. What of it as long as it has popular appeal? This is the reason for Garvey's success with the people. O yes, he may look outlandish, loud to you, but the people respect him because they know that

he is using his own head and is master of his own art. No, gentlemen, I don't think I would be so smug if I were you. The
authorities are already talking about outlawing VooDoo in Harlem.
These are your last great days, Herman, packing them in for
60 nights as you do your prestidigitation. A new generation is
coming on the scene. They will use terms like "nitty gritty," "for
real," "where it's at," and use words like "basic" and "really" with
telling emphasis. They will extend the letter and the meaning of
the word "bad." They won't use your knowledge and they will call
you "sick" and "way-out" and that will be a sad day, but we must
prepare for it. For on that day they will have abandoned the
other world they came here with and will have become mundanists
pragmatists and concretists. They will shout loudly about soul
because they will have lost it. And their protests will be a shriek.
A panic sound. That's just the way it goes, brothers. You will be
just a couple of eccentric characters obsolete out-of-date unused as
the appendix. Funny looking like the Australian zoo. But me and
my Griffin politics, my chimerical art will survive. Maybe I won't
be around but someone is coming. I feel it stirring. He might even
have the red hair of a conjure man but he won't be 1. No, he will
get it across. And he will be known as the man who "got it
across." And people like you will live in seclusion and your circle
will be limited and the people who read you will pride themselves
on their culture and their selectiveness and their identification with
the avant garde.

Well, Abdul says, looking at his watch, I have to get back to the
office. I have an anthology that's really going to shake them up when
I get done translating it.

What language is it in? LaBas asks.

Hieroglyphics. Abdul starts to shake hands with Herman and
LaBas but seeing a couple arriving at the doorway his friendly
face becomes a scowl and he withdraws his hand.

He wags his finger in their face. And if I ever see you characters
hanging around my mosque I will have my men take care of you,
Abdul says, his back turned to the 2 people. He winks at LaBas
and Herman and then nearly knocks over the 2 people on the
way out of the room; standing in the doorway are a high-yellow
woman and her bespectacled light-skinned unsteady harassed-look-
ing male escort.

Watch out with your old short Black ugly self, she scornfully shouts as Abdul flies by the 2 and out the door.

Julius? Why don't you do something, Julius? When these niggers manhandle me like that?

Yes dear my lovely Nubian queen, the man says meekly as he and the woman turn about and head for the other rooms. (Julius was a well-known Black doorman for a quality Gentlemen's club, hired to bounce the literary bad niggers who might become rowdy. He was W. E. B. Du Bois' Boswell, but Du Bois was always in conference to him.)

PaPa LaBas and Black Herman move from the room and down the hall of the Townhouse now filled with people.

You know, maybe he's got something, Herman.

Maybe so but I don't think that he should experiment in public this way. He's doing a lot of damage, building his structure on his feet like this. That bigoted edge of it resembles fascism. An actor . . . We'll see.

PaPa LaBas reflects. Do you think we're out of date as he said?

I know that the politicians of this era will be remembered more than me but I would like to believe that we work for principles and not for self. "We serve the loas," as they say. Charismatic leaders will become as outdated as the solo because people will realize that when the Headman dies the movement dies instead of becoming a permanent entity, perispirit, a protective covering for its essence. Yes, Abdul will become surrounded by people who will yield inches of their lives to him at a time; become the satellites rotating about the body which gives them light; but that's ephemeral, the fading clipping from the newspaper in comparison to a Ju / Ju Mask a 1000 years old. No, LaBas, the New York police will wipe out VooDoo just as they did in New Orleans, but it will find a home in a band on the Apollo stage, in the storefronts; and there will always be those who will risk the uninformed amusement of their contemporaries by resurrecting what we stood for.

The 2 men, PaPa LaBas and his guide Black Herman, walk into the 1920s parlor of the Townhouse. People are standing about a light-skinned-appearing man.

Well I'll be damned, Black Herman says. It's the President Elect, Warren Harding.

They move into the center of the room where Harding stands beneath some white chandeliers. He is on the tail end of some remarks he is making to the gathering. The Hostess stands off to the side, next to a society interviewer from the Race press. Her party is made: an unannounced visit of the next President.

As you know, Mr. James Weldon Johnson visited me in Muncie and gave me information concerning the nasty war taking place in Haiti the administration was attempting to conceal.

The guests move in as Harding reaches into his hip pocket and removes a plug of tobacco.

I think we made a good shot with the Haitian material and the administration was put on the defensive. They were hard pressed to explain why a horrid war with Marines committing so many atrocities was allowed to continue. I promised Mr. Johnson that on the way to Washington I would drop by and see him and it was he who suggested that if I attended your little party I could hear some of that good music. The sounds Mr. Daugherty my Attorney General and Florence my wife keep hidden from me. So if you don't mind a gate crasher I think I'll just go and dip my fork into some of those chitterlings and pigs' feet I know you're cooking down in the basement kitchen.

The President Elect followed by 2 of his aides walks down the steps leading to the basement as titters fly through the room.

Well I have to go, LaBas says to Herman.

Wait, I'll walk you down the stairs.

Herman puts on his black top formal hat and black cape. They walk down the Townhouse steps. Black Herman and LaBas shake hands when they reach the sidewalk.

Keep in touch, PaPa; there are some people in the harbor who want to meet you.

Good. Call me. LaBas walks toward his car. T Malice has the night off. He turns to Black Herman, the other man approaching the end of the block.

Herman, can I give you a ride?

The man turns around. No that's O.K. I'll walk.

Herman?

Yes?

These young kids these days know how to give a party, don't they?

You can say that again, Herman agrees before vanishing around the corner.

●   ○

Biff Musclewhite has reduced his status from Police Commissioner to Consultant to the Metropolitan Police in the precinct in Yorktown in order to take a job as Curator of the Center of Art Detention. (More pay.) He is sitting with 1 of his old colleagues, Schlitz "the Sarge of Yorktown," nicknamed affectionately by the police station he so often visited over the years.

They are sitting at the table of the Plantation House located in the Milky Way of Manhattan, the area of theaters and night clubs. The Southern Belle chorus line is promenading on the stage (the background of which is a riverboat) in their multipetticoated skirts, carrying parasols and wearing bonnets. Banjos strumming. Black waiters stand against the wall dressed as if they were in some 18th-century French court. White powdered wigs, frilled cuffs and shirts. The deep, blue lighting fills the club.

Gonna miss ya, Biff, remember the bags I use to bring to ya, ya got real rich outta that; the only guy retiring at $3000 per as a millionaire. I'll bet you have 1,000,000s in stocks and bonds inside your shoeboxes.

Yes, I've come a long way, hobnobbing with the rich out on Long Island . . . Curator of a museum . . . a long way from that punk kid you use to cover, down in the Tenderloin. Musclewhite laughs.

Yeah, remember when you went off to war and the whole gang turned out to say goodbye and sing "Over There." You really gave it to them Huns, Biff. We were proud of you.

. . . You know, Sarge, some would think that this was a plot for a Cagney movie. You and I brothers, you become a gangster and I become a cop . . .

Only you didn't go straight. I was always dumb but you were smart, taking more money from us than I would ever make in policy or bootlegging liquor, and now Curator of the Center of Art Detention which is kind of Big Cheese for us crooks. There you are taking bigger than me and getting away clean; how did you swing it?

Some of my friends over at the Plutocrat Club said there was an opening. I asked them how I could get the job if my only experience was as police commissioner. They said I had to learn the art of making a simple oil portrait resemble a window dressing in heaven. They said it was the gab that was the art. How you promoted it . . . So I've been learning these art terms from reading the New York *Sun*. And you know, I'm getting good at it.

Similar to my business. That's what I mean, Biff, you've always had a head on your shoulders. Your silver hair, the expensive clothing, hanging out with all the swanks. A good cover. You got it made, pal. The pressures I have . . . Buddy Jackson is muscling in on my operation in Harlem; we tried to get him the other day but the nigger seems to have 9 lives. My man hurled a bomb at him and a dame.

[*The curtain opens, revealing Charlotte's Pick, who is about 4' 1". He is in what appears to be a slave cabin and the stage foliage indicates that the cabin is in a forest. There are roots lying on a wooden table and an old tattered book. We can see by the way Peter is mixing things, the greenish-yellow candles, the black cats walking about, and a black bird looking sinisterly down upon the whole affair, that Peter is impersonating a cunjah man. He removes a tattered book and begins to mumble words from it. The slave master's wife Charlotte materializes; she tantalizingly removes her hoop skirt and petticoats until she is down to a brief flapper's skirt. Bloodhounds approaching in the background. The audience begins to chuckle as Doctor Peter Pick goes through the motions of putting her down. Charlotte makes even bolder more suggestive overtures to him. The closer the noise of the bloodhounds comes to his cabin the more the audience laughs at the Pick's Predicament. The bankers, publihsers, visiting Knights of Pythias and Knights of the White Camelia, theatrical people, gangsters and city officials who frequent the club are getting a big kick out of this. An angel in a Green Pastures getup passes by. Pick invites him in and asks him to read the words. Nothing happens as Charlotte now begins to remove her blouse. The angel leaves the cabin, puffing on his cigar and tipping his black felt derby with ribbon band. The bloodhounds are closing in on the cabin as Peter Pick makes more attempts to send her back from where he conjured her. A local demon passes by and Peter Pick yanks its tail and pulls it into the cabin. It too reads from the magic book, the* grimoire, *and nothing happens. Charlotte is removing her brassiere and has unpinned her hair. The bloodhounds are heard crossing the swamps and some can be heard coming up on the ground a few yards from the Pick's cabin. Well, in desperation Pick passes the book to the planter's wife and asks her to read from it. She reads. Pick disappears!*] The curtains close upon thunderous applause and laughter.

So this was the Charlotte his friends, Masons in the know, at the Caucasian lodge talked about. Her apartment where one was initiated into certain rites. They were calling it the Temple of Isis. The rites, it suggested, were of a sexual nature, Muses Biff Musclewhite, who resembled the white-mustached Esquire symbol. Wellheeled. Dirty old man.

Some act huh!

Yes, Musclewhite distantly replies to Schlitz the Sarge; *the beauty, the enchanting body of this woman,* Musclewhite thinks. A . . . why don't we order.

The "Sergeant" snaps his fingers.

Hey Pompey! Cato! come over here, he calls to the 2 Black waiters standing against the wall of the Plantation House.

They respond smartly, approaching Biff Musclewhite and Schlitz the Sarge's table, bedazzling in their resplendent uniforms. The Police Commissioner now Curator of the Center of Art Detention is examining the menu.

Schlitz the Sarge, about to give an order, raises his head when he gets it shattered.

The 2 men put the guns back inside their vests and hop some tables until they disappear through the door. The patrons scream. Faint. Panic. Screaming.

Shocked!! Musclewhite rises from the table and pursues the waiters. His friend's leaning back in the chair. Eyes staring straight ahead, about ⅓ of his head from the brow up scattered into the neighboring diners' dinner plates and on their clothes.

Outside the club the 2 men are nowhere to be seen. Only white powdered wigs lying on the sidewalk.

●   ○

PaPa LaBas, noonday HooDoo, fugitive-hermit, obeah-man, botanist, animal impersonator, 2-headed man, You-Name-It is 50 years
old and lithe (although he eats heartily and doesn't believe in the
emaciated famished Christ-like exhibit of self-denial and flagella-
tion).

He is contemplative and relaxed, which Atonists confuse with lazi-
ness because he is not hard at work drilling, blocking the view
of the ocean, destroying the oyster beds or releasing radioactive
particles that will give unborn 3-year-olds leukemia and cancer.
PaPa LaBas is a descendant from a long line of people who made
their pact with nature long ago. He would never say "If you've
seen 1 redwood tree, you've seen them all"; rather, he would reply
with the African Chieftain "I am the elephant," said long before
Liverpool went on record for this. The reply was made when a
Huxley had the nerve to warn him about the impending extinction
of the elephant—an extinction which Huxley's countrymen were
precipitating in the 1st place.

(*Freud would read this as "a feeling of an indissoluble bond,
of being one with the external world as a whole," which poor Freud
"never experienced," being an Atonist, the part of Jealous Art
which shut out of itself all traces of animism. When Freud came
to New York in 1909 LaBas sought him out to teach him The
Work; but he couldn't gain entrance to the hotel suite, which was
blocked by ass-kissers, sychophants similar to those who were to
surround Hitler and Stalin later, telling the "Master" what they
wanted him to hear and screening all alien material meant for their
master's attention. They had told LaBas to take the back elevator
even though some of them prided themselves on their liberalism. 42
Professors of New York University or people from Columbia
University.*) (The 1909 versions of Albert Goldman, the "pop"
expert for *Life* magazine and the *New York Times* who in a
review of a record made by some character who calls himself
Doctor John [when the original Doctor John was described by
New Orleans contemporaries as a "huge Black man . . . , a Sengalese
Prince . . .] made some of the most scurrilous attacks on the Voo-
Doo religion to date—I. R.)* *Humiliated, PaPa LaBas had left the*

---

* No one called him an anti-Negro vulgarian, however.

hotel, the laughter of these men behind him. He didn't get to see Freud, much to Freud's and Western Civilization's loss.

He could have taught Freud The Work. Give him a nook of the Nulu Kulu and maybe his followers would not have termed such sentiments "abnormal" or "pathological." For next to Black Herman he was 1 of the few in the Northeast who could summon a loa when he wished.

It is customary for the followers of the great man, being prigs and inferior to him, to distort and cheapen the techniques of the master.

LaBas sits in court awaiting the clerk to call his case. He has been summoned for allowing his Newfoundland HooDoo dog 3 Cents to soil the altar at St. Patrick's Cathedral. PaPa LaBas couldn't comprehend the charge. He was merely fulfilling an old civic axiom: that of keeping the city streets clean.

This is 1 in a long series of annoyments that have been launched against him by the Manhattan Atonists. They know that he was in contact with Jes Grew.

There were suspicious mailmen. A nasty fat-cheeked Black cat sat on the fence all day below his office, staring up at his window. A human hand had been sent through the mail. Barbarous? Maybe, but this wasn't a case of conjugating Greek words, or cumbersome footnoting; this was cash. Their livelihood.

Their patients were flocking to his methods. Irene Castle, in a book, had seemingly given 1 of his techniques her endorsement:

> Nowadays we dance morning, noon and night. What is more, we are unconsciously, while we dance, warring not only against unnatural lines of figures and gowns, but we are warring against fat, against sickness, and against nervous troubles. For we are exercising. We are making ourselves lithe and slim and healthy, and these are things that all reformers in the world could not do for us.*

This had saved him at 1st. This endorsement by Irene Castle, a woman whose personal fetish was that of dressing as a nun. After her endorsement the vicious campaign aimed at him had

* *Castles in the Air*—Irene Castle.

abated. The harassment from the bulls, the constant inspections of his Mumbo Jumbo Kathedral by the Fire Department, the reviews of his tax records.

Irene Castle's clients were tycoons and captains of industry—Harriman Astor Vanderbilt she taught for 100 dollars an hour to do a diluted version of Jes Grew, during the day they paid blue-nosed deference to the Atonist creeds. Somehow like the Haitian elite pays homage to Catholicism but keeps a houngan tucked away in the background.

At night they would wallow up to their bankbooks in the Charleston at Irene's Caves. No ordinary gin mills but high hat joints where they danced to Jim Europe's "Black Devils," the first jazz band to play on 5th Ave.

With such powerful backing, PaPa LaBas had been able to stave off their attacks—the attacks of the Manhattan Atonists. Many of their "patients" were relatives of these tycoons and they couldn't risk a dollar by irritating someone whose techniques had been endorsed by Irene Castle.

But recently she had moved to the right of Jes Grew and was consulting the Government on the Epidemic. The hostility had been renewed. PaPa LaBas knew the fate of those who threatened the Atonist Path. They would receive the wrath of its backbone: the Wallflower Order which attends to the Dirty Work.

Their writings were banished, added to the Index of Forbidden Books or sprinkled with typos as a way of undermining their credibility, and when they sent letters complaining of this whole lines were deleted without the points of ellipses. An establishment which had been in operation for 2,000 years had developed some pretty clever techniques. Their enemies, apostates and heretics were placed in dungeons, hanged or exiled or ostracized occasionally by their own people who, due to the domination of their senses by Atonism, were robbed of any concerns other than mundane ones. PaPa LaBas did not proselytize. Not even those who worked with him, Earline, Charlotte; all he requested was that they feed the loas. A debt be owed to their influence upon his experience. A precaution.

The clerk interrupted his thoughts by calling his case. He is summoned and asked to swear upon the only book the judge will allow in "his court." PaPa LaBas won't dare touch the accursed thing. He demands the right to his own idols and books. It reminds PaPa LaBas of the familiar epigram: "Orthodoxy is my Doxy, Heterodoxy is the other fellow's Doxy."

The late Teens and early 1920s are a bad time for civil liberties. In Bisbee Arizona, 1917, 1,100 members of the Industrial Workers of the World (Wobblies) are subjected to the tortures of a vigilante mob. January 23, 1920, 5,000 "Reds" are routed from their beds, imprisoned or deported. At the beginning of the Jazz Age, February 20th, 1919, in Hammond Indiana, after deliberating for 2 minutes a jury of his peers acquits Frank Petroni who had murdered in cold blood a man who yelled "To Hell with the United States."

Fear stalks the land. (As usual; so what else is new?)

While PaPa LaBas has been haggling with the judge the prosecutor has been conferring with the bull. The prosecutor requests to approach the bench. After a short conference, the judge dismisses the case.

They really don't want him in jail. They want to wear him down, pique him, enthrall him, tie him up by burdening him with petty court appearances so that he won't have time for Mumbo Jumbo Kathedral.

Outside PaPa LaBas climbs into the back seat of his 1915, 2-passenger Town Coupe Locomobile. It is a car designed to accommodate the philosophy "small numbers make for distinction, quantity destroys" and its production is limited to 4 per day. He reaches into 1 of the wooden vanity cases and removes a sky blue colored cigarette. His own brand, Mumbos.

His driver T Malice, so-called as a result of his penchant for the practical joke, is a tall lanky youth pursuing a degree in librarianship at Lincoln University.

People are running in the direction of Wall Street.

What's up? PaPa LaBas asks, picking up the tab to read.

Seems that the Sarge of Yorktown sent some of his Torpedoes to take Buddy Jackson but failed. Buddy and his woman weren't touched. What happened with your case?

They dismissed it again. Another stalling action. We'll probably find a fire inspector when we reach the Kathedral. Since Irene condemned The Work, the Department of Public Health has also been hassling us. The lies put out about the place by these men with degrees from the Atonist cause. Whenever sophistry and rhetoric fail they send in their poor White goons. They don't have the guts of real gangsters. The letters after their names are their tommy guns and those universities where they pour over syllables in the many cubicles, their Big House.

Well, you know how these fagingy-fagades are, pop. Mr. Eddy's very screwy these days.

Fagingy-fagade? What's that?

White people, pop. Ofays.

PaPa LaBas, conscious of the contemporary since Berbelang's attack, writes this into his black notebook. He asks T Malice to repeat it several times so that he can ascertain the correct spelling, having become a student of auditory phonetics. The big car moves from 100 Center Street toward uptown. They detour to make room for ambulances arriving at the scene of the explosion.

The Locomobile with the 2 men and dog occupants moves toward the vicinity of the explosion. When they reach it they see people milling about. The fire trucks, police and cars are parked haphazardly about the street. PaPa LaBas notices an object that has been blown to the pavement. He emerges from the car after signaling T Malice to halt. It's the brokers "ugly" fetish: a wood-carving of Ghede. Isn't that strange, PaPa LaBas thinks. PaPa LaBas re-enters the auto. Desiring privacy as he examines the Ghede, he pulls down the backseat's silk roller shades. It is an easy ride; the rear of the car contains 50-inch springs.

● ○

PaPa LaBas' Mumbo Jumbo Kathedral is located at 119 West 136th St. The dog at his heels, PaPa LaBas climbs the steps of the Town house. He moves from room to room: the Dark Tower Room the Weary Blues Room the Groove Bang and Jive Around Room the Aswelay Room. In the Groove Bang and Jive Around Room people are rubberlegging for dear life; bending over backwards to admit their loa. In the Dark Tower Room, artists using cornmeal and water are drawing veves. Markings which were invitations to new loas for New Art. The room is decorated in black red and gold.

A piano recording plays Jelly Roll Morton's "Pearls," haunting, melancholy. In the Aswelay Room the drums sleep after they've been baptized. A guard attendant stands by so that they won't get up and walk all over the place. PaPa LaBas opens his hollow obeah stick and gives the drums a drink of bootlegged whiskey. Stunned by Berbelang's attack upon him as an "anachronism," he has introduced some Yoga techniques. In 1 main room, people are doing the Cobra the Fish the Lion the Lotus the Tree the Voyeurs Pose the Adepts Pose the Wheel Pose the Crows Pose and many others. There is a room PaPa LaBas calls the Mango Room, so named to honor the great purifying plant. On a long maple table covered with splendid white linen cloth rest 21 trays filled with such delectable items as liqueurs, sweets, rum, baked chicken, and beef. The table is adorned with vases containing many types of roses. This room is the dining hall of the loas, and LaBas demands that the trays be refreshed after the Ka-food has been eaten. His assistants make sure that this is done. The room is illuminated by candles of many colors. On the tables sky-blue candles are burning. In the other main room attendants have been guided through exercises. Once in a while 1 is possessed by a loa. The loa is not a daimon in the Freudian sense, a hysteric; no, the loa is known by its signs and is fed, celebrated, drummed to until it deserts the horse and *govi* of its host and goes on about its business. The attendants are experienced and know the names, knowledge the West lost when the Atonists wiped out the Greek mysteries. The last thing these attendants would think of doing to a loa's host is electrifying it lobotomizing it or removing its clitoris, which was a pre-Freudian technique for "curing" hysteria. No, they don't wish it ill, they welcome it. When a client is handled by an especially vigorous loa the others stand around this person and give it encouragement. Smiling PaPa and T see that everything is really Jake.

PaPa LaBas walks into his office. His lamp glows. Incense is burning. Sandalwood, myrrh and many other formulas which survived the ban when the Catholic Church decreed that only frankincense be used in ceremonies. He inspects a rejected manuscript from London, the editor says he liked his article on "lost liturgies in New Orleans" but feels "it doesn't fit in with our format." PaPa LaBas reviews the editorial board. Just as he expected.

All Atonists. He looks down the hall. Earline is emerging from 1 of the rooms. Strange. He never noticed that before, her walk. She is serpentine and her hips move tantalizingly under the thin, white short dress.

Thanks for inviting me to your party, Earline. I hope I didn't upset your guests like that, the argument between me and Abdul. It occurred after you left but I'm sure you heard about it.

O we're accustomed to Abdul's bunk. He gets on his soapbox and goes on for hours. I have heard that he is receiving money from the Knights of the Ku Klux Klan.

PaPa LaBas reflects. I rather like him though, at least he has his own flag, not like these Black Marxists who merely mimic the words of the "Internationale," somebody else's thought, and somebody else's song. Abdul is just an irritated lyricist who can't seem to get his music sung. I am eager to read his book when it's out.

Charlotte wants to see you.

She does? I thought it strange that she wasn't giving you assistance out there.

I can manage. I think she's quitting.

What's up?

I don't know, you'd better ask her.

PaPa LaBas walks into Charlotte's office and finds her sitting on her desk. She is dressed quite spiffy. A black-felt hat adorned with ostrich feathers. Pearls, a black suit with flapper skirt. She raises her eyes from the magazine *Vanity Fair* when she sees LaBas. She is inhaling from a Fatima Turkish cigarette held in an ivory holder.

What's wrong, Charlotte?

O pop, I don't want to hurt you but I'm leaving. You know Berbelang had some good points; after he left the clientele, his followers dropped off. He influenced your approach, which at 1st I thought was O.K. but, pop, you know you developed a cultish thing about this New HooDoo therapy, I mean, I have learned all of the dances and everything . . . I feel . . .

You mean you've gotten an offer . . .

Well yes, I am going on the stage, the Plantation House wants me to star in their new review *The Witches' Pick*. I tried out a few months ago and have gone back on amateur nights. Now they want me for a long run. I'm gaining quite a following.

Congratulations. That's good news.

O you mean you approve? She asks in her characteristically sultry voice.

Yes of course, if you have a break like that, just so you don't become 1 of those Gold Diggers as Irene did.

She glances at the floor.

There's more?

The manager wants me to entertain some of the selective clientele. The diamond stickpin trade. You know, teach them diluted versions of the dances I have observed here.

Charlotte, you shouldn't attempt to use any aspect of The Work for profit.

Why not? I helped translate the French works and took Berbelang's place when you were short of help, pop. Pop, you can't keep something as wonderful as your techniques a secret. They will benefit the world.

Charlotte, I think we should be careful. I don't know the extent to which the Haitian aspects of The Work can be translated here. Suppose the loas have followed the features of their work I have borrowed. This means that they have to be appeased. That's why I require that the 22 trays be fed just in case. The 22 trays dedicated to the Haitian loa. I know you all think it's silly but we have to observe these precautions. People didn't believe me when I warned of the Jes Grew epidemic; but now here it is.

O pop, they just invented that to sell the tabs, you know how outrageous the newspapers are getting to be.

I still think you ought to wait, Charlotte. It might be dangerous. Upset a loa's Petro and you will be visited by troubles you never could have imagined.

Charlotte rises from the desk, walks over to LaBas and puts her arms around his neck.

Look, pop, I want to take the benefits of all of the beautiful things you and Earline and Berbelang have taught me and give it to everyone.

PaPa LaBas pauses for a moment.

I hate to let you go but I guess you know what you're doing.

Charlotte picks up her things and walks toward the door. She turns, kisses LaBas goodbye and walks out. LaBas hears her conversing with Earline outside the door.

She had been hired as a translator. Sometimes, the mail being so slow, she would be his messenger. Taking packages to his clients on her way home. He was worried about her. There was always the precaution he had developed because he had "been called" and awarded himself the Asson which was as good as inheriting the ability to Work. But he felt obligated to warn his technicians of malevolent side effects of the field lest they pick up a loa they didn't want. If this was considered conservatism or orthodoxy then that's what it would have to be.

He phoned the florist. He would send Charlotte a mixed bunch of roses. She could choose the variety she wanted. She liked to choose.

13 Earline is quite cheerful when she arrives home. She has bought this marvelous scarf which bears a design of a stylized heart pierced by a dagger. She amuses herself by thinking this an apt metaphor for her present affair of the heart. She removes the mail from the box. She then picks up the New York *Sun* which lies on the doormat. The headline is about Haiti. VooDoo generals. Something about Marines. She has heard PaPa LaBas speak of Haiti. He wanted to visit there but wasn't able to. PaPa LaBas had quipped, If I don't visit Haiti perhaps Haiti will come to me. Earline enters the apartment and goes into the living room. She undresses for a bath. She takes a luxurious bath in basil leaves and strange aromas. Her black skin glistens like a glazed piece of pottery. It affects the touch like satin. She lies in the tub, the folded newspaper in her hand. *What was this about doughboy zombies? The tabs were becoming outrageous; as if the scandals of Hollywood weren't enough they were playing up this matter on Haiti. Recently 1 of the reporters had sneaked into a big house chamber and emerged with a picture of a woman undergoing execution—ghastly but fun.* The picture showed a zombie Marine surrounded by men in white coats. The door opens.

Hi.

Looking through the open bathroom door into the other room,

she sees Berbelang. Hi? You've been gone for 3 days, all you got to say is hi?

Hello.

Berbelang, what is happening to you?

Berbelang opens the refrigerator and takes out a piece of barbecue from a bowl. He removes the wrapping and eats a short rib.

O I've been busy, you know, hanging out.

He wears a black hat featuring a white silk headband decorated with black scarabs and a long woolen black frock coat which hugs him about the ankles. He wears these impeccably shined high black boots of blunt-toed Civil War style. A very fat knotted and hand-painted tie under a white vest decorated with black orchid designs. It isn't new but he's clean and he wears the stuff well. He is known by the fellows as a Lounge Lizard for his way with women. But he doesn't pursue it. He isn't 1 of these Drugstore Cowboys or Creepers who hang out, ogling every Jazz Baby who walks by. Berbelang is serious.

Look baby, soon I will be through and able to tell you everything but now, sugar, you have to trust me.

Earline stands in the doorway with an elaborately decorated towel covering her body.

Berbelang glances at the painting on the wall. It was done by J. B. Bottex, a Haitian. A Black Mary Magdalene and Jesus. The 1st thing you see is the woman's effulgent rump covered by a lime dress. She wears pearls, a string around her neck, and her hair is tied in a bun. She is watching a procession, some Haitians following Christ . . . Christ has eyes for her. He has stopped and is staring at her as she leans over the banister of her porch.

Berbelang's trousers sag a bit at the knees. He removes his coat and hat and tosses them across the table. Earline has moved over to the bed and, legs crossed, is sitting on its edge.

What's that pretty thing lying next to you?

A scarf I bought today.

Berbelang approaches the bed and handles the scarf. Fondles the silk in his hand and smiles.

Some very serious things are happening baby, Berbelang confides, lying down next to her. You will see that Jes Grew is no dream of an old man but . . . dynamic, engrossing —

Earline rises, supports herself by leaning on her hands. She starts to defend PaPa LaBas.

O Berbelang, he admires you so, why can't you be—
But Berbelang has other ideas. He puts his hands about her waist and they begin some furious necking. He switches off the lights so that only the *Fire of Love Brand Oil* candles burn. Sputtering candles whose poles have been anointed.

At 3:00 in the morning Earline awakes. She feels warm under the covers, a contentment like bathing in the rich soap, the basil leaves. She turns to her lover. The pillow shows the imprint of where his head once was.

14 Hinckle Von Vampton resembles the 4th Horseman of Apocalypse as depicted in a strange painting by William Blake: a grey-bearded figure of whom it was written: "Behold, pale horse and its rider's name was Death and Hades followed him . . ." Von Vampton works in the copy room of the Atonist voice, the New York *Sun*, administered by members of the Wallflower Order. He lives in a rooming house located in the Chelsea district of New York City. Never married, he sits with his companions in an Automat on 23rd Street, night after night, discussing European history, drinking coffee and eating bean pie. His companions get into heated arguments as numerous cups of coffee are fetched from the Automat's spigot. Hinckle Von Vampton, steady, a black patch on his eye from an old war wound, is often referred to by the disputants as "The Grand Master."

● ○

1 night, Von Vampton's nosy landlady, who constantly interrupts his meditations by sweeping about the door of his room, peers through his keyhole and finds the man staring at an ugly, hideous bejeweled object: a little black doll. Hinckle Von Vampton is dressed as she is to report later, "like 1 of them Knight fellers. And began kissing some ugly nigger doll." Spaced-out, his good pupil dilating, sitting in a ragged uniform marked with a Red Cross emblem, a coat of lamb's wool, he utters a strange cry.

And then in reverie he leans back into his chair.

It is A.D. *1118—the Burgundian knight Hugues de Payens is conducting a ceremony before the Temple of Solomon. He is founding the "Knights Templar," the "poor fellows of Christ." They are a scraggly bunch who look as if they haven't bathed in months. They are a kind of Tac Squad for Western Civilization; a mighty highway patrol assigned to protect the pilgrims en route to the Holy Land from attack by infidels and robbers.*

1 day Hinckle Von Vampton forgets to keep a headline in the present tense. Word comes from the chief copy editor that "the old man is losing his grip." He begins to bring Thermos bottles filled with gin to the job.

● ○

That night Hinckle Von Vampton enters his room only to find it ransacked. His clothes have been dumped about. His books lie on the floor, the trunk is empty as are the drawers. Hinckle Von Vampton questions his housekeeper.

"She don't know nothin."

Hinckle Von Vampton's housekeeper, intrigued by the scene she stumbled upon—the scene of her tenant kissing this strange looking "statoot"—has invited her Mah-Jongg club to come up and "see the show."

Their vantage point is a skylight above the studio. The quality of the glass is such that they can look down without being detected. This time he is standing on the statue of a dog. Lifting his drink and sword and whirling the sword about his head, he utters strange words which 1 of his landlady's friends is later to associate with "Araby."

The reputation of the Knights Templar grows as men who won't bug out and avoid their obligations. No softies or jellyfish they. No indeed. They are the militia templi, *the protectors of the Temple of the Wizard Solomon and all the treasures within. They save the Second Crusade (1146–1150) from annihilation by "Islamic hordes."*

15 The particular edition of the New York *Sun* which is now a collector's item certainly paid its dues to the Atonist order which demands that it devote so many column inches per month to the glorification of Western Culture. "The most notable achievements of mankind." A story concerning the authentication of a Rembrandt jumps to page 60 where it runs parallel to a column describing Afro-American Painting which is described by the Atonist critic as "primitive," at best "charming" and "mostly propagandistic."

The managing editor has been meeting all day with "higher ups." They are deciding what their particular tab can do to crush the Jes Grew epidemic which has now reached Chicago. When he walks into the office and inspects the edition of the newspaper which was done without his supervision, he grits his teeth and blows his top, rushing from the office like a bellowing Bull. There is a colossal mistake in the headlines. 1000s of copies are in the streets and others are en route. It is too late to call them back. Heads with roll.

He storms into the copy room to find the makeup man drunk on gin. His head on his desk. The managing editor fires the makeup man on the spot. As the man picks up his things the managing editor asks who was responsible for the error.

"That furriner," says the makeup man. "Hinckle Von Vampton, that furriner."

They have sent Hinckle Von Vampton to the headline clinic to cure him of his dead and broken heads but Vampton has been unredemptive. Hinckle Von Vampton is sitting in his chair in the little room adjoining the copy room lost in his thoughts:

Private castles are the Knights Templar' for the asking. It is rumored that they possess hidden seaports from where they sail to unknown continents. They arouse the envy of Europe's monarchs who, jealous of their service to the pope, would like to curb their power. They have powerful friends among the royalty however. King Richard 1 of England is a patron and King Alfonso of Aragon and Navarre wills his countries to them; but this plan is foiled by the Moors. King Baldwin 1 grants the Templars his palace as their headquarters.

16   Von Vampton?

Hinckle Von Vampton's 1 blue eye blinks and then fixes upon
the swarthy form before him. A man in trousers a few sizes too
large, suspenders, hair pasted down with a bad smelling grease.

We tried to give you a chance, pops, but now you are through.
We had orders from the Occupation Forces that no news of this
war would be printed on the mainland. You give it a full banner
headline. **VooDoo Generals Surround Marines at Port-au-Prince.**
We warned you, pop, but now you've really done it. Your style
was too fancy anyway. We like strong lively short verbs and
present tenses and you can't adapt to this American style, pops.

Damn you.

The people outside, listening through the glass window, are
shocked at this use by Hinckle Von Vampton of abusive pro-
fanity.

You are as boorish as your newspaper. Every managing editor
is his newspaper. You use ketchup at every meal, you don't change
your clothes and you are a slob, therefore your newspaper is a
slob. You put hifalutin stories on the cover but in the rear you
carry ads for the cheapest Bijou, scandalous stories about Hollywood and photos which titillate, that despicable cover you carried
of the woman's execution your reporter smuggled from the big
house.

Hey wait a minute buster, s'matta with you?

You are as lurid as your every page. Your concept of briefness
will lead to inaccuracy and ultimately destroy the "boobooise" you
represent. You will entice the monsters of your twisted dreams
and they will surface like dead fish. Moreover, my friend, your
style book is a racing form.

Red in the face as a baboon's ass, the managing editor swallows
a couple of pills.

Look Hinckle, I don't want to argue with you. We have our
orders about this Haiti thing. Americans will not tolerate wars
that can't be explained in simple terms of economics or the
White man's destiny. Your headline has done considerable damage.
Our switchboard is overloaded with questions from the populace
concerning Haiti. Some of them don't even know where it is.

Haiti is 21° latitude by 72° longitude, Von Vampton supplies.

Yes, right . . . Anyway mobs are checking out books from the 42nd Street Library on Haiti and the lions have been taken indoors for their protection. This is a can of worms you've given us and you will have to go.

The Haitian thing has asked the Cockatrice and Sea Monsters of the Western Psyche to move over.

Hinckle Von Vampton examines the man. Jowly. A gin-inspired pallor. He glances at the cuff links. A Knight in armor wearing the Red Cross on his breast.

Where did you find those cuff links?

I found them around the corner on 42nd Street, why?

Not only are you a louse but you are a desecrater as well. Death to defilers.

Hinckle Von Vampton reaches for a short bronze dagger and is about to plunge it into the managing editor's chest when other employees rush into the office and take him off the managing editor.

THAT DOES IT. YOU'RE CRAZY. GO PICK UP YOUR PAY AND GET OUTTA HERE BEFORE I CALL THE BULLS.

With pleasure, Hinckle Von Vampton says, brushing off his immaculately starched collar. You should be able to manage them very well the way you ignore their corruption.

With dignity, Hinckle Von Vampton gathers his newspapers and walks out of the offices of the New York *Sun*.

In the streets, little boys wearing soul caps and knickers are shouting out the headlines.

VooDoo Generals Surround Marines At The Poor Prince

Hinckle Von Vampton smiles. That's America for you. Rumor stacked upon rumor like bricks in the Mason's Tower of Babel. "Gamalielese," as Mencken described Harding's prose. A prose style so bad that it had charm.

S.R.: A LATE BREAKING DEVELOPMENT IN HAITI.

RUMORS CIRCULATE THAT A SOUTHERN MARINE IS VICTIM

OF CANNIBALISM. THE ACTION IS TERMED BARBAROUS,

GHASTLY, HEINOUS, AN AFFRONT TO THE ENTIRE
"CIVILIZED" WORLD. KONGRESS DEPLORES HAITI IN A
RESOLUTION WHICH MEETS LITTLE OPPOSITION. WHEN
ASKED TO COMMENT JAMES WELDON JOHNSON SAYS:
  THE QUESTION AS TO WHICH IS MORE REPREHENSIBLE,
  THE ALLEGED CUSTOM IN HAITI OF EATING A HUMAN
  BEING WITHOUT COOKING HIM OR THE AUTHENTICATED
  CUSTOM IN THE UNITED STATES OF COOKING A HUMAN
  BEING WITHOUT EATING HIM. THE HAITIAN CUSTOM
  WOULD HAVE, AT LEAST, A UTILITARIAN PURPOSE IN
  EXTENUATION.*

17 Unemployed Hinckle Von Vampton hobbles through the
streets. His hat is turned down. It had become too much. He didn't
mind setting heads for the rubbish Americans called a newspaper.
Tabs, with their "Torch Murders," "Love Nests," "Sugar Daddies,"
and "Heart Throbs." He didn't mind the cheap stock, the lack
of eloquence, the inclination for synonyms, he had accomplished
what he set out to do. Now his ancient employers would have to
turn to him. If the Jes Grew thing didn't convince them they
would trace the Haitian leak to him and then they would want
to bargain. Heh heh. He laughed. Heh heh, Hinckle laughed.
Passersby stopping to watch this man double up on the street
HEHEHEHEHEHEHEHEHEHEHEHEHEHEHEHEHEH

  Dance is the universal art, the common joy of expression.
  Those who cannot dance are imprisoned in their own ego
  and cannot live well with other people and the world. They
  have lost the tune of life. They only live in cold thinking.
  Their feelings are deeply repressed while they attach
  themselves forlornly to the earth.†

* *Along This Way*—James Weldon Johnson.
† Joost A. M. Meerloo, *The Dance: from Ritual to Rock and Roll, Ballet to
Ballroom* (Philadelphia: Chilton, 1960), p. 39.

That night, bubbling with success, a happy Hinckle Von Vampton attends a lecture at the Knights Templar building which boasted such distinguished charter members as De Witt Clinon, 1-time Governor of the State. The members give him a standing ovation and invite him to the platform where he quietly sits in a hard back chair as a lecturer describes the tributes paid the ancient discredited Order by a grateful Europe. The burial grounds, churches, farms and villages and pastures that were awarded to them. They become the bankers of the Mediterranean and trade with both Christians and Muslims. Serving no monarch, they answer only to the pope himself. At 1 point their income amounts to $90,000,000 sterling and by A.D. 1128 they are declared by the pope immune to excommunication.

That night, joyously weeping over his victory, Hinckle Von Vampton says praises. Ancient words spoken by only 10 people in the whole world to the little black doll with the black curly hair. "He who made us and has not left us." The landlady giggles so she almost reveals her strategic position outside the door.

● ○

That morning Hinckle Von Vampton is on the way to the
bank to withdraw money to pay his rent. A car pulls up and
before the startled daylight shoppers, its occupants leap out and
whisk Hinckle Von Vampton away by gunpoint. The witnesses
are not able to give clear descriptions of the men. Later that
afternoon when Hinckle Von Vampton's housekeeper lets herself
into his room to clean she finds it in disarray. She is surprised. "He
may be nuts but he's neat," she says to a Mah-Jongg companion
later on.

Christianity has never been worldly nor has it ever looked
with favor on good food and wine, and it is more than
doubtful whether the introduction of jazz into the cult
would be a particular asset.
Carl G. Jung, *Psychology and Religion: West and East*

. . . the African deities were fond of food, drink, battle
and sex.
David St. Clair, *Drum and Candle*

The headquarters of the Wallflower Order. You have nothing
real up here. Everything is polyurethane, Polystyrene, Lucite,
Plexiglas, acrylate, Mylar, Teflon, phenolic, polycarbonate. A gal-
limaufry of synthetic materials. Wood you hate. Nothing to remind
you of the Human Seed. The aesthetic is thin flat turgid dull
grey bland like a yawn. Neat. Clean, accurate, and precise but 1
big Yawn they got up here. Everything as the law laid down
in Heliopolis 1000s of years ago. (Heliopolis, the Greek name
for the ancient city of Atu or Aton.) You eat rays and for snacks
you munch on sound. Loading up on data is slumber and recreation
is disassembling. Transplanting is real big here. Sometimes you play
switch brains and hide the heart. Lots of marching. Soon as these
Like-Men disappear walking single file down the hall here comes
another row at you. The Atonists got rid of their spirit 1000s of
years ago with Him. The flesh is next. Plastic will soon prevail over
flesh and bones. Death will have taken over. Why is it Death you
like? Because then no 1 will keep you up all night with that racket

dancing and singing. The next morning you can get up and build, drill, progress putting up skyscrapers and . . . and . . . and . . . working and stuff. You know? Keeping busy.

Now some problems. Jes Grew. *Mu'tafikah*, Teutonic Knights who've done it again making such a mess of things that Carl Jung wrote:

> The catastrophe of the first World War and the extraordinary spiritual malaise that came afterwards were needed to arouse a doubt as to whether all was well with the white man's mind.

18 The headquarters of the Wallflower Order, backbone of the Atonists is, due to the Jes Grew contagion, bustling with activity. Aides run about like ants scurrying across a white telephone. They use a new invention Television to scan the U.S. for Jes Grew activity at this moment stirring Chicago.

Wearing sandals and dressed like a Cecil B. De Mille extra, Hierophant 1 paces the floor, his long, grey beard touching his waist. His yellow eyes dart from screen to video screen as he watches the progress of the epidemic. Watching it Fade Out of Kansas City only to Fade In in St. Louis. Various wooden, metallic and plastic figures shaped like human beings, pet zombies and creatures whose mothers were scared by computers speak to 1 another in code. Gibberish. Sounds of tape recorders of its human voice at high speed. Jes Grew is compounded by the *Mu'tafikah* who are responsible for art thefts now ravishing the private collections of Europe and America. 1 of their number, an international *Mu'tafikah*, has lifted the sacred Papyri of Ani stored in the British Museum and returned it to "Brothers in Cairo," so read the "illiterate" "contradictory" "scrawls," product of "a tormented mind," which was left behind at the scene of the theft.

The Far Eastern Museum of Cologne has discovered several items from its Chinese collection missing. To add to this, the war launched by the Order against the Haitian nation has been exposed by a well-planted headline in the New York *Sun*. More books concerning Haiti have been checked out of American libraries in a week than in the previous history of the library system. To add to that, people walk all over New York speaking Creole and wearing tropical clothes; the women long white dresses, the men linen suits. As the war drags on it arrives upon American shores. The Wallflower Order launched the war against Haiti in hopes of allaying Jes Grew symptoms by attacking their miasmatic source. But little Haiti resists. It becomes a world-wide symbol for religious and aesthetic freedom. When an artist happens upon a new form he shouts "I Have Reached My Haiti!"

Dance manias inundate the land. J. A. Rogers writes, "It is just the epidemic contagiousness of jazz that makes it, like measles, sweep the block."* People do the Charleston the Texas Tommy and other anonymously created symptoms of Jes Grew. The Wallflower Order remembers the 10th-Century *tarantism* which nearly threatened the survival of the Church. Even Paracelsus, a "radical" who startled the academicians by lecturing in the vernacular, termed these manias "a disease."

The Wallflower Order is well aware of what Jes Grew wants and what Jes Grew needs. In case they're wrong they have other techniques. Their diagnosis is the same as PaPa LaBas', a "so-called" astrodetective they have under surveillance.

You must capture its Celebration and then it will dissolve. It's a new age. 1920. Sword fighting only interests the kids who attend the matinees. Douglas Fairbanks can sell Liberty Bonds and act but he is of no aid to you. The Teutonic Order is of no use. You must use something up-to-date to curb Jes Grew. To knock it dock it co-opt it swing it or bop it. If Jes Grew slips into the radiolas and Dictaphones all is lost. Luckily your scientists are working on microorganisms; minuscule replicas of yourself capable of surviving the atmosphere of any planet. Your inventors are preparing a Spaceship that will transport these microorganisms to 3 planets you've had your eye on. You wish all of your subjects were like them. Loyal, passive, "just doing our jobs."

You must get your hands on Jes Grew's hunger. That text. Last reported in the hands of a surviving member of the Knights Templar, that discredited order which once held the fate of Western Civilization in its hands until the scandal.

* *The New Negro*—Alain Locke, editor.

When Hinckle Von Vampton is shoved into the round revolving room he interrupts the Hierophant's speculations.

This round room's ceiling is a dome of glass through which the Hierophant can keep track of the Heavens. The 1st thing Hinckle sees is a man suffering from a condition know as kyphosis angularis standing on a ladder marking a huge map. It is his species count; the name and number of life near extinction. Dots of a dead white color are placed in Birds Reptiles Amphibians and Fish. The phone rings. The man climbs down and answers. The man grins, resumes his position, then places a dot in the watercress darter.

A huge magic snake of electric bloodless dots, and potentially deadly or benevolent depending upon how you look at it, clusters from New Orleans to Chicago on a map of the United States. Rashes are reported in Europe as well. Jes Grew begins to become pandemic, leaping across the ocean but generally forming a movement which points from Chicago to the East. On another wall are the symbols of the Atonist Order: the Flaming Disc, the ⚡1 and the creed—

> *Look at them! Just look at them!*
> *throwing their hips this way, that*
> *way while I, my muscles, stone,*
> *the marrow of my spine, plaster, my*
> *back supported by decorated paper,*
> *stand here as goofy as a Dumb Dora.*
> *Lord, if I can't dance, No one shall.*

Hinckle Von Vampton, arms held by the interrogators of New Orleans' late mayor, stands before the Hierophant 1.

Why have you removed me from the City?

Jes Grew has gripped the vitals of America, the Hierophant replies to his prisoner. You placed that headline in the New York *Sun*, our Atonist organ. We traced it to you. You knew what the script was. What we were doing in Haiti; we've all been through this before. And you have the nourishment of Jes Grew without which it will soon wane. Hand it over.

O I see, Hinckle replies, freeing his arms from the assistants who begin to struggle with the captive.

Leave him alone, the Hierophant orders.

I see, Hinckle says with obvious relish. Now that the Teutonics have fumbled the latest crusade you want me, a Templar, to bail you out.

The Hierophant bows his head. You know we're in trouble, don't you? You've seen the young men wearing slave bracelets, sitting in the cafés quoting nigger poetry. The young women smoking Luckies, wearing short skirts and staying out until 3:00 in the morning. If you know that we are desperate then you must know that we will go to any extreme to stop it. Therefore if you don't yield the Text we will rub you out.

Rub me out . . . Hinckle smiles and begins to strut about the room. Rub me out. Gone is the rhetoric, the convoluted sentences

300 words long with many parenthetical elements and modifying clauses separated from their objects, the logic and reason you were always so pleased with. Anxious about this Jes Grew epidemic, you speak like the common bootleg merchant or heist artist.

I . . . I don't want to be difficult with you, Hierophant 1 says pressing the button so that 3 weird-looking dudes in 3rd Man Theme trenches enter through doors leading to the round room. One carries the ritual dagger on a pillow . . .

This development doesn't deter Hinckle.

You have a body of Thugs now who kidnap innocent people at noon time and "rub them out." Enforcers. Torpedoes. Hoods. No longer do you quote Plato or the other obscurantists . . .

That's true, the Hierophant concurs. We leave all of that to New York intellectuals with Black maids. You have 5 seconds to tell us where you put that Text or it will be your last 5 seconds.

The man with the dagger, as if prompted by some military impulse, marches to the center and snaps to attention before the Hierophant.

I don't have it.

You what?

I can be of no assistance to you. You should have thought of the Text the dark day October 13, 1307, your King Philip 4 and the pope, Clement, he hired to do his "Dirty Work," brought the charges against my Order, rounded up our leaders and executed them. After all we did to defend your wretched tails.

The guards exchange surprised glances. Never before have they heard Hierophant 1 addressed in such a manner.

You are still the Grand Master of the surviving Knights Templar. Arrogant, proud. We had no choice but to bring you to trial. Your Order became so powerful that it threatened ours. We are not in a position to share power. I am merely the curator, the chief janitor, the custodian of a hierarchy which extends to the very top. I was given my orders and I had the pope and my king execute them. The charges they brought against you were all proven, even "worshiping the devil in the form of a cat," "spitting, stamping, urinating on crucifixes" as well as participating in acts in which Arabs' pharmacopoeia was used. You were accused of sodomy and kissing the tail of the black god Baphomet

. . . you had to be dealt with for the sake of Christendom.

Christendom? Without our Order there would have been no Christendom. We wanted to expand and we were acquiring African powers as a result of our contact with the Arabs. You should have known when your King Philip the 4th was eaten by a boar on November 29, 1314, the month after our executed leader Jacques de Molay cursed him, and when Pope Clement the 5th died on April 20, 1314, after yelling, "I'm burning up, I'm burning up," that we learned more from the Saracens than to play chess or smoke hashish. Your Christendom was for serfs, for underlings and the peasants. You, the pope and the king, were allowed to practice ceremonies which "deviated" from the rules of us as your flunkies. "Flatfoots," you used to call us behind our backs . . . You arrested us but some of us escaped. I came to America where I have been able to hold our little band together now scattered all over the globe waiting for this day . . . this day when you would be forced to remit your errors. And now it has arrived.

The guards exchange glances again. They can't believe what is occurring before them. The Hierophant knows the value of maintaining mystery between him and his guards.

Please leave. We want to be alone, he says as the guards salute by bringing their fists against their chests and leave the room.

What did you do with the Text, Hinckle?

O the Text. You want the Text. You fool. Did you think that the rivals of Atonism would be quelled by giving them fellowships and grants-in-aid? Didn't you realize that the "pagans" would refuse to be Milled and Humed at your Universities, would return to the tribes, don the Robes of the Leopard Skin Priests and purge the Atonist from their minds, girding themselves to do battle against your thing?

Hinckle, we can make a deal. The Text. Please, think of the Cross, the Virgin.

Think of the Virgin, he says. We fought and died for the Virgin the Cross and the Cup and what kind of reward did we receive? Our lands burned, our property confiscated and a humiliating trial.

We need the Text, Hinckle, I implore you, the Hierophant remonstrates, his eyes brimming with tears.

If you really must know, it's in the hands of 14 J.G.C. individuals scattered throughout Harlem for now. Only I can call it in and anthologize it. Janitors, Pullman porters, shoeshine boys, dropouts from Harvard, musicians, jazz musicians. Its carbons are in New York, Kansas City, Oakland, California, Chattanooga Tennessee, Detroit, Mobile, Raleigh. It's dispersed. Untogether. I sent it out as a chain book.

So that's why my men weren't able to find it when they ransacked your apartment?

Yes. If J.G. is indeed seeking its Text I will be able to help you out. If it's not I will also be able to aid you; but on 1 condition.

What is the condition?

Put my Order in charge of the 2nd phase as well as the 1st. Give us a chance to redeem our good name before the world.

Out of the question, the Hierophant answers. Higher-ups will never permit such an arrangement.

Very well then. Jes Grew is inclined toward New York, because it senses that the key to its Book is there. All it needs is the list of 14. It merely will have to be told what to do and then . . .

All right! All right! You win. The Knights Templar will be in charge of the anti-Jes Grew serum. I have no choice. The Black Tide of Mud will engulf us all. What do you need . . . ?

Now you have come to your senses. 1, I will collect the Text and it will be burned. 2, I will create the Talking Android so that New York resistance will be firm if J.G. decides to make a foray into the city. A few tricks I learned at the New York *Sun* will come in handy. You see, the J.G.C.s have no control over who speaks for them. It's in the hands of the press and radio. What we will do is begin a magazine that will attract its followers, featuring the kind of milieu it surrounds itself with. Jazz reviewers, cabarets, pornography, social issues, anti-Prohibition, placed between acres of flappers' tits. Here we will feature the Talking Android who will tell the J.G.C.s that Jes Grew is not ready and owes a large debt to Irish Theatre. This Talking Android will Wipe That Grin Off Its Face. He will tell it that it is derivative. He will accuse it of verbal gymnastics, of pandering to White readers. He will even suggest it abandon the typewriter completely

and create a Black Tammany Hall. He will describe it as a massive
hemorrhage of malaprops; illiterate and given to rhetoric. And
if the Talking Android is female she will shout before the Caucasian club, "They just can't write, they just can't write," but
then when pressed she might break into her monologue—you
know the one—"My no good nigger husband who left me with
these kids." So that won't do.

I will accomplish this within 6 months or . . . or . . .

Or what?

I will imbibe the sacred poison.

Fair enough. It sounds like an excellent plan, Hinckle. A precaution in case the Text isn't what the plague needs and a Talking
Android who will Knock-It Bop-It or Sock-It.

The Hierophant smiles. Now you're catching on. You're groov-
ing with the jive, H.

The Hierophant rises to shake Hinckle Von Vampton's hand.

Of course you will work with our people there. They will
provide you with all of the assistance you need. Their names are in
this little black book.

The Hierophant hands Hinckle the little black book and for
a moment Hinckle thumbs through it.

Warren Harding?

Yes, we had problems trying to get him nominated. It took 10
ballots. Some of the delegates at the convention called him a
"He-Harlot" and a "Black Babylonian." They called the convention
"boss controlled" and said that his nomination was the result of a
"Senate Cabal." H. L. Mencken, the writer, termed him "a series
of wet sponges," but we groomed him from the beginning by
surrounding him with a man who is now his Attorney General.
It took an advertising agency named Lord & Thomas to sell
him to the American people. The charges of the convention
had to be somehow dealt with. If they only knew. Hard-headed,
these descendants of indentured servants and criminals. 30,000
felons, I understand, were sent to Georgia alone. Bloody para-
doxical place, that country. The J.G.C.s shipped there to harvest
cotton and rice surrounded by the descendants of 2-bit hoods,
loan sharks, and Atonists of the most fundamental variety. Os-
tensibly pragmatic, the place's characteristic fiction is "dark ro-
mance."

Center of industrialism but at the same time the home of the Fox sisters, the founders of Spiritualism . . . well anyway Harding is just a Mason so you may use him as you wish; there is another man, the 1st entry in the book under M, who you may call upon in an emergency but be careful he isn't revealed because he is the most sensible contact we have.

I don't think that I will be needing any additional help. I will use my old friend Hubert "Safecracker" Gould . . .

"The only man of his generation who didn't go to jail?"

Yes, I need him at my side for this . . . this Crusade.

I think it's going to work out fine, Hinckle. Perhaps if we had called upon you earlier we could have regained the Holy Land before 1917. We will destroy the Knights Templar' trial records, the 36 feet of long scrolls decorated with those strange symbols your Order was so fond of. They will be burned tonight at the Vatican . . . And Hinckle, . . . Hinckle if your Order is successful we will put you in charge of the next Crusade, World War 2 a bigger extravaganza than 1. Beyond the dreams of Lubitsch and De Mille, which is being choreographed at this very moment.

Hinckle's eyes shine . . .

What are you going to call the magazine, Hinckle?

The *Benign Monster*. Give it the Freudian angle.

Hinckle carrying the little black book and his orders begins to leave the room for the transportation that will convey him to this mysterious country's harbor where awaits the World War 1 submarine he will use for his journey to the Templars' private, secluded estate on Long Island.

I have 1 more request, Hierophant 1.

Yes Hinckle, anything, anything. You name it.

Summon your men, I wish to say our old Templars' chant.

Not here Hinckle, before my men; they won't understand after all the vilification they've heard against your Order.

SUMMON YOUR MEN!!!

Hierophant 1 presses the buttons and here they come. Marching. Hut Hut Hut Hut Hut. Hut. Hut. Hut Hut Hut. Soon the men are all gathered about the famous horseshoe-like desk where the Hierophant stands. They raise their mugs and begin to shout Beascauh after the name of the Templars' 1st piebald horse.

19   A talented grave-robber and 2nd-story man, Hinckle Von Vampton arrives for his assignment 1 moonlit night in an old rusty World War 1 surplus submarine, part of an arsenal the Wallflower Order keeps on hand in case its underlings kick up; mostly presidents the likes of the twangy New Englander Calvin Coolidge, kings with brain disease, 44-year-old Eagle Scouts with set jaws, maharajahs who have heart attacks while playing polo, unemployed actors who married the brain surgeon's daughter, African presidents who are out of the country a great deal. So as Fats Waller once remarked, "One never knows, do one."

On the shore his new household awaits him as the craft surfaces from a large pool of oil slick. It resembles a posh ad for whiskey. A few of the maids, their black skirts and white aprons and their hair blowing in the breeze, hold cocktails on trays. Hinckle Von Vampton arises from the sub and is rowed onto the beach. He steps out of the boat. He inspects the cooks, chauffeurs and the maids and the gardeners and grooms.

●   ○

That night he dines with his staff at the head of a long table beneath a ceiling which has a mural commemorating the ceremony of the Knights Templar' immunity from excommunication (the Hierophant had it painted as a surprise). Hinckle lays down the rules of the house.

●   ○

The next morning Hinckle Von Vampton calls his old comrade-in-arms Hubert "Safecracker" Gould, 1-time carpetbagger, now "radical education expert" who lives in a penthouse high above the streets of New York purchased from the proceeds he has received from the scribblings of little colored waifs and the income from a downtown cabaret on East 3rd Street—a sweatshop for Black musicians—of which he is silent partner.

Hubert?

Yes, who is it? The voice at the other end belongs to Hubert "Safecracker" Gould, standing holding his cigarette holder between his fingers.

O Hinckle, hi sport, I am told you successfully carried through the plan to embarrass the Wallflower Order. I saw the headline. Calls came in from our little band distributed all over the world.

That's not all . . . I was interviewed by the Wallflower Order and we made a deal. We're exonerated. The Order. They burned the evidence from the trial and we're in charge of the epidemic.

How were you able to swing that?

Let me explain that later. I used the headline and the Book.

That worked?

Yes, of course it did.

If there's a deal what are we to do?

They gave us a staff. Their North American contacts have been buzzed that the power has passed from the Teutonics to us again. Listen, here is the plan . . .

20 Guess who's outside the reporter cries excitedly, rushing into the city room of the Atonist sheet the New York *Sun*. Hinckle Von Vampton, dressed like a banker or tycoon with a chauffeur outside. All the brass is down there . . . and they're coming this way . . .

Does the old man know?

No, he . . .

The 2 reporters resume their seats and return to clattering away at their typewriters as the managing editor returns from his 2-minute coffee break. A little less gabbin' and a little more tabbin', you guys, he says.

The door leading to the city room opens and the party starts through on their way to the executive offices of the New York *Sun*. Well when the managing editor sees Hinckle Von Vampton he nearly drops dead.

You! But before he can say anything the editor-in-chief and the chairman of the board of the *Sun* begin to pass by his desk.

Of course, you know the managing editor, don't you, the executive pauses, turning to Hinckle.

O yes of course I do, Mr. Elm. Please put him on the agenda of topics we will be discussing over sherry and cake upstairs.

The editor-in-chief extends his hand to Hinckle's elbow, leading him through the city room and out. The managing editor sits down. He makes a gesture associated with the comic Leon Errol, gradually rubbing his open palm down over his red face. The reporters exchange grins.

That night the managing editor resigns. Apparently the decision occurred in a meeting at the top which Hinckle Von Vampton had held to "get acquainted" with his contacts.

21   Dypsomaniacs, those who take it from behind by german shepherds, those delighted by pin pricks at the bottom of the feet, whippersnappers, vibrators, Free Love advocates, ex-I.W.W. intellectuals, an art director who likes Aubrey Beardsley, a flagpole sitter whose record is 10 days, 10 hours, 10 minutes, and 10 seconds, people whose feet fall asleep, 3 or 4 inside dopes, and muckrakers of Tammany Hall. The staff of the *Benign Monster*.

The cover is splendid. Some kind of head in the mush. No . . . A Fat Lady atop a Whooping Crane . . . No . . . A Cow? It's very hard to make out the cover. It's in the avant-garde style. Adolf Hitler has an article on the future of Germany. He's the young lad who killed 14 at a Protestant Bible Study camp. His tousle-haired lawyer was seeking to free him by appealing to German Psychology. Wotanian seizure is the diagnosis underneath this "Christlike" looking young man. A nude flapper 1 page, deathwhite skin with black circles around her eyes. Another page carries a picture of a lynching. Bulging eyes. Entrails. Delighted sheriffs licking chocolate-covered ice cream sticks. There is a hot story about a woman who used to go down to meet the trains. "The Drawers of Wa-Wa." They expect this feature to get the magazine across.

The phone rings. Hinckle Von Vampton and Hubert "Safecracker" rush into the office. Hinckle Von Vampton picks up the phone and the fixed tight-lipped expression on his face widens into a grin.

We've been banned in Boston! We've made it. (As a journalist in the 1932 movie *Doctor X* said, "Sensationalism? Why the sons of guns love it.")

While the staff celebrate, Hinckle Von Vampton contemplates his next move. He glances at the poll he devised as a feature for the newspaper. The Jazz Poll. Bix Beiderbeck wins the Trumpet category. Paul Whiteman the Big Band. Something is missing. Something colored. It will take time to get the Talking Android. In the meantime they need a Negro Viewpoint.

22 Across town the city room of the New York *Tribune* is in stitches. The reporters, rewrite men and managing editor are on the floor convulsed with laughter. Woodrow Wilson Jefferson stands in the middle of the room barefoot, his bags dropping chicken feathers, his cuffs the length of what are called "high waters." He is bewildered at the response he is receiving.

The cherubic-faced balding man sitting at the desk prods Jefferson. Tell us again who you want to meet?

Why . . . why Karl Marx and Friedrich Engels.

Another round of laughter. But when the editor-in-chief walks into the room they stop.

What's going on here? Don't you know we got an edition to get out. You. C'mere.

Jefferson points to himself.

Yeah, you. C'mere.

Jefferson walks up to the man.

Now, what's on your mind, Mac?

I want to meet Karl Marx and Friedrich Engels.

Well they don't work here no more, they were promoted. Now get outta here.

The city room breaks up. Woodrow Wilson Jefferson slowly walks out, undaunted. He is an ambitious man. If he wasn't going to find these men here, he was going to return to the room he rents above Frimbo's Funeral Home and look them up in the phone book. He is walking down University Street in Greenwich Village when he comes upon the sign in the window.

NEGRO VIEWPOINT WANTED

As soon as Woodrow Wilson enters the office of the *Benign Monster* holding the sign, Hinckle Von Vampton starts licking his chops.

Yes young man, what can I do for you?

I came about the Negro Viewpoint job.

Yes, what is your experience?

I have read all the 487 articles written by Karl Marx and Friedrich Engels and know them by heart.

The perfect candidate, Hinckle Von Vanpton decides. *He doesn't mind the shape of the idol: sexuality, economics, whatever, as long as it is limited to 1.*

You're hired.

But don't you want to hear about my contributions to the County Seed packages, my descriptions of the bulbs and the germs?

That's enough. You've convinced me.

Hinckle Von Vampton informs Woodrow Wilson Jefferson of his salary and the other terms of the position as Negro Viewpoint.

We've an office for you in the rear of Spiraling Agony, my estate, and you will also be required to perform certain chores in addition to your responsibility as a columnist. We are doubling-up due to our very limited resources.

Well what will my double-up be? Woodrow Wilson asks, overjoyed at having found a job the 2nd day in New York.

Ask the cook when you reach Spiraling Agony.

Hinckle Von Vampton summons 1 of his drivers to take Woodrow Wilson to a rented room above Frimbo's Funeral Home in Harlem to gather his things and then go on to Long Island.

1 thing, Mr. Von Vampton?

Yes, what is that Woodrow?

Can you introduce me to Karl Marx and Friedrich Engels?

. . . Hinckle thinks *he would have to really mold this 1 but it would give him good practice for when he discovered the Android.* Come into my office just 1 moment, Woodrow. I'll explain.

S.R.: IN HAITI IT WAS PAPA LOA, IN NEW ORLEANS IT
WAS PAPA LABAS, IN CHICAGO IT WAS PAPA JOE. THE
LOCATION MAY SHIFT BUT THE FUNCTION REMAINS THE
SAME. CREOLE BANDS CONCEAL JES GREW FROM
CHICAGO'S PSYCHIC DEPARTMENT OF PUBLIC HEALTH.
ERZULIE WITH HER FAST SELF IS SHELTERED IN A
"VOCALISING" TRUMPET WHICH SINGS FROM MUTE TO
GROWL. LEGBA TAKES REQUESTS FROM BEHIND THE
DERBY-COVERED BELL OF A "TALKING" SLIDE-TROMBONE.
(He is a loa who has always worked for his keep.—
I.R.)

A few months later Hinckle Von Vampton has familiarized
himself with Afro-American literature of the 20s. He has written
the 14 people who are sending the book about in a chain. None

has answered however. The mails are terribly slow. Often it seems that the U.S. government service national state and local is in a state of collapse. (In Boston there is a police strike.) But as soon as he received the book he would burn it. And if that didn't dissolve it the Talking Android would certainly remove its steam.

He has already interviewed 3 candidates for the position of Talking Android, the 2nd phase of the plan to stamp out Jes Grew. They had declined; explaining that as potential victims they did not feel that they would be immune to its drawing power. Well, there are 3 months left; surely someone will turn up. Hinckle's disguise in Manhattan circles is that of Negrophile, patron-of-the-arts and of course controversial publisher of the *Benign Monster* magazine. He has attended many parties and come in contact with the poets, novelists, even being invited to a reception at Irvington-on-Hudson, and finding the Hostess "charming" and "vivacious." The circulation of the magazine has soared since the article or story about Wa-Wa who went down to the railroad station and was handled by all of those conductors.

Tonight, he sits in his dressing gown, picking at a snack of tiny non-poisonous snakes, crocodile eggs and Nile crabs, provided for him by W. W. Jefferson's other duty. As he sits enjoying this meal, he thinks about his next plans in recruitment.

Don't know what to do with W.W. If he wasn't so good at gathering these er . . . er . . . delicacies. What's this? mmmmmmm-mmmmmmmmmmmmmm-MMM! Weeds gathered at the grave site of a recently dead infant? Why I haven't savored this since . . . well since those parties we used to have many many years ago in our private guarded Chapter House . . . W.W. would be all right if he'd just avoid those Marxist-Engelian and sociological clichés. Economics, integration, separation . . . capitalism. No one took this seriously. Why, this Soviet business would blow over. Each day the New York Times experts were predicting that the monarchy would be returned to power and when this happened then his magazine would seem out of step with the times which was ½ of its appeal—being-in. His column only did 1 thing . . . confuse the state of Black letters which was good because then they would be isolated and he could be like the wolf approaching the sheep who wanders away from the variegated herd. Yes indeed W.W.'s column which pitted 1 writer against the other called "The Pat Juber" . . . saying each new writer made the former resemble . . . how had W.W. put it, "resemble interlocutor in a minstrel show?" This column had its good points, but W.W. didn't seem to have that razzle-dazzle. That jargon he used bored people . . . A . . . here comes the dope now.

Hinckle Von Vampton is content. He daubs his 2 faint pink lines where lips should be.

I don't know what I would do without you, W.W., he says between jawfuls to W.W. who is refilling Von Vampton's cup of tea. Where were you able to find these morsels which so intrigue my palate?

I'm glad you like them, Mr. Von Vampton. When you told me you had the junkie tongue for these types of food I sought them out. It turned out that they were near me all the time. You see when you told me that Mr. Marx and Mr. Engels were dead it was such a blow to me I went to this potter's field out in the country to meditate. There was a swamp near by the tombstones and there I found many crawling things.

Well, they are indeed delicious, W.W., and I must advise you that many people like your column "The Pat Juber." It really stirs things up. But there's 1 thing though, W.W.

What is that, Publisher Von Vampton? W.W. says, standing before Hinckle's desk.

You know our readership isn't as bright as you are. The books you read and all of those articles. You quote Kant, James and Hegel very well but don't you think that you ought to liven it up a bit with some of that raggle-taggle. A little ingredient of scandal . . .

The next issue, Mr. Von Vampton, there will indeed be some spice. I am going to get some of these niggers who are writing these nasty plays like Wallace Thurman. He wrote some play called *Harlem* in which these bonzos be rubbing up against each other.

Why would you object to that, W.W.? Why any month we might run a picture of a nice boyish young disrobed thing. We've been banned in Boston for pornography. Why would you want to include your material in our magazine but then abhor the same freedom when it occurs among your playwrights.

Look, Mr. Von Vampton. It comes down to this. If I have to be contradictory using the real 1 time and ideal the other then that's the way I would be. I will use any vehicle at all so that I won't have to return to that farm and spend the rest of my life milking cows and distributing feed.

Excellent, W.W., excellent. I never thought of it that way . . . of course I should have known.

I have some more articles to write for the forthcoming issue, Mr. Von Vampton, I will retire to my office in the rear.

Most impressive, Hinckle thinks. *Perhaps . . . no that was out of the question . . . W.W. was too dark. This was the 1920s, black is out, colored is in. Besides Jes Grew absorbs Black as Black does Jes Grew. Others must try harder. But this was a marvelous thing he had just witnessed. A Black Pragmatist. Perhaps soon the slave-master will learn that he doesn't have to use his offspring mulatto children to curb and refine Jes Grew activity. He can use White talking out of Black instead of the Brown or White talking out of Black. No 1 will be wise. A new kind of robot. The mulattoes were always held in suspicion by the Blacks anyway, but a Black Prag-matist could be anything he chose to be. Why that was freedom, wasn't it?*

W.W., before you leave, I have been reading Abdul Sufi Hamid. I can't decipher some of the dialect and the esoteric references. What is your assessment of him?

O he writes stirring poems. Apocalypse. Moors triumphant, riding elephants as they conquer southern Europe. Black women whom he equates with the Queen of Sheba! He is really a dynamo, Publisher Hinckle Von Vampton.

What do you think he is saying, Woodrow? Hinckle moves the tray to the center of his long desk topped with a gas lamp.

He's telling them niggers that they will never be ready and that nothing will come of them and that if they take a drink from time to time it will enervate their brains and every time they go to bed with a woman that the corners of the room will fill with nests of Gog and Magog.

Excellent, now I understand those lines of his very well. What's his views on the plague?

He says it involves too much dancing and should be stamped out, with force if necessary.

Good. Good. I will give him an entire page in the next issue. Accompanying photo. The works. Maybe some flappers kicking up their legs beside his scowl. *Maybe even the Talking Android!*

He's a little off though, Publisher Hinckle Von Vampton.

Look W.W., will you cut out that Publisher Von Vampton nonsense. You're up North now. Call me Hink. Now what's this about him being mad?

He's going about telling everyone that he is compiling some sort of anthology that will upset the nation. Some strange text he's assembled about this Jes Grew thing. He said it would be the anthology of the century.

Hinckle Von Vampton staggers to his feet, the patch nearly slipping from the black hollow where his left eye used to be. The eye had been dislodged when the ancient foe drove a lance through it.

He what?

He says he has this anthology the nigger says has hieroglyphics and strange drawings written all over it. He says only 14 other people have seen it and that some crazy White man has paid them monthly checks to keep sending the anthology around. For some strange reason 1 of the 14 gave the anthology to Abdul.

Hinckle Von Vampton rises, drags himself to the fireplace and leans against the wall above it. He is wheezing, gasping for breath. His respiratory system feels jammed with something so thick that had it been a plumbing system all of the Drāno in the world couldn't relieve its burden.

Is there anything wrong, Hink?

These old war pains, W.W. I get them from time to time. Old war wounds.

O I didn't know that you fought in the last war, sir.

I didn't. I received them in another, loftier crusade.

What war was that, Hink, the Spanish-American War?

I . . . I . . . How do you think that this Harding election will affect the Negroes, W.W.? Hinckle says in at attempt to change the subject.

Why . . . it's funny that you should mention it, sir, they all call
him the Race President.

What?

He was at a Rent Party I hear and was dipping his fork into the
chitterlings and drinking liquor along with everybody else. Why
that man is copacetic with me, Publisher Hink.

Hink?

Hinckle Von Vampton, sir?

Publisher Hinckle Von Vampton?

W.W. runs from the room to obtain aid for his employer who is
stretched out on the floor, cold.

23   The *Mu'tafikah* are holding a meeting in the basement of
a 3-story building located at the edge of "Chinatown." Upstairs is
a store which deals in religious articles. Above this is a gun store;
at the top, an advertising firm which deals in soap accounts. If
Western History were a 3-story building located in downtown
Manhattan during the 1920s it would resemble this little archi-
tectural number.

3 men, under an almost maroon red light, kneel on the basement's concrete floor. Berbelang and Thor's raincoats hang from a
coat rack near the door. Propped against the wall are their dripping,
black umbrellas. Some of the women *Mu'tafikah* in Garbo hats
and speaking in brittle unadorned voices are standing around a
long wooden table in the rear of the basement. Under a soft lamp
they are coolly planning excursions into the Cloisters the Frick and
the Met.

On the table lies a Nimba mask made of Guinea wood they've
seized from a private collection belonging to a society woman on
Park Ave. Other *Mu'tafikah* are carefully packing items. They are
to be sent to a contact "Frank" somewhere in the Pacific Islands
who will in turn ship them to their rightful owners in Asia. "Tam"
a Nigerian musician and writer will return 5,000 masks and wood
sculpture to Africa. He had begun by lifting a Benin bronze
plaque with leopard from the Linden-Museum in Stuttgart, Germany. Before museum heads could warn their continental col-

leagues of his presence in Europe, he and his aides, posing as innocuous exchange students, had repatriated masks and figures —carried to Europe as booty from Nigeria, Gold Coast, Upper Volta and the Ivory Coast—from where they were exhibited in the pirate dens called museums located in Zurich, Florence, England and in a private collection in Milan. The Tristan Tzara collection, Paris; the Rietberg Museum, Zurich; Berlin's Museum für Völkerkunde; Budapest's Néprajzi; the Náprstkovo Museum, Prague; the Rijksmuseum voor Volkenkunde, Leiden—none are spared invasions into their "primitive" collections by these cool soft-spoken, colorfully dressed Africans. Moving swiftly about Europe with the aid of sympathetic White students and intellectuals (yet unaffected by 1 of America's deadlier and more ravaging germs: racism), they reap a harvest of their countrymen's stolen work. (Their task is in many ways easier; for example, they don't have to lift heavy sculpture or canvases. Some pieces are only a few inches.) The Jean-Pierre Hallet Collection of Kongolese sculpture is picked clean.

So effective is Tam that respectable, opulent chiselers must protect collections, locked up in their villas, with round-the-clock guards. Another man, a South African trumpeter, "Hugh," is in L.A. transmitting Black American sounds on home. He realizes that the essential Pan-Africanism is artists relating across continents their craft, drumbeats from the aeons, sounds that are still with us.

Seneca masks are lying on another table. A delegation from the Cayuga and Onondaga Grand River Reservations in Canada are arriving shortly to return these to their tribes.

In another corner, some other Mu'tafikah are planning to invade the forthcoming Pre-Cortesian exhibit to be held at a leading museum. They want the Pulque Beaker, the Plumed Serpent with the controversial human face, some terra-cotta water spirits and mosaic knife handles. They repeat the names of the items aloud, the sound resembling subdued chanting. Berbelang always requests that the items to be liberated be committed to memory. In this way not a single item will be left behind. This group is also dealing with a momentous engineering feat—that of removing the 4½ ton Olmec head. They must think of a way to deliver it to Central America.

Berbelang, Yellow Jack and Thor Wintergreen are awaiting the arrival of another member of their team, José Fuentes. Soon there is a knock at the door. They hear Fuentes give the password.

Fuentes enters, shaking the rain from his seaman's cap. He brings in a package that's 6 feet 8 inches high, 2 feet 1 inch across.

What is it, Fuentes? Berbelang asks as the other teams look up from their work and toward Fuentes who, after hanging his raincoat on the rack, begins to open the package.

"The Hermit of a Chasm of the Forest" done delicately on rice paper. I relieved it from the Philadelphia Museum where it was on loan from the Cologne Museum of Far Eastern Art. I walked right past the guard.

Berbelang, Yellow Jack, Thor and Fuentes begin to examine the map of the Center of Art Detention that's spread out on the floor. They pass a drinking vessel shaped like an Inca warrior's head and filled with good old California vermouth; it'd been given by South American *Mu'tafikah* to the North American branch in recognition of their work and devotion to the cause.

Berbelang moves the pointer to the North Wing of the Center of Art Detention.

Here we pick up lapis lazuli, turquoise, carmelian, the blue fäience hippopotamus, and some jewelry. 2 teams will relay scarabs, gold sandals, headdresses, brooches, pendants, and don't forget the bronze coffin and the mummified cat.

"Sabu say, 'Those who defile the tombs of Egypt must die.'"

Berbelang quickly glances at Fuentes, the source of the remark, a wide grin on his Mayan face.

Quit clowning, Fuentes. There are only a few weeks before our performance and we must have everything perfect. This is our most ambitious haul.

Berbelang moves the pointer to the Center of Art Detention's North Wing corner.

Here you will find a set of alabaster canopic jars belonging to a Princess Sithathroyunet. That ends the small stuff. We will need some big men to take out the tombs of Peryneb, a Lord Chamberlain of the 5th Dynasty, and his wife Mitry, and some other heavy items belonging to Meketre, a noble of the 11th Dynasty. We must also retrieve the diorite sphinx statue of King Senwosret 3 from the 12th Dynasty and a sphinx of Queen Hatshepsut. The most important item will be handled by the 3 of us, a pottery vessel decorated with antelopes.

Berbelang moves the pointer down the hall to another room. Here is the Peruvian collection where you will lift many items of Mochica art from the North Coast and on the other side Paracas from the South.

How do you plan to gain entrance to the museum, Berbelang? Thor asks.

That will keep until later, Thor!

We wouldn't tell you anyway, gringo. You just joined the group and how do we know that you won't tell. Your father is on the board of several museums, you might squeal on us, Fuentes threatens the white boy.

Knock it off, fellas. We have to get this done, time is running out!

Berbelang moves the pointer farther down the Center of Art Detention's hall.

Here is the ancient Near East stuff. A number of strong men will have to get those 2 glazed brick lions.

They ain't doing Nebuchadnezzar no good.

Berbelang, Thor and Yellow Jack smile at Fuente's remark.

Be sure to get the pottery ceramics, the painted antelopes, and a small gypsum statue from the Tell Asmar square temple here. Now Yellow Jack will take over.

The man with the mandarin mustache takes the pointer.

Here are the Chinese, Korean and Japanese galleries. The principal items are the seated Buddha and the scroll paintings. They've 30,000 items. I have been going up there for 3 weeks and on the night of the heist I will have a list of the most important smaller items.

Berbelang picks up the pointer again.

Lastly, we come to the Islamic Art collection. It's a long gallery adjoining the Chinese sculpture hall. We take the incense burners and a small casket dated the 12th century which you will recognize by the drawings of mythological animals. What we especially want is the page of a manuscript dated 1600: *The Concourse of the Birds*.

The real *Concourse of the Birds* is there? Thor remarks, surprise showing in his blue eyes.

Yeah, gringo. The real 1 your swine Robber Baron of a father and his fellow Copper King rats lifted as they sailed the world on their pirate ships.

Obviously stunned, the White boy's face flushes.

A slight smile appears on Yellow Jack's face.

Look, if you don't trust me now, you never will, Fuentes. I've tried to prove myself. Make sacrifices.

Sacrifices, huh? Liar like Cortez, Pizarro, Balboa and the rest of your "virile" Conquistadors who raped our motherlands.

But what have Cortes and Pizarro or the others to do with me?

You carry them in your blood as I carry the blood of Montezuma; expeditions of them are harbored by your heart and your mind carries their supply trains. You've changed your helmet for a frontier hat while I have changed my robes for overalls and a black leather jacket. The costumes may have changed but the blood is still the same, gringo. If it wasn't for Berbelang you wouldn't be here.

Leave him alone, Fuentes. He's done his work well since he's been here. He's the only 1 among us who's able to enter a museum without arousing suspicion, says Berbelang.

You know, sometimes I think that an African friend of mine was right, Berbelang.

Right about what, Yellow Jack? Berbelang asks, now fixing a stare on him, his brows coming together.

Well the White man came into China, exploited our lands, raped our women, plundered our art but then came the Boxer Rebellion and we fought back. They went into South America but then came Bolivar who struck a blow for Indian autonomy. But they've done everything to you: raped your women castrated you burned your homes massacred you and yet . . .

And yet what? Berbelang asks as the people around the other tables begin to take notice of the argument.

Look, let's go on with the plan, Thor says.

Shut up gringo, Fuentes says, moving in Thor's direction.

Finish it, Yellow Jack. And yet what? Berbelang insists.

You just don't seem to be militant like Marcus Garvey and Abdul Hamid and some of the others from the West Indies . . . I mean this African said that the reason you North American Blacks were docile was that the strong ones were left behind in South America . . .

Why you! Berbelang springs toward Yellow Jack and grabs him by the collar. Yellow Jack grins.

Forget it, Berbelang says, returning to the pointer. Let's continue with this. We'll argue later . . . We finish the Islamic collection by lifting the Mihrab and a fäience mosaic.

Berbelang rises.

Yellow Jack, wearing his black silk jacket with the velvet buttons reaching to the top of his neck and matching black pants, has put on his flat black hat. He walks over to Berbelang who is standing in the corner.

Look, Berbelang, I know about Posser Turner and Walker, I was just trying to get your goat. It's him, Berbelang, Yellow Jack says, pointing to Thor who looks down to his feet knowing that he is being discussed. They can't be trusted. You know.

Give him a chance, Yellow Jack; at least we are talking to 1. A great deal of our success depends upon at least a few like him. You remember in that Art History class at City College. The pact that we made that day . . . that we would return the plundered art to Africa, South America and China, the ritual accessories

which had been stolen so that we could see the gods return and
the spirits aroused. How we wanted to conjure a spiritual hur-
ricane which would lift the debris of 2,000 years from its roots
and fling it about. Well, we are succeeding with these raids into
the museums, for what good is someone's amulet or pendant if it's
in a Western museum. But ultimately we need to recruit him or this
will mean nothing.

Well, it's your 3 months to lead but as soon as my turn comes
up, out he goes, Yellow Jack said. You know in China we used to
call them devils.

You used to call us devils too.

Yellow Jack is surprised by this remark.

Berbelang smiles at him, walks over to the Pre-Cortesian table
where the invasion of the museum is being planned.

Figured out how to get the Olmec head yet?

The man responds in the negative.

Keep trying.

Berbelang lights a Chesterfield, wrings his right hand until the
match is out and puts his raincoat on. He leaves the basement.
He wants to call his former colleague Charlotte and request a
favor.

Berbelang?

Someone is calling. Berbelang turns around and sees Thor following, his unkempt blond hair blowing. He seems a bit tanner than Berbelang had remembered him. Perhaps it was the recent trip around the Gulf of Mexico on his father's yacht.

Look, Berbelang, if I am going to cause trouble maybe I'd better leave, he says walking alongside Berbelang.

O so it's getting a little rough for you? Not like that cushy job on that radio station. How many did you have? 500 subscribers? The elite of the city but O yes, committed. Went up to Harlem once in a while to see what the new steps were. "Frolicing among the darkies," as slavemasters used to say. After all, European artists are flocking to it, Stravinsky writing Ragtime pieces . . . Picasso painting like an African. Theodore Dreiser stealing one of Paul Lawrence Dunbar's plots.

Look, I was sincere when I volunteered for this, B. I wasn't just another 1. Up there slumming. I just don't think that I am of much help . . . if it's going to cause this much dissension. I mean Yellow Jack and Fuentes. I feel out of place, the remarks about my father. I'm not my father, can't they understand?

Look, Yellow Jack's father himself is a rich silk importer and Fuentes' has a degree in medicine. It's when we met at the University at the Art History class that we decided to do this. We vowed. We began to see that the Art instructor was speaking as if he didn't know we were in the room. We felt as if we were in church, stupid dull sculpture being blown up to be religious objects. Have you ever seen people line up outside a Van Gogh exhibit? When they get inside there are so many they can't even see the paintings, they just pass by like sheep or like mourners passing the tomb of a fallen hero, a bier, with the same solemnity. And the extent of their knowledge concerning Van Gogh is that he "cut off his ear." Man, it's religion they make it into. We decided that we would be their desecraters, that we would send their loot back to where it was stolen and await the rise of Shango, Shiva, and Quetzalcoatl, no longer a label on a cheap bottle of wine but strutting across the sacred cities near the mysterious lakes of huge snakes like a cock. A proud cock.

I agree with all you say . . .

No you don't, Berbelang says, turning to him as they reach the corner. Come on in here and have a cup of coffee.

They enter a diner near Houston Street. Sam's Eats. They sit down. A beefy man, tattoos spelling M.O.M. on his arms, stubbled face and in a dirty apron, walks over to the table. He giver Berbelang an evil stare.

Whatta yooz want? he asks in the voice of a 33 rpm record player at 16 speed.

2 coffees, Berbelang says. The man spits the toothpick out of the side of his mouth.

How familiar are you with the Faust legend?

O as familiar as most . . . he sold his soul to the devil.

Yes that's true enough, he sold his soul to the devil for pleasure, prestige and position. Did you ever think about it?

No, I never gave it much thought. About as much as any intelligent person. The waiter walks over to the table. He slams down the coffee. Some of it spills.

That will be 3 cents.

Berbelang glances at Thor. He knows that the coffee should be 1 cent a cup. Berbelang removes a nickel from his pocket and calmly places it on the table. The waiter picks it up, examines it and then walks away from the table.

. . . Faust was an actual person. Somewhere between 1510 and 1540 this "wandering conjurer and medical quack" made his travels about the southwest German Empire, telling people his knowledge of "secret things." I always puzzled over why such a legend was so basic to the Western mind; but I've thought about it and now I think I know the answer. Can't you imagine this man traveling about with his bad herbs, love philters, physicks and potions, charms, overcharging the peasants but dazzling them with his badly constructed Greek and sometimes labeling his "wonder cures" with gibberish titles like "Polyunsaturated 99½% pure." Hocus-pocus. He makes a living and can always get a free night's lodging at an inn with his ability to prescribe cures and tell fortunes, that is, predict the future. You see he travels about the Empire and is able to serve as a kind of national radio for people in the locales. Well 1 day while he is leeching people, cutting hair or raising the dead who only have diseases which give the manifestations of death, something really works. He knows that he's a *bokor* adept at card tricks, but something really works. He tries it again and it works. He continues to repeat this performance and each time it works. The peasants' begin to look upon him as a supernatural being and he encourages the tales about him, that he heals the sick and performs marvels. He becomes wealthy with his ability to do The Work. Royalty visits him. He is a counselor to the king. He lives in a castle. Peasants whisper, a Black man, a very bearded devil himself visits him. That strange coach they saw, the 1 with the eyes as decorations drawn to his castle by wild-looking black horses. They say that he has made a pact with the devil because he invites the Africans who work in various cities throughout the Empire to his castle. There were 1000s in Europe at the time: blackamoors who worked as butlers, coachmen, footmen, pint-sized page boys; and conjurors whom only the depraved consulted. The villagers hear "Arabian" music, drums coming from the place but as soon as the series of meetings begin it all comes to a halt. Rumors circulate that Faust is dead. The village whispers that the Black men have collected. That is the nagging notion of Western man. China had rocketry, Africa iron furnaces, but he didn't know when to stop with his newly found Work. That's the basic wound. He will create fancy systems 13 letters long to convince himself he doesn't have this wound. What is the wound? Someone will even call it guilt. But guilt implies a conscience. Is Faust capable of charity? No it isn't guilt but the knowledge in his heart that he is a *bokor*. A charlatan who has sent 1000000s to the churchyard with his charlatan panaceas. Western man doesn't know the difference between a *houngan* and a *bokor*. He once knew this difference but the knowledge was lost when the Atonists crushed the opposition. When they converted a Roman emperor and began rampaging and book-burning. His sorcery, white magic, his *bokorism* will improve. Soon he will be able to annihilate 1000000s by pushing a button. I do not believe that a Yellow or Black hand will push this button but a robot-like descendant of Faust the quack will. The dreaded *bokor*, a humbug who doesn't know when to stop. We must purge the *bokor* from you. We must teach you the difference between a healer, a holy man, and a duppy who returns from the grave and causes mischief. We must infuse you with the mysteries that Jes Grew implies.

Thor stirs his coffee. The waiter's huge veined eyes stare at them both contemptuously; above his head, on the wall behind the counter, is a naked woman with some filthy caption. He looks at the stale cakes in the case, the 3-week-old piece of pie, flies swarming about a puddle on the counter.

Why would you give me such responsibility? I'm just 1 man. Not Faust nor the Kaiser nor the Ku Klux Klan. I am an individual, not a whole tribe or nation.

That's what I'm counting on. But if there is such a thing as a racial soul, a piece of Faust the mountebank residing in a corner of the White man's mind, then we are doomed. It always seems that we talk to the many and then the few and then we are down to 1 man and just as the war between the races is about to begin that 1 man becomes a few and then the many until the next time around and we turn our back on 1 another before the whole procedure begins again. Perhaps 1 day it will be the many and stay there.

Berbelang rises from the counter under the scrutiny of the counterman's wet crocodile eye. The eye which peered above hot primal mud.

Where are you off to, Berbelang?

I have to get back to the basement. I have some more thinking and planning to do. Maybe in a few days I can get back home. I haven't seen Earline since the day before yesterday.

Berbelang leaves Thor sitting at the table; as he leaves, the counterman spits on the floor.

Thor hasn't seen Earline since the night of the Rent Party. He can't understand why Berbelang never permitted Earline in the *Mu'tafikah* plans. *Why did he wish to protect her?*

The counterman turns to Thor.

1 thing I can't understand is guys like you mixing with the likes of these niggers.

My father owns the chain.

What?

My father owns the restaurant chain. He's your employer.

The man's lips begin to twitch as rapidly as butterfly wings flutter. The wet toothpick drops to the floor.

There is silence as Thor watches Berbelang walk down the street toward the basement hideout. Long gliding strides as if he were wafting toward the basement door.

. . . The counterman walks over to the table. Cleans it off.

There's a little more coffee in the pot, sir, would you like some?
Thor deep in thought looks up.
O yes . . . Right, I'd like some more.

Nevertheless necromancy persisted, and on occasion . . . it
no longer lurked in dark corners and obscene hiding-holes
but flaunted its foul abomination unabashed in the courts
of the Palace and at noon before the eyes of the superstitious capital.

Montague Summers
The History of Witchcraft and Demonology

24 After meeting with top aides, Attorney General HARRY
M. Daugherty faces the newsreel cameras and microphones. He
reads recommendations in a bill to be sent to Kongress. A way of
allaying the Jes Grew crisis which threatens our National Security,
survival and just about everything else you can think of. He adopts
a plan based upon the ideas of Irene Castle, the woman who in 1915
inspired a generation of young women to cast aside their corsets
and petticoats. He delivers the Plague edict. Pelvis and Feets Kon-
trols.

> Do not wriggle the shoulders.
> Do not shake the hips.
> Do not twist the body.
> Do not flounce the elbows.
> Do not pump the arms.
> Do not hop—glide instead.
> Drop the Turkey Trot, the Grizzly Bear,
> the Bunny Hug, etc. These dances are ugly,
> ungraceful, and out of fashion.*

From the bedroom of the White House, where he sits sipping
whiskey, Warren Harding glares down at his Attorney General.
A mere Mason, he is helpless to prevent what is about to take
place. Raids on Washington Speaks go on until dawn. No DANCING!
signs of huge black letters and exclamation points are posted

---

* *Modern Dancing*—Mr. and Mrs. Vernon Castle.

throughout the city. Anybody caught Doing it! Doing it! Doing it! is a federal crime.

● ○

It has been a busy day for reporters following Jes Grew. The morning began with Dr. Lee De Forest, inventor of the 3-element vacuum tube which helped make big-time radio possible, collapsing before a crowded press room after he pleaded concerning his invention, now in the grips of Jes Grew.

> "What have you done to my child? You have sent him out on the street in rags of ragtime to collect money from all and sundry.
>
> "You have made him a laughing stock of intelligence, surely a stench in the nostrils of the gods of the ionosphere."*

25 It is 2:00 A.M. Rain has fallen and created many water puddles in the streets of Harlem. Moving on an invisible cord, H.V.V. climbs the steps, a spider swollen on snake venom, of the building where Abdul's office is located. All wormy and creepy-like, H. "Safecracker" Gould follows behind. The strange pair reach the top of the landing and are confronted with the glass door of Abdul's office. It has the name of his magazine on it. They knock. Abdul comes to the door; he is putting his magazine together.

What do you want?

I would like to talk to you, Mr. Abdul. I am the publisher of the magazine the *Benign Monster*.

Hey man, what was the idea of you putting my picture there last week without my permission. Those weren't my views and you know it. And I didn't like the lewd photos that accompanied the article.

O we were merely trying to give you a friendly overture, perhaps boost the circulation of your magazine. According to our ratings we've climbed to 10,000 circulation. We plan to double that

---

* *This Fabulous Century: 1920–1930*, Vol. 3—Time-Life Books.

within a short time. We thought we could run some of the anthology you have . . .

What anthology are you referring to? Abdul says, eying the pair suspiciously.

Why the 1 you have. Woodrow Wilson Jefferson said so . . .

O him. Well I don't have it . . .

What do you mean, you don't have it?

I mean just that the words were unprintable.

But the tune was irresistible . . .

I don't think so. I don't like the lyricism. That kind at least. No, I don't have it.

"Safecracker" whispers to Hinckle Von Vampton. Let me talk to him, I know the jargon.

Look man, let's us cop the anthology; we may lay something on you.

Who is the corny guy you brought with you? Abdul asks, raising his head from the desk where he had been assembling the mag. Look, I don't have it.

We can have you arrested. The building code. I saw 14 violations downstairs myself. We can close down the magazine and your office. We have friends downtown.

"Safecracker" Gould reveals a pistol.

Move over, let's look into that safe. No use reasoning with this hothead, H.

Gould points to a safe located behind Abdul.

Gould struggles with Abdul in an effort to reach the safe.

Hey man, what are you doing? Abdul swings Gould around but cries out in pain as the dagger pierces his back. After he falls to the floor mortally wounded, Hinckle Von Vampton removes the dagger from his back.

What's the procedure now, H.?

Open the safe.

"Safecracker" Gould puts his nimble fingers to work and soon the safe swings open.

Empty!!

Well it's not here.

Let's leave, Hubert S. Gould nervously remarks.

No wait, I have to cover my tracks. Take care of this, he says, pointing to Abdul's corpse.

● ○

The phone rings in Biff Musclewhite's office. Musclewhite talks after the person on the other end has identified himself and spoken.

O I thought you'd never call . . . I've been wanting to meet you but of course realizing you would be busy with phase 2 . . . A corpse you say to remove? Of course I will remove it at once, Grand Master. It will be done at once.

26   Tapping his obeah stick, PaPa LaBas climbs out of his Locomobile. He walks into Abdul Hamid's headquarters. His name appears on the glass door.

In the outer office is a desk, upon which lie magazines and newspapers including the newly published *Fire*. Its editor is Wallace Thurman; Langston Hughes and Zora Neale Hurston are associates. Countee Cullen, Langston Hughes and Gwendolyn Bennett have contributed poetry. Woodrow Wilson Jefferson has written a review in which he said that the magazine was pretty good but the contributors would have to go a long way to catch up because "their work didn't make you feel like you wanted to go out and pineapple a necktie store." The review has been clipped and filed.

Ornamenting the desk are amusing lampoons carved in wood, ivory, and cast in bronze by African sculptors. They depict Whites who went into Africa seeking skins, ivory, spices, feathers and furs. The subjects are represented giving bribes, drinking gin, leading manacled slaves, wearing curious, outlandish hats and holding umbrellas. Their chalk-faces appear silly, ridiculous. Outstanding in the collection is the figure of a monkey-like Portuguese explorer, carved by an Angolan. He is obviously juiced and is sitting on a barrel. What side-splitting, bellyaching, satirical ways these ancient craftsmen brought to their art! The African race had quite a sense of humor. In North America, under Christianity, many of them had been reduced to glumness, depression, surliness, cynicism, malice without artfulness, and their intellectuals, in America, only appreciated heavy, serious works. ('Tis the cause,

Desdemona.) They'd really fallen in love with tragedy. Their plays were about bitter, raging members of the "nuclear family," and their counterpart in art was exemplified by the contorted, grimacing, painful social-realist face. Somebody, head in hands, sitting on a stoop. "Lawd, I'z so re-gusted." Bert Williams had captured the Afro-American mask with Northrop Frye's inverted U lips. But the figures on the desk, these grotesque, laughable wooden ivory and bronze cartoons represent the genius of Afro satire. They had been removed to Europe by the slavers, traders and sailors who had taken gunpowder and uniforms to Africa. They did not realize that the joke was on them. After all, how could "primitive" people possess wit. LaBas could understand the certain North American Indian tribe reputed to have punished a man for lacking a sense of humor. For LaBas, anyone who couldn't titter a bit was not Afro but most likely a Christian connoting blood, death, and impaled emaciated Jew in excruciation. Nowhere is there an account or portrait of Christ laughing. Like the Marxists who secularized his doctrine, he is always stern, serious and as gloomy as a prison guard. Never does I see him laughing until tears appear in his eyes like the roly-poly squint-eyed Buddha guffawing with arms upraised, or certain African loas, Orishas.

LaBas believed that when this impostor, this burdensome archetype which afflicted the Afro-American soul, was lifted, a great sigh of relief would go up throughout the land as if the soul was like feet resting in mineral waters after miles of hiking through nails, pebbles, hot coals and prickly things. The young poet Nathan Brown, LaBas felt, was serious about his Black Christ, however absurd that may sound, for Christ is so unlike African loas and Orishas, in so many essential ways, that this alien becomes a dangerous intruder in the Afro-American mind, an unwelcome gatecrasher into Ifé, home of the spirits. Yes, Brown was serious, but the rest were hucksters who had invented this Black Christ, this fraud, simply in order to avoid an honest day's sweat.

Papa LaBas looks over the figures again. He grins widely. Also on the table lies a book, *Bronze Casting In Benin*. Abdul had announced to the Race press his intention to teach a course on African sculpture to the neighborhood children. He was a hard worker. Some said he could learn a language in a week. In his own land, the land from which his ancestors had been captured during

Africa's decline, Abdul would have been royalty. A prince. Here he was ridiculed and considered eccentric, even a dangerous character. No wonder he was so bitter. Who wouldn't be?

It was when PaPa LaBas walked into the room that he saw Abdul lying head down on his desk.

There is a letter on the desk. A pink rejection slip.

Dear Abdul:

We have read with interest the manuscript entitled "The Book of Tat," the sacred anthology. We have decided, however, things being what they are, that we cannot publish this book. It does have that certain panache, that picaresque characterization and zestful dialogue. I was also attracted to the strange almost mystical writing. But the market is overwrought with this kind of book. The "Negro Awakening" fad seems to have reached its peak and once more people are returning to serious writing, Mark Twain and Stephen Crane. A Negro editor here said it lacked "soul" and wasn't "Nation" enough. He suggested you read Claude McKay's If We Must Die *and perhaps pick up some pointers. Whatever, thanks for permitting us to take a peek. Later Daddy*

                                                        S.S.

PaPa LaBas notices a piece of paper in Abdul's fist. He removes it. "Epigram on American-Egyptian Cotton"

> Stringy lumpy; Bales dancing
> Beneath this center
> Lies the Bird.

PaPa LaBas picks up the phone and calls the police. Just as he hears the 1st ring on the other end a man bopadoped into the room. It is one of the local fences. LaBas places the phone in its receiver. The man is stunned when he sees Abdul's corpse.

Hey what's wrong with Abdul?

He's been murdered.

The fence's eyes pop.

Murdered? I was just talking to him this morning and he said he had some boxes he wanted me to look at. Said the boxes were covered with jade, emeralds, jeweled bugs, birds and snakes. That Abdul . . . strange dude. Who do you think did it?

I don't know, PaPa LaBas says, dialing the phone once again.

Well I guess the bulls are going to be here. I'd better leave.
The man exits.

It must have been something to do with the anthology. Disgruntled contributor or something, LaBas thinks.

The authorities answer.

Would you please send an ambulance to Abdul Sufi Hamid's office on 125th St. and Lenox Ave.

We've already sent an ambulance to that place, buddy, answers the voice on the other end.

Strange, LaBas thinks, *perhaps someone has already discovered the corpse and phoned.* In fact he could hear the attendants carrying stretchers climbing the steps.

Monotonously, PaPa LaBas answers some routine questions. His mind is on other things.

Harlem! . . . The City that Never Sleeps! . . . A Strange, Exotic Island in the Heart of New York! . . . Rent Parties! . . . Number Runners! . . . Chippies! . . . Jazz Love! . . . Primitive Passion!

a handbill for the play Harlem *by Wallace Thurman*

---

27 Hinckle Von Vampton reads of PaPa LaBas' grim discovery on the front page of the New York *Sun:*

HATE MONGERER MEETS
WELL-DESERVED END
HINT WAR BETWEEN BLACK FACTIONS
NO SUSPECTS IN MURDER OF CULTIST
MU'TAFIKAH QUESTIONED

Later Hinckle Von Vampton's car pulls to the front of Buddy Jackson's cabaret. It is 1 of the more famous 1s in New York City along with Percy Brown's Gold Grabbers, Edmund's, Leroy's and Connie's. The basement is an Indonesian soul food restaurant featuring such exotic numbers as:

CHICKEN IN COCONUT MILK
BAR-BE-CUED FISH
BREGEDEL DJAGUNG
FRIED PINEAPPLE.

On the 2nd floor is a theater where all the young Black actors come to recite Shakespeare, dreaming of becoming a 2nd Ira Aldridge, the famed Negro thespian.

W.W., Hubert "Safecracker" Gould and Von Vampton alight from the car and head toward the entrance of the cabaret where the review is in progress. The mulatto doorman halts their progress.

What's wrong? queries Hinckle Von Vampton.

That man, sir, he's a mite too dark.

Too dark? an astonished Hinckle Von Vampton replies, but isn't this Harlem where the darkies cavort?

They cavorts, sir, but on stage; we cater to Brown Yellow and White.

That's ridiculous, Hubert "Safecracker" Gould remarks. I've seen Buddy Jackson in this place and he is as black as anthracite as black as ebony as black as the abyss, an Ethiopian if there ever was.

That's different, sir.

What do you mean different? Hinckle Von Vampton asks.

He's the owner.

I see, Hinckle Von Vampton says, turning to W.W. You will have to wait outside in the car. Here is 3 cents, go and buy yourself an August Ham.

An August Ham, Hink? What's that?

Dammit, W.W.! An August Ham is watermelon. Don't you know your own people's argot? Get with it, Jackson, maybe it will enliven your articles a bit. You still haven't made a transition from that Marxist rhetoric to the Jazz prose we want.

Once inside Hinckle Von Vampton pornographic publisher begins to relax, drink champagne and savor the high-yellow chorus as they go through some dandy routines. They end their review with the internationally famous Cakewalk which already the French are calling "poetry-in-motion."

There is a hubbub at the door. A party of people, Brown, Yellow and White enter. They are directing their attention at a Brown man in the middle of all of this. Vampton recognizes him as Major Young, a young man who is gaining a wide audience. The interracial revelers are having a good time. Langston Hughes, writing of this period, said: "We liked people of any race who smoked incessantly, drank liberally, wore complexion and morality with loose garments, made fun of those who didn't do likewise . . . After fish we went to two or three in the morning and drank until five." Abdul had accused them of "womanizing" and said they were merely trying to "show out" and should cultivate discipline by perhaps fasting sometimes: living off carrots and grasshoppers or even lying upon a bed of nails.

Hinckle Von Vampton, recognizing Major Young, ambles Hubert over to his table where Hubert places a note under his glass.

Major Young rises, excuses himself and walks over to Hinckle's table. He shakes hands with Hinckle, who rises slightly. "Safecracker" Gould "the only man of his generation who didn't go to jail" is too busy, writing down the "nigger mumbo jumbo words" he is hearing from the surrounding tables.

Safecracker! Hinckle says and the startled "Safecracker" turns to him.

We have a guest, say hello to Major Young.

They all sit down and Hinckle orders some more champagne and a Black, trucking waiter comes to his table.

I have read your poetry, my friend, and I must say that I am immensely impressed. Why it soars and it plumbs and it delights and saddens, it sounds like that great American poet Walt Whitman.

Major Young looks at him suspiciously. Walt Whitman never wrote about Harlem.

Well . . . let's just say it is polished as Whitman's attempts are.

Polished? I don't understand. Is writing glassware?

Insolent coon on my hands, Hinckle thinks. Well, let's just say that I enjoyed your work, my friend. The poems were quite raw and earthy; Harlem through and through.

Young smiles wryly.

I happen to run a little risqué sheet called the *Benign Monster*. It's to get White Americans a little loose. I've read Freud very much and my little sheet brings it all out into the open. Allows it to all hang out. We need a contribution from someone like yourself Mr . . . er . . . Mr . . . something in dialect with lots of razzledazzle in it.

Yes I've heard of your magazine, it employs that W. W. Jefferson, he's really dopey and glib. And why does he use that jargon so?

O don't worry about him. We just keep him around as a Go-Get.

As a Go-Get? I don't understand.

Well Go-Get cigarettes and coffee; if you wish we can easily dismiss him.

No, that won't be necessary because I haven't decided to submit anything. I didn't like those drawings you put on somebody's poems in the 1st issue. They were racist and insulting.

O you mean those. O they were just to perk up interest. Whatever you decide, we'll publish it. It will be an excellent welcome relief from that Nathan Brown. He's so arid and stuffy with his material that Phi Beta Kappa key must have gone to his head. Does he know what those references mean? Or is that just half-digested knowledge. He seems to pretend a good deal.

Nathan Brown happens to be a very accomplished poet and a friend of mine. Is it necessary for us to write the same way? I am not Wallace Thurman, Thurman is not Fauset and Fauset is not Claude McKay, McKay isn't Horne. We all have our unique styles; and if you'll excuse me I think I will join my friends.

Well here let me give you my card. Keep in touch.

If I was in my own territory Perry Street in Greenwich Village I'd give that nigger the caning he'd never forget. Who is he to tell me things like that? Hinckle thinks.

Gould lifts his head as Hinckle raises his voice.

Did you see that, "Safecracker"?

What do you expect from these New Negroes or whatever they call themselves. Uppity. Arrogant. If they were real Black men

they would be out shooting officials or loitering on Lenox Ave.
or panhandling tear-jerking pitiful autobiographies on the radio,
wringing them for every cheap emotion they can solicit. They
would be massacred in the street like heroes and then . . . why I
could snap pictures of the corpses and make a pile of dough. That's
why they should do this if they were real Black men.

Did you get what you wanted, "Safecracker"? The evening is
not entirely lost?

Yes, the dances were difficult to write down though. Eccentric
and individual. But soon I will have stolen enough to have my
own Broadway musical. I think I'll call it *Harlem Tom-Toms*.

Hinckle laughs as he leaves the quarter. You know, "Safecracker,"
what we used to call you in the Templars. What . . . O yes . . .
the "Caucasian blackamoor."

28 Charlotte has struck it wealthy with her Plantation House
routine. She possesses a richly endowed apartment as a result of her
ability to Stop the Show. The bathroom features a dresser, the
color of ivory, with gold trimmings; a sunken marble tub which
has steps leading down into it. Doctor Peter Pick, her "Lucky
Piece," has phoned that morning. He desires to "call on you" for
the purpose of discussing changes in the routine. Charlotte lounges
on her green-velvet American Empire sofa. On a table are the
liquors Charlotte enjoys. Cream-colored ones made with banana,
vanilla beans, and her favorite liquor Crème de Rose. There are
many types of roses located in vases throughout her apartment.

The doorbell rings. Her Irish maid Suzie Mae answers. It is
Doctor Peter Pick dressed in his Moorish outfit, featuring baggy
pants and a fez. He kisses Charlotte's hand and then takes a seat in
a chair facing her. The maid serves him a drink of whiskey
Charlotte's stashed out of sight of the feds. The little fellow seems
troubled. There is a "disconcerting expression on his countenance,"
as they say. He's a Pick but even Picks have emotions.

What's troubling you, Peter?

Well Charlotte, in order to understand you must realize that before I joined your act I had a past. Before becoming a familiar adhesive to you, your insurance, the electric blanket which covers the long winter nights of your act, my sperm really got around.

Get to the point Peter, the heart of the matter.

Charlotte, it's not that I don't think we're a good team. With my struts, grinds, and shuffles and your torch and palmistry we are going a long way. I received the Craw Tickler of the Year award from the Drama critics; and millionaires call on you for you to teach them dilute dances of The Work. Why, all the Fat Cats, Swells, and S.O.B.s out on Manhattan's Milky Way catch our act. I am the best Pick on the T.O.B.A., better than Sophie Tucker's Picks, or Gussie Francis' Picks. Why, the other Picks call me a Pick's Pick, thus my name Doctor Peter Pick . . .

Peter please, what's the matter? Charlotte asks, seeing tears well in the little fellow's light-brown eyes.

Charlotte, I have been all kinds of Picks to you. I've been your Sore Pick your Happy Pick your Vicious Pick. I have made stage love to you as well as made denigrating remarks regarding your morals and your anatomy in the presence of bankers with diamond stickpins on their chests, Rotarians, and visiting knights. Why, we leave them in the aisles, Charlotte. But Charlotte, I think that we ought to turn the act around. Stand it on its head. Upside-down the Plantation.

How's that, Peter?

Why don't you conjure me and go through the motions of putting me down. The Angel will pass and he will be of no assistance. The demon will also pass and he too will be of no help. Then you whisper into my ear, I read the words and then you disappear. And for those who missed the first act we can have a summary of the preceding show done in the beginning, as they do on the serials . . .

You certainly keep up, Peter. Why, I think that's a wonderful idea.

You mean you like it?

Of course Peter, we will begin tonight.

O thank you Charlotte . . .

And wait here. Charlotte goes into the bedroom and returns with a tattered little blue-covered book.

This is PaPa LaBas' *Blue Back: A Speller*, required reading at

Mumbo Jumbo Kathedral. Perhaps there's something that you can use when sending me back to make it appear more convincing.

O thank you Charlotte! You know I always wanted to be a choreographer but with Jes Grew about no one would heed my labanotations. Maybe Stagecraft will be a new career for me. Perhaps it is easier to switch the conflicts about than educate the masses to a new melody.

Peter, you do have a gift.

Let's drink to our new act, Charlotte.

Upon Charlotte's call the maid enters the room.

O there you are, Suzie Mae. Would you please serve Doctor Peter Pick another drink.

The Irish maid, who ain't been in the country long enough to learn good English, replies in her semiliterate manner. Why natural, Miss Charlotte. Natural.

S.R.: UPON HEARING ETHEL WATERS SING "THAT DA-DA-STRAIN" AND A JAZZ BAND PLAY "PAPA DE-DA-DA" EUROPEAN PAINTERS TAKE JES GREW ABROAD. IT HAS BECOME WHAT THE WALLFLOWER ORDER FEARED: PANDEMIC. AT HOME, YOUNG PEOPLE CHEER THE BAYERDOFFER DEVILS WHO'VE CHALLENGED GRAND OPERA TO A DUEL AT THE METROPOLITAN THEATER IN LOS ANGELES . . . THOUSANDS BOO VERDI'S TRIUMPH AS A HOMETOWN DECISION . . . THE LOOTING CONTINUES UNTIL DAWN . , . WORLD-WIDE MU'TAFIKAH GIVE JES GREW ENCOURAGEMENT BY PUTTING IT UP TAKING IT IN AND HIDING IT OUT . . . ON WALL STREET SAXOPHONES MAKE A STRONG RALLY WHILE VIOLINS ARE DOWN. THE BALLET LINGERS ON DEATH ROW AND . . . THIS JUST IN!

OUTBREAKS OF JES GREW 60 MILES FROM NEW YORK CITY. 30,000 CASES REPORTED INCLUDING COWS, CHICKENS, SHEEP AND HORSES, DISPROVING

SPECULATIONS THAT ITS EFFECTS ARE CONFINED TO THE
HUMAN SPECIES. EVEN THE SAP IN THE MAPLE TREES
MOVES NASTY. LOCAL CHURCHES SCHEDULE LAST-MINUTE
MIDNIGHT SERVICES TO INDULGE IN PRAYERFUL
ANTIDOTES AGAINST THE PLAGUE. <u>Mary Lou Williams</u>
<u>composed a "Roman Catholic Jazz Mass" while</u>
<u>outside in the rain, on the night of the</u>
<u>performance, J.G.C.s chanted, "Mary Lou, Mary Lou,</u>
<u>what's wrong with you?"</u>—I.R.)

29 There is a knock at the *Mu'tafikah* basement door. A
husky Black man of about 45 with folds in a hanging jaw accompanied by 2 others of similar physical mold enters the basement
headquarters. He wears a camelhair overcoat; black kid gloves and
light-colored snap brim hat with a creased top and narrow black
pointed-toe shoes covered with arabesque pattern.

His eyes wander about the ceiling. He then stares straight ahead
at the people working at the tables. Packing masks, wood sculpture
and other amulets.

The trucks you can have for a few days. Then there are some
barrels of booze to go to Chicago and we will need them. The
costumes havta be back tomorrow night, he says to Berbelang.

Other men wheel wardrobe closets into the basement. They con-
tain boxes of shoes, formal dresses, jewelry, stockings, tuxedos,
black silk top hats, white silk scarves.

The other stuff has to be back at the theater tomorrow for the
opening of that musical he's backing. The Studebakers tomorrow
morning. He's got 18 funerals scheduled by his various Harlem
undertaking establishments. And listen pal, he says jabbing a black
gloved finger into Berbelang's chest, be sure to get them back . . .

The man, 1 hand still in a huge pocket, readmits a cigar to his mouth and begins to walk out of the basement. He turns around and as if this was a signal the men follow his motions.

O the most important thing I forgot to tell you. The boats are down at the harbor. The ships are waiting out at sea. And good luck he told me to tell you, he said you'd understand. He said the only reason he's giving you these things is he's a Race Man.

The man approaches Berbelang and gives him a strange handshake. Berbelang looks puzzled.

O, I thought you was 1 of us and that was why he was givin' you some code. Well so long. The man turns and he and his partners begin to leave.

As he prepares to turn the knob Berbelang stops him.

Hey! Listen! How did Buddy Jackson get the ships and boats?

He said some fellow named Black Eagle, a monoplane flyer, has international connections.

The man left the basement.

The men and women put on their costumes. They pile into the Studebakers parked against the curb. You can still see the influence of the carriage upon this automobile's design, this Studebaker which was characterized by its vendors as "Knight Motored."

30 Hard-boiled Biff Musclewhite, "the man who tamed the wilderness" and much decorated combat officer of World War 1, now curator of the New York Center of Art Detention and part-time consultant to the Yorktown police. He is relaxing his head upon Charlotte's lap as she sits upon the sofa. Charlotte strokes his grey hair. 1 leg dangles over 1 of the sofa's arms. His sword touches the floor and his hand embraces a glass of fizz water which rests next to a champagne bottle on the table. 1 boot on, the other on the floor near the sofa, he continues to speak, his blouse unbuttoned in 2 places.

. . . And then my dear, I single-handedly led this charge into German lines before we encircled their men . . . and it was then that I realized that the fate of my men was in my hands.

Major Biff Musclewhite has finally convinced Charlotte to allow him to see her. He has brought some roses which the maid Suzie Mae has placed in vases. Charlotte, bored, stares at the ceiling as she listens to him talk on and on about World War 1.

. . . I like the décor in this apartment, it shows that distinctive taste. You certainly are selective, my dear, in lesser hands the style would be gaudy almost Africanesque . . . I should like you to permit me to contribute to the maintenance of the apartment. As a combat veteran I am accustomed to doing my bit. Kiss me, my dear.

The Major springs from his lying position and suddenly grips Charlotte's long arms at the same time pinning her against the sofa's back and kissing her violently.

Just then, the door bell rings.

Patting her hair and smoothing her dress, she is released from the Major's vice-like hold. As the Major waits in the other room, buttoning his shirt, Charlotte rises to open the door.

A minute goes by before Major Biff Musclewhite inquires about what is happening in the other room.

Do you have company, my dear?

Berbelang, Thor, Yellow Jack and Fuentes enter the room; they wear Chesterfield coats over their tuxedos and black top hats which they wear cavalierly.

Why . . . why what is the meaning of this? Charlotte, who are these men?

They said they were friends of yours and forced themselves in, Charlotte replies.

Take it easy, Musclewhite. We're taking you for a spin in our Studebakers. A little trip down to the C.A.D., you cad. We're going to have a little opening, Fuentes adds.

The Major rises from the sofa and suddenly spins about and leaps for Yellow Jack who flips him over, landing him on the floor with a thud.

The Major reaches for his sword but Berbelang reveals this magnificent long razor, its handle encrusted with diamonds and emeralds . . . It was designed after an ancient ceremonial knife.

Major Biff Musclewhite thinks better about his resistance. They escort him into the other room. Charlotte stands in the hall, seemingly petrified.

Don't worry, my dear. I shall deal with these rapscallions.

O move! Yellow Jack says, pushing Biff Musclewhite out of the apartment and down the hall toward the elevators.

Major Biff Musclewhite rides silently with his apprehenders to the basement of the apartment building. *How did they know he was at Charlotte's? The Mu'tafikah had excellent intelligence. The authorities would have to put the Dictaphones to work to protect themselves in the future. He would suggest this to the Mayor of New York if he could ever get him out of a night club or away from the baseball diamond.*

They slowly walk out of the apartment building and Musclewhite is forced into the car. The fleet of cars, headlights blinking, then forms a procession which moves to the Center of Art Detention located at 82nd St. and 5th Ave.

● ○

The 2 guards are amazed when they see the party of men and women mount the steps of the museum.

No 1 told us of an opening tonight, 1 guard said to the other.

When they see Biff Musclewhite, this Black man following close behind, they open the door.

Sir . . . there's no opening scheduled in the catalogue.

Of course there is, Musclewhite said. Open the door and admit these people.

But that's against the rules, sir; it's 10:00 P.M. This's never happened before. Besides we ain't seen no new show put up, sir. This is highly unusual.

Musclewhite felt the razor cut through his coat and then felt a tiny trickle moving slowly down his back.

Do what I tell you, open the door and let these . . . these . . . ladies and gentlemen in.

The guards oblige and the people enter the museum; Berbelang stands next to Biff Musclewhite at the entrance as the *Mu'tafikah* file by.

You 2 can have the rest of the night off, Musclewhite says after Berbelang whispers the instructions in his ear.

Mumbling, the guards resignedly put on their coats and leave the premises.

The men and women *Mu'tafikah* methodically go about their work; the husky men removing the larger items to trucks parked in the rear of the Center for their journey to the boats waiting down at New York harbor. A few hours later the job is complete.

Berbelang, Yellow Jack, Thor, Fuentes and the remainder of the party start for the museum's exit. They've figured out a way to obtain the Olmec head. As they walk through the main gallery of the museum Berbelang pauses before Goya's painting of Don Manuel Osorio de Zúñiga, 50×40 in. (127×101.6 cm.). The little boy in a bright scarlet outfit among cats and birds. He sees the child as the Goat-without-horns; the famous sacrificial White child of the Red Sect rites. He removes his razor and is about to slash the child in the painting. Yellow Jack grabs his wrist. Berbelang turns to Yellow Jack.

Remember the vow, Berbelang, we are just going to return the things, not pick up their habits of razing peoples' art. It isn't Goya nor is it the painting's fault that it's used by Atonists as a worship.

Of course, Berbelang says. I haven't had much sleep.

The party exits from the museum with their hostage Biff Musclewhite.

● ○

Over Fuentes' strenuous objections Berbelang has left Thor to guard Biff Musclewhite who is bound and gagged, hands tied behind his back and sitting in a chair near 1 of the basement walls of the *Mu'tafikah* headquarters. They've decided that there's no other way of obtaining the Olmec head, therefore they've kidnaped Biff Musclewhite to hold for ransom, instead of releasing him after the haul as planned.

Musclewhite stares straight ahead at Thor who paces up and down the middle of the room, fidgeting and inhaling a Havana cigar.

May I have 1, son?

Thor turns, walks toward Biff Musclewhite, removes a cigarette from his shirt pocket and puts it in Musclewhite's mouth. He then takes a match and lights it.

Musclewhite drags on it and speaks out of the corner of his mouth. Thanks.

Thor sits on the bench of 1 of the tables within hearing

distance but on the other side of the room. He examines the agenda for forthcoming art heists. An exhibit of "primitive" art is encircled meaning that Berbelang wants it "touched."

How old are you, son?

Thor looks up from the exhibit handbill lying on top of the bench.

You talking to me?

Yes, I asked your age.

Thor rises, walks over to where the man sits and shakes his finger in his face.

What's it to you? The only reason I have to be in your company is because they are going to exchange you for a promise that the Olmec head will be shipped back to Central America. Frankly, I don't think you're worth it.

Musclewhite smiles.

What's so funny? Thor says, becoming angry at the hostage calmly sitting there in the chair.

Nothing funny, son. You remind me of myself. I went off to war and was going to save the world but look now, already the war clouds are forming again. The disarmament conference; they always talk of laying down their arms before they resume fighting. The German tribes are restless. And here at home society is coming apart at the seams.

Why do you old people love clichés so. Coming apart at the seams, all of that phony hypocritical language . . . I hate it! Thor says, agitated, clutching a fistful of his hair.

Hypocritical? I don't know about that. If you think we are hypocritical why don't you have your father pay those donors for their artwork and then there would be no need for your nigger spic and chinaman friends to risk their necks for it.

Hey look, you. Thor starts for the man but then the comment registers.

How did you know? I mean, about my father?

The many times I saw you when your father brought you into the yacht club; a little child dressed in a fashion after Gainsborough's Blue Boy.

You in a yacht club? Don't make me laugh.

I know you look down on me because I come from one of the European countries under domination by stronger Whites than my people. We were your niggers; you colonized us and made us dirt under your heels. But in America it's different. There is no royalty in the European sense. Only money counts. Guggenheim, Astor, Ford, Carnegie . . . people you would spit upon if you had them at home in Europe. We're saving our dough and soon we will be able to purchase our own heraldry cheap and then maybe our values will be your values. We've learned, you see by joining your clubs and making our way from Police Commissioner to Curator of the Center of Art Detention. We've learned to bullshit the way you do, build up an aura of sacredness about the meanest achievement, allowing "the Sunlight to intrude upon Royalty" as 1 of your queens said. 1 of these days 1 of our sons, perhaps the son of a Polish immigrant, will emerge from some steel town in Pennsylvania and mount a turd on the wall of a museum and make it stick . . . and when you ask him what it is he will put on his dark glasses and snub you the way you did us. And on that day we will have overtaken you.

That'll be the day.

So you see you still have loyalty to your elite. Look son, we are trying to save you. Your class. We used to run alongside your carriages in barefeet when you drove through our neighborhoods, and you would splash mud in our faces violate our sisters, flog our fathers; but we kept coming for more because we loved your beautiful clothes, your clean hair, the charming ladies riding beside you, the way you talked . . . Fascinated by the man's talk, Thor sits down slowly . . .

You are all we had. Against them. Against the Legendary Army of Marching Niggers against the Yellow Peril against the Red Man. We didn't have what you had and so when you appeared before the world with your coronations and your ritual they imitated you all over the world and marched like you talked like you and made their national anthems "Finlandia" or "God Save the Queen."

But . . . but . . .

Musclewhite won't allow Thor Wintergreen to say a word.

It was then that we realized you were all we had, the way you had cultivated a theater to keep us from them, a theater with scene shifts and a changing cast of characters but always squeezing out the Bronx cheer from your bought-off claque. Then we found out what you were doing. But we didn't let on, we decided that we would imitate you. America was our chance, a caste built upon money. We want to protect you though, you are our finest. Son, why do you make it hard for us?

Because this looting of the world's art treasures can't go on. That's why. When I was in Egypt a guide told me that the Egyptians would never think of removing their dead like the foreign museums had. How would you like it if someone disturbed your dead, dug up their bones and put them on display, melted down the sacred jewelry of your ancestors as they did in Mexico, and destroyed your stone idols.

Now you listen to me, Musclewhite fires back. If it's a bunch of precious stiffs you think you're after, then my name is Joe E. Lewis. Look pal, it's time we came clean with each other. Don't you think I know why you're in this? Don't you think I used to listen to that fancy radio station you were on. The Franz Liszt Birthday Specials, the Tolstoy Marathons, you never did that for the nigger musicians or writers. No, they died in the East River while you talked about some great books and serious works of art, a code for White. Right? So come off of your high horse, buster, and stop this pretending . . .

Look, Thor answers, rising. They are my friends. I believe in their way and reject yours. I can't sleep at night for the thoughts of your foul deeds. Feeding the Tasmanians to dogs, for food . . .

Nerts! So you'd just say why bother about a civilization which is in need of young men? So you'd just fink out upon our glorious Western civilization; you would say why bother putting it back in stock? It makes me so mad I want to cry. You, a young Prince of Our Ways, running with a band of . . . of . . . of *Mu'tafikah*. Them loafers, ne'er-do-wells, nihilists throwing pineapples at us. Look son. Don't you think I want to see every man a king, a chicken in every pot, every child fed clothed and sheltered in America? Warren Harding himself presided at a celebration of their achievements the other day at the Lincoln Memorial. Son, we don't mind digging in our pockets and pitching in for the underprivileged, the insulted and injured, but son, this Berbelang is different. This is a nigger gone berserk. A nigger the planters kept from other niggers so they wouldn't catch what he had. The insolent freeman who will sit in the front of the bus and look about as if to say "Who don't like it?" Berbelang was on the ship the *Flying Dutchman*, the slaver under the cruel master captain. He put something on the captain so his sailing around the world forever became legendary. Berbelang's not 1 of these automatons marching well dressed in an anti-lynching parade; he is aware of his past and has demystified ours.

Son, this is a nigger closing in on our mysteries and soon he will be asking our civilization to "come quietly." This man is talking about Judeo-Christian culture, Christianity, Atonism whatever you want to call it. The most noteworthy achievements of anybody anywhere in the . . . the . . . whole universe. A . . . haha . . . haha . . . hahahaha.

His head in his hands, Biff Musclewhite begins to sob quietly.

Stop it stop it, Thor says, pacing the room nervously.

I've seen them, son, in Africa, China, they're not like us, son, the Herrenvolk. Europe. This place. They are lagging behind, son, and you know in your heart this is true. Son, these niggers writing. Profaning our sacred words. Taking them from us and beating them on the anvil of BoogieWoogie, putting their black hands on them so that they shine like burnished amulets. Taking our words, son, these filthy niggers and using them like they were their god-given pussy. Why . . . why 1 of them dared to interpret, critically mind you, the great Herman Melville's *Moby-Dick!!*

Stop it! Thor sits down on the bench and begins to cry.

Musclewhite, seeing that he has made a dent, continues. That's what it comes down to, son. They're the 1s who must change, not us, they . . . they must adopt our ways, producing Elizabethan poets; they should have Stravinskys and Mozarts in the wings, they must become Civilized!!!!

Thor, crying, continues to sit at the table.

Musclewhite. Softly. Gently. Son come and untie me, son, and together my young valiant prince we will do battle with the dragons of Jes Grew, Helen and *Mu'tafikah* too. You know how she is: fickle, unreliable. You remember what Goethe said: Helen goes the way of Euphoria.

No, he said Euphorion.

Yes of course son, you know the bitch. My Great Book hasn't arrived this month. The mails are slow.

Thor finishes untying Musclewhite. Musclewhite rises from the chair and begins to massage his wrists.

O.K. son, I'm going to call my bulls. We'll wait here until he returns. When is he due?

Thor is crying at the bench where he has returned to sit. 8 o'clock . . . , he answers.

Musclewhite walks over to the bench and removes from his pocket a key chain. The charm on the key chain is Charlemagne. The Crowned Head of Charlemagne done in gold.

There, son. It will soon be over.

He gives the chain to Thor who begins kissing it and handling it as the devout do that Sufi invention, the rosary.

S.R.: THE WALLFLOWER ORDER INDUCES ITS RUNNING DOG MEDICAL SOCIETIES AND ITS JACKANAPE PUNK FREUDIANS TO ISSUE A REPORT WHICH "SCIENTIFICALLY" PROVES THAT JES GREW IS HARD ON THE APPENDIX . . . THE SHIMMY, THAT DESCENDANT OF THE NIGERIAN SHIKA DANCE, IS OUTLAWED . . . DOCTORS IN YAKIMA WASHINGTON ANNOUNCE THAT "THE SOURCE OF MAN'S WICKEDNESS IS A 'TORRID ZONE' IN THE BRAIN, AN INCH AND A HALF THICK FROM THE EARS UP. . . ;"*

Jazz did a number of things to popular music as well as to metropolitan life. It sped up the tempo of things. Whether it was a cause, or the effect of a still more general cause, is here beside the point. Once the new musical spirit had come, it rapidly spread into daily—and nightly!—activities. It was not long before the old type of musical comedy began to appear outmoded. "Pep" was heard in the land. Once we had "ragged" words; now we "jazzed up" everything.

Isidore Witmark & Isaac Goldberg
From Ragtime to Swingtime

* *This Fabulous Century: 1920–1930*, vol. 3—Time-Life Books.

31   Slight-of-build, wiry, sinewy and melancholy, resembling
the drawings of Charles Cullen, Nathan Brown walks down the
steps of Salem African Methodist Episcopal where he comes to
meditate about the Black Christ. Black-caped, he is impervious
to the rain. The poet whose work commingles Death and Nature
in haunting ways reaches the corner of the street. He sees upon a
building's wall a foreboding shadow closing in behind him. He
turns to see a regally dressed, elderly gentleman wearing a black
seal coat. He is carrying a cane and wearing a top hat.

I didn't mean to startle you . . . I admire your collection of
poetry *Dark Crepuscule*. It's solidly in the Western tradition and
convinces me that you are the foremost bard of your race. It's
about time they produced such a bard!

If you will excuse me, sir, I have another engagement, answers
Brown, rather embarrassed, looking down at the pavement.

But surely you will sign this autograph to your volume of
poems. I would be most grateful, Hinckle continues, extending a
pen for Brown's use.

Nathan Brown interrupts his walk to stop and sign an autograph for this stranger. He then resumes his walk, moving along
the street, the stranger alongside him.

Do you reside in Manhattan? Nathan decides to inquire of the
gentleman who persists in accompanying him on his journey.

I have a modest place . . . a cottage . . . on Long Island.
Spiraling Agony. It's where I spend my time during my declining
years, courting the muse and feeding sea gulls. I am what you
could consider a gentleman editor. I publish a magazine called the
Benign Monster. You've heard?

Haven't I! It has a bad reputation in these parts . . . lurid,
tasteless like an overgrown glossy tab.

We're short of staff but we do the best we can. That's why
we need someone like you to give it class, taste.

I am committed to teaching school. I wouldn't be in any
position to help you . . .

But your vast knowledge of civilization, Christ, Abelard, Pros-
pero, your word order, Think Not instead of the vulgar Don't
Think, your consciousness of your Black heritage but never allowing it to become a mystification as J. A. Rogers, Hughes, McKay

and some of that contingent; the way you recorded that Simon, the servant, the servant who carried our Lord's Cross, was colored.

I have been educated in both cultures and so I use the advantages of both.

That's why you would be such an addition to our staff, the publisher of the *Benign Monster* insists to this poet whose biographer has written "[his problem] was that of reconciling a Christian upbringing with a pagan inclination . . ."

You never become bogged down in Marxist clichés and nationalism: all of these qualities are needed with the plague occurring. Look, we can make you the dominant figure in Negro literature today: King of the Colored Experience.

"All Coons Look Alike to Me," mutters Nathan Brown vacantly, examining the trees which lined the street, uncomfortable as he listens to the stranger's extravagant praise.

What was that?

I think that when people like you, Mr. Von Vampton, say "The Negro Experience" you are saying that all Negroes experience the world the same way. In that way you can isolate the misfits who would propel them into penetrating the ceiling of this bind you and your assistants have established in this country. The ceiling above which no slave would be allowed to penetrate without stirring the kept bloodhounds . . . I'm afraid that I won't be able to help you, Mr. Von Vampton. I am teaching school to Harlem youngsters so that they won't be influenced by people like you . . .

Hinckle is desperate; there is only another month remaining and if he doesn't create this Android, according to the bargain, he'll have to drink the poison.

Look, you little yellow bastard; we can make you powerful, Striver's Row, Sugar Hill, you name it . . . don't you think that people are sick of this Jes Grew thing, this malady that's hanging over America like a black . . . cloud?

It may be a malady to you but many of us are attempting to catch it. Now if you will just remove your hand from my shoulder I want to continue my walk. I have an appointment with someone who will perhaps make me vulnerable to it.

He leaves Hinckle Von Vampton standing on the street in Harlem.

He would get even with him. He would call his friends and tell them that they will publish more work from this poet at their peril . . .

Hinckle Von Vampton returns home and spends a night dreaming of things too horrible to repeat. New Jersey. Things like that. He awakes the next morning and after bathing goes downstairs to fetch the newspaper. The headline causes his ancient wound to feel. Cab Calloway had startled a Cotton Club audience by announcing his candidacy for President on the strange Jes Grew ticket. Then he outlined his platform in some kind of strange Satchmo language. The show was headlined by a group known as the Dancing Bales. Was this some kind of nigger code?

A telegram arrives. From the Wallflower Order. It consists of 1 word.

WELL?

Time was running out. He would have to come up with something, Knock It Dock It Co-opt It Swing-It Bop It or Rock It were the orders.

. . . But the woman he really loved was a voodoo queen
From Creole French market, way down in New Orleans
—Stackalee

32 The trolley car faces the Hudson River. A strange ship has been docked there, a huge black freighter which, although appearing shabby, distinguished looking Blacks, many of them well dressed, have been boarding and disembarking. Funny that the ship should be anchored at this particular pier because it had been closed down and in the many years of his route he hadn't noticed any other ships using it. It rested there in the water which undulated, shining like black silk. It was a yellow moon with spots of red appearing as if they had been left by the wild brush strokes of a painter. After the cloud passed the bright, full moon remained, as white as cocaine. The ship flying the black and red colors wasn't any of his business.

He was 1 of the few trolley car operators of his race. After the riots of 1900 when Whites ran amuck and murdered or assailed every Black in the streets of New York City they could lay their hands on he had been hired as a concession to the sentiments of a protesting Black committee. They still wouldn't give him a holiday and he wanted to have this 1. He and his wife had been married for 20 years. He wanted to be home with her and the 3 children. As he sat in the trolley resting for 2 minutes before resuming his route he removed a wallet and smiled upon the photos of his family. He put it back in his pocket. Across the street was an illegal blind pig. It would be 2:00 A.M. by the time he returned home and maybe he would just stop in after this last round and have a drink. A drink of King Korn and then home. This night was special. His wife had gotten some "wine" for the occasion from one of Buddy Jackson's boys. He was going to get his head spifflicated. He looked in the rearview mirror hanging above his steering equipment. That passenger was still on the trolley. He had picked her up on the corner each day in Harlem and brought her downtown, but this time she hadn't got off. And she was giving him the eye. No mistake about it. He had been around; even served in the 1st World War. But she didn't seem to be a harlot. He had seen harlots on his journeys around the country and Europe and recognized the signal from their waist up. Man, if he wasn't a married man! The perfume enticed him. He had noticed it when she got on the trolley. She wore the long skirts the fresh white bandanna the tropical blouses all the women were wearing now. His wife even had 1. Tonight she was going around in the circles of his route. Maybe she was lonely. Well, wasn't his business; he would have a drink when he returned to his stop, then on to the carbarn and home.

33   Berbelang has decided to return to the basement to relieve Thor who's been watching Biff Musclewhite, now object of a city-wide manhunt. The street is unusually quiet as he enters the block. He feels a tingling at the nape of his neck. Something's wrong but he doesn't quite know what. He starts to enter the basement . . . Those cars across the street. When he turns around Biff Musclewhite orders his men to open up. Between the eyes. Berbelang grabs his forehead. But the blood pours out like fire hydrants gush water into the summer street. Strange, he feels O.K., he doesn't feel a thing. He's just getting weaker, losing consciousness. Biff Musclewhite climbs from the police car and with 2 other men walks across the street. They stare down at the corpse. Berbelang's mind has rushed out to the pavement: Yellow, Red, Blue. Fire Opals.

34   The final run completed, he stops the trolley car. A funny sweet odor comes from that ship. Lavender lights beam from her portholes. Still on the trolley, huh? Well she would have to get off now.

Lady, you haffta get off. This is the last stop.

Earline rose from her seat and walks, swinging her hips, down the aisle of the trolley car. She gives him a look the nature of which would force a man to divorce his wife, sell his home, hang around the blood bank, offer his skin for grafting, donate his eyes to an alligator, hit the banker on the head to give her what she wanted.

That . . . feeling swept over his abdomen and then worked its way up. She didn't come on like a whore. He had served in the last war, you know. He couldn't figure out. What she was up to?

Would your husband mind you having a drink with me? Man, he didn't mean for it to come out like that. He was getting rusty . . .

All Black men are my husbands, she answered seductively.

The music came from the blind pig, heavy, thick, gummy like a quagmire; mud, the rich ancient soil of the Black-belt South with its climate, swamps, swarming with birds, snakes, bugs, wildflowers. Egypt of America, someone said. When they open the door, her arm in his, the funk hits them so hard it almost knocked them out. The air is surfeit with smoke: yellow, billowy; couples dancing as if in trances doing the Slow Drag, Grind and other intimate dances. On the wall is a torn ancient poster of a Jack Johnson fight. The guitar player with the band looks as if he was asleep but his guitar sounds like a tiny evil venomous snake would sound if it could sing. His hair is parted down the middle and is wavy from vigorous applications of Tuxedo. They stand at the bar.

Would you like a drink, miss?

You can call me Earline, and she eases closer to him and through her skirt he could feel her body. He gets hard as a rock and he isn't even embarrassed.

35 You killed him. You didn't give him a chance, Thor yells as Biff Musclewhite got back into the car. It wasn't necessary to shoot him like that. Like . . . like an animal.

O, so you didn't like the way we handled your friend, huh? We'll see that yours will be quiet and traditional. And then Musclewhite laughs, all weird and sick-like. Early Richard Widmark; *Kiss of Death* (1947). 1st the opening, his nervous mouth baring a few front teeth and then a little more teeth until he is grinning widely; all the way to the station his eyes are fixed.

The detectives on each side of Thor exchange puzzled glances. Thor sobs holding his head in his hand.

36 Earline awakes the next morning; her head is bad. She supports herself, raised in the bed. Lying next to her is the nude trolley car man sound asleep. Snoring. A smile on his face that people must bear when they witness the Christian's Glory.

She gets up, the expression on her face a mischievous smile, frowning. She goes into the kitchen and puts on a pot of coffee. When it begins to boil, she pours herself a cup of coffee and reaches for the newspaper.

● ○

Major Biff Musclewhite is about to phone Charlotte to tell her that he has survived the "excruciating ordeal" at the hands of the *Mu'tafikah* and perhaps ask her to dine with him. A sort of celebration. He had told her that he would deal with these rapscallions and by golly giminy he had.

He is dialing the number GR 3-4822 when an assistant comes in and places some items on his desk. The phone rings once.

Chief, here are some objects belonging to that black *Mu'tafikah* Berbelang: his billfold, razor and dice . . .

The phone rings a 2nd time.

Musclewhite moves the things lying on the desk.

. . . Cards, a strange-looking tangled root.

The phone rings a 3rd time.

Hello?

Yes my dear, this is Biff, I was able to extricate my person from the *Mu'tafikah*.

Say it again, I just awoke. The last thing I remember was going on the stage of the Plantation House . . . I don't remember how I got home . . .

O that's all right. He comes upon the picture of the Mumbo Jumbo Kathedral group: there is Earline, Berbelang, PaPa LaBas and . . . and . . .

I was going through the last routine with my Pick and then I must have fainted. I don't know how I got here . . .

It must be something in the air, Biff Musclewhite says. You know, this Jes Grew thing has reached Dunkirk New York. Maybe I will come over and see you, Musclewhite says, brows furrowing. Half hour?

Yes, do come over.

37 Charlotte walks to the window. She removes some rose petals that had been placed in saucers resting on the sill. Much of the soft water has evaporated and a film is floating on the top. She removes the film and pours it into little vials. It would sit there for a few days until all of the water evaporated, leaving behind the aromatic essence of the rose.

Charlotte picks up the newspaper which is lying on a table. She sits on the sofa. It is the maid's night off, so she goes to the kitchen and pours herself a glass of milk. Then she walks into the living room and picks up the newspaper. And she screams and drops the newspaper to the floor. BERBELANG SHOT BY BIFF MUSCLEWHITE!!

MUSCLEWHITE BAGS COON
War Hero Slays Art-Napper
Depraved Black Mu'tafikah *Dead*
More Arrests Predicted

Manhattan, the 1920s—Today Biff Muscle-white, fearless curator of the Center of Art Detention and consultant to Yorktown Police, shot and killed Berbelang the bad, cute Black bandit, and leader of a gang of dope-sniffing self-styled *Mu'tafikah*.

The shooting occurred shortly after he freed himself from a hideout where he was being held for ransom in the gang's wild scheme to exchange the well-known city father for the ugly sausage-lipped big-headed Olmec head.

> **Musclewhite escaped by subduing Thor Wintergreen, misguided tycoon's son who had joined the band of freaks and their scantily clad flappers.**
>
> **Trapped inside his headquarters the demented coon chose to shoot it out with the World War 1 combat veteran and hero who once told Nature where to go. "Come in and get me, coppers," the spade shouted, followed by his wild, bizarre laughter.**

The doorbell rings. Charlotte opens it upon Biff Musclewhite . . .

You . . . you killed Berbelang.

Buff Musclewhite forces himself into the room.

O you seem concerned. I didn't know that you knew the man, Biff Musclewhite says, removing the cord from his pocket. You were always irresponsible. Fickle. Never loyal and always looking askance at them as they picked cotton fanned you in the mosques, fetched your horses and scratched your alabaster back. You can't be trusted.

What are you going to do? Charlotte says, alarmed, walking backwards.

She reaches a table and knocks the gas lamp to the floor.

Biff Musclewhite brings the cord about her neck and puts all of his strength behind it, squeezing it, until Charlotte drops lifeless to the floor.

38   When the rookie cop arrives, Musclewhite is calmly sitting and drinking some bootleg whiskey.

The rookie comes into the room and finds Charlotte on the floor, dead. What happened here?

I had to bust her for possession, see this booze? Musclewhite points to the liquors on the table. Found it in her cabinet. Not bad either. Well when she saw that her number was up she offered resistance and I had to, er . . . well, you know, she was resisting.

But you know no 1 is being arrested for that any more; besides, she looks as if she's been strangled.

I had to . . . you see she had a gun.

But there's no gun here, sir.

Well a man, he was her accomplice; he escaped through the fire escape.

Could you describe him, sir.

He was a muscular Black, a huge stud if I ever saw 1.

The rookie walked over to the window from which 1 could look down upon the alley separating Charlotte's building from the next 1 over. There were huge white feathers lying on the sill of the ½-opened window as if a large bird had struggled to get through.

But there's no fire escape here, sir.

Look, are you disputing my word, Biff Musclewhite says, squeezing the glass in his hand.

No, sir, no sir. I'm going to call the coroner.

The rookie leaves the room.

Biff Musclewhite thinks *I should have called the coroner in the first place. He was a bowling partner; he'd see that this rookie was transferred. He'd fix him; he'd transfer him to Harlem.*

VooDoo Generals Routed
Peralte Slain By
Valiant Marine
Hunt What's His Name

39 What did all of these things mean? She grins and takes a sip of coffee. A knock at the door. PaPa LaBas and T Malice enter the room.

Earline, have you heard? Berbelang . . .

She doesn't know what they are talking about. She collapses to the floor. T Malice lifts her and takes her into the other room. LaBas lifts the phone and calls Herman.

Herman?

Yes, what's up?

Earline. I think she picked up one . . . the one with the red

dress on. The one known in Brazil as Yemanjá; you know what
W. C. Handy called her: St. Louis woman.

Be right down. I'll bring some sisters and some food.

LaBas gives him the address and hangs up.

T Malice is standing in the door leading to the bedroom.

Pop, there's a man in there asleep.

O brother, let me talk to him.

He went into the bedroom, T Malice following close behind.

40   Earline is asleep but her eyelashes are fluttering which
means that the 1 she picked up would soon be active again. He
hopes that Black Herman will hurry.

Hey man? LaBas said, shaking the sleeping trolley car operator.

Wha . . . wha . . . The man begins to open his eyes.

Hey man, wake up, hurry.

The trolley car operator wakes up slowly and looks about the
room. Hey man, if it's your wife . . . look, she flirted with me.
I didn't . . .

No need to explain but you'd better leave. We have an emergency with her, no questions asked.

The man climbs out of the bed and begins to put on his clothes.
You know, nothing like this never happened to me. I'm happily
married and have 3 children. I've never laid an eye on another
woman.

You couldn't help yourself. If you hadn't given in to her requests
she would have destroyed you.

I don't understand.

Look, I'm PaPa LaBas, here's my card, LaBas says, giving the
trolley car operator his card. The trolley car operator walks toward
the door, self-conscious and embarrassed.

Come by my office sometime when you get a chance. I'll explain
it all to you. The trolley car operator nods to LaBas and leaves.

Just as the trolley car operator leaves the room, the sisters and
Black Herman enter. They talk, and then leave T Malice in the
living room to answer the telephone and to keep out friends who

might come to inquire about Berbelang. The others go into the bedroom.

The old sisters, steady, sober professionals that they are, gather about Earline's bed. They are dressed in white uniforms: white dresses white stockings and white shoes. They wear white nurses' caps.

A lavender mixture of High John Conqueror compound, orris root, sandalwood, talcum plain, is floating up from the incense burners they've placed about the room. The shades have been drawn. The designs on the window shades are those of hearts pierced by daggers. 1 sister is sprinkling oil of white rose about the room. Another is in the bathroom drawing hot water into a tub while an assistant sprinkles it with basil leaves. Black Herman is in the kitchen wearing a white apron, mixing a solution of rice, flour, eggs, crême de menthe, juices of 2 pigeons and 2 chickens, Madeira wine, raw brought to a liquified boil.

It will be ready in a few minutes, Herman yells to LaBas, standing in the bedroom. Then I will prepare the cocktail.

Earline was beginning to stir.

Earline, LaBas calls. Can you hear me?

She gives him a smile so wicked in its content that it makes his flesh crawl. He touches the back of her left hand softly; she digs her nails into his right hand, she is tense like a cat. LaBas plays it cool; he withdraws his hand and a sister wraps a white bandage about it. The sisters, although they have not seen anything like this before, do not reveal their surprise but keep on doing The Work.

Girl, LaBas begins to speak. Why don't you leave Earline alone? The child has enough troubles. Her man is dead and she loved him. You understand that, don't you? You got 1 man to flirt with you and make love to you, now why don't you return to where you came from. There's no need to worry her like this. Pick somebody else.

Earline slowly moves back from the edge of the bed. She smiles at the sisters who look at 1 another and return the gesture.

How did you know it was me?

Look, we may not have the legitimate Assons but we've been called and we can Work-It-On-Out too.

Man, Earline says, waving him away in a high piercing West Indian accented voice, there ain't nothing no American HooDoo man or whatever you call yourselves can do for me.

I wouldn't be too sure about that, Black Herman says entering the room carrying 2 huge glasses containing his recipe on a tray.

What's that that man has in his hands? Earline asks, reaching for the glasses on the tray from where she lies on the bed clad only in a black slip and panties.

Herman recoils, setting the tray supporting the cocktails on a table in the room.

O no you don't. You don't lay your hands on this until you promise to depart from this girl's body.

A sister has entered into another phase of the ceremony. Clarence Williams is singing some mellow blues. She has placed the record on a Victrola. People begin to sway a bit along with the music.

What's that sound? Earline asks Black Herman.

It's a loa that Jes Grew here in America among our people. We call it Blues.

It sounds nice, Earline says, climbing from the bed in her barefeet and approaching Herman. LaBas and the women move out of the way. She puts her arms about Black Herman's neck and starts to move with him. As they dance about the table where the tumblers of the drink rest, cherries held by straws leaning on the rim, she tries to reach for the cocktail.

Herman pushes her hand away.

You better let me have that, nigger, before I put a hurtin' on you you won't like.

Black Herman walks to the bed, picks up her scarf, and casts it to the floor where it becomes a snake. He moves a fingertip in a teasing manner about the snake's head. A snake with sufficient deadly venom to fell an elephant.

Anybody can do that, Earline taunts. You don't have what it takes, Black American man, she says, moving again toward the tray.

Black Herman grabs her by the arms and flings her onto the bed. She starts to spring at him but before she can he swiftly moves the spread of hearts-and-daggers design out from under her and she lies curled-up, in thin air, about 2 feet between her and the top of the bed. Black Herman known as "an international heartbreaker," the man who while on the trip to Africa hypnotized a lion, is now the first American to give a Crisis de loa to a loa.

Earline twists in the air, confused.

Put me down! Put me down!

Black Herman reaches over to where she is suspended and puts his arm about her waist, gently bringing her body toward him like an intelligent fisherman reeling in, causing only a slight ripple in the water, enchanting the fish. Black Herman is a Fish Bewitcher.

He bends over, holding her there and kissing her. She begins to struggle but suddenly kisses him back, passionately hanging on to him as he holds her from the waist up, her bottom half suspended there like a mermaid in water.

Black Herman signals for the sisters and PaPa LaBas to leave the room. They quietly leave, turning the lights down to a dark red glow, the music a quiet piano moving through the room. Herman takes over where LaBas has failed.

Before LaBas exits he hears Black Herman whisper to Earline.

Softly, a husky whisper. Now you know you want to leave this girl now, don't you?

She cries passionately almost inaudibly Yes! Yes! You know I will; but first . . . please . . . please feed me! Then I will leave her . . .

The door closes shut.

41   About an hour later Black Herman emerges from the room. LaBas and the sisters are seated about the kitchen table drinking tea.

How is she? T Malice asks.

She'll be all right. When she wakes I want you to give her the magic bath; she will be herself again. But don't tell her about Berbelang, she won't remember anything from the last 24 hours or so. Just stay with her until she comes out of it and don't mention who visited her. 1 of the sisters nods.

LaBas sits a minute; Black Herman joins the rest at the table. How did you succeed where I failed, Herman?

Well it's like this, PaPa. You always go around speaking as if you were a charlatan and putting yourself down when you are 1 of the most technical dudes with The Work. Abdul was right that night . . . I didn't want to say. You ought to relax. That's our genius here in America. We were dumped here on our own without the Book to tell us who the loas are, what we call spirits were. We made up our own. The theories of Julia Jackson. I think we've done all right. The Blues, Ragtime, The Work that we do is just as good. I'll bet later on in the 50s and 60s and 70s we will have some artists and creators who will teach Africa and South America some new twists. It's already happening. What it boils down to, LaBas, is intent. If your heart's there, man, that's ½ the thing about The Work. Even the European Occultists say that. Doing The Work is not like taking inventory. Improvise some. Open up, PaPa. Stretch on out with It.

Maybe I'm a bit too rigid. 1 of Berbelang's friends, Jose Fuentes, called me a repressed Negro.

There was silence for a moment.

Don't you think we ought to check with Earline to see if the other 1 has completely left.

O pop, I don't believe that a little Erzulie ever did anybody any harm.

The sisters smile. T Malice smiles too.

42   The next morning LaBas receives a call from Black Herman, indicating that "visitors in the harbor" are anxious to meet with him. He also indicates that Earline is in good hands and that she is "coming out of it."

About a ½-hour later Herman's President straight 8 pulls up to Mumbo Jumbo Kathedral and LaBas enters.

Who are we to meet?

I am not at liberty to say—it's secret, but the people want very much for you to meet with them. Did you hear of Abdul Hamid's murder? Herman asks.

Yes, I forgot to say I discovered the body.

Was there anything to indicate how he got his?

I found something I didn't show to the police, but as you will recall he mentioned something about an anthology, the archives of an ancient people. I found a crumpled piece of paper, an epigram in his fist concerning Egyptian-American cotton. I can't connect it to anything but I have a nagging suspicion that it has something to do with the missing anthology. I can't put it out of my mind.

Strange, very strange, Black Herman said, steering the car toward the Hudson River pier. You know the night before he died I had a vision of him attired in something which resembled a night club floor, he was whirling about the center like a dervish, in the center, he wouldn't move away from that center . . .

LaBas hasn't paid attention to the last remark. He had picked up a copy of the New York *Sun*. It was folded to the society page and a red pencil had circled the picture of a distinguished looking grey-haired man above the caption "Patron-of-the-Arts." It was Hinckle Von Vampton, publisher of the *Benign Monster*. He wore a black patch over his eye but what was even stranger was the pendant he wore about his neck. The pendant depicted 2 Knights riding upon 1 horse.

A very interesting pendant; do you have it encircled for any particular reason, Herman?

I just want to keep my eye on him.

Once at the pier they approach the freighter *The Black Plume*. The ship's searchlight swings in their direction. It blinks on and off 3 times. 2 of the Host's assistants—Python men—both over 6 feet tall emerge from a room and lower the ramp. Black Herman and PaPa LaBas board. The men escort them into a stateroom where they are invited to sit upon some chairs. Outside the ship may be tugboat-shabby but the interior is beautiful. On the floor are loa signatures drawn with cornmeal and water. Rada Drums hang from the ceiling. The colors of the room are black and red, the walls are red, the floor is black. A flag hangs from the ceiling upon which has been sewn the words *Vin ' Bain Ding*, "Blood, Pain, Excrement." On a table are handbells, descendants of instruments Egyptians called (ancient) sistrums found in their Temples of Osiris and Isis. The central post is red. Incense composed of hot iron is burning.

On the walls are oil portraits of Toussaint L'Ouverture, and Jean

Jacques Dessalines, heroes who had expelled Napoleon's troops from Haiti and brought about the Independence of 1803. Next to these are portraits of Henri Christophe and Boukman, the Papa Loi, who rallied the Haitian countryside to the banner of VooDoo, and the mulatto general André Riguad.

A tall Black man enters the room. He is wearing a red robe and a long necklace made of beads and snake bones. On his finger is a ring upon which a Dark Tower is ensconced.

B. Battraville invites the others to sit. He sits, crosses his legs and lights a cigarette.

I must give you the background, gentlemen. As you well know we surrounded the Marines at Port-au-Prince but the action wasn't entirely successful because they had been tipped off by the mulatto secretary.

The *New York Times* called you bandits.

Benoit Battraville smiles as a tall Python man serves them rum.

Charlemagne Peralte was hardly a bandit. Our leader was a member of the Haitian elite. He did not invite the American Marines to land in our country on July 28, 1915. The U.S.S. *Washinton* landed uninvited. They came on their ships without an Act of your Kongress or consent of the American people.

We didn't learn about it until recently and that was when you surrounded the Marines . . .

We were lucky to hear even then, Black Herman, Battraville replies. It was made as a signal to someone. It was a telegram, a message by headline from 1 man to a secret society located in a "neutral country."

PaPa LaBas is startled . . . You mean?

Yes you were correct in your book *The Forest Within*. People thought it was merely a far-out work but we read what you were saying . . . At the foundation of the aesthetic order which pervades this country is a secret society—an ancient society known as the Atonist Path which is protected by its military arm the Wallflower Order, those to whom no 1 ever asked, "May I have this 1?"

Herman chuckled.

Why I'll be damned. I figured something like this was at the bottom because everyone is wondering why we were down there.

Economics didn't make sense, although, in his excellent *Nation* articles James Weldon Johnson did speak of the influence of the National City Bank.

Yes, that figured into it, but we saw it as merely an upsurgence of a Holy War they've waged against us and others like us for 1000s of years. They wanted to bring it to a head because they saw us as a beachhead for their ancient opponents and responsible for the Jes Grew crisis in your country.

Strange, the press claimed that you had dissected the President Vilbrun Guillaume Sam's . . . head.

They are required to yield their column inches to the Wallflower Order if they are to survive. What for us are heroes are for them robbers, killing a man who could not do malice with style is considered barbarism or cannibalism, worshiping out of doors in the woods instead of in a cathedral is a sign of unculturedness.

I don't follow, malice with style?

Yes, LaBas, certainly as a matter of course, there are to be political prisoners but not whole families randomly massacred in prison as Sam did. The U.S.S. *Washington* saw the punishment of the President as their excuse. They marched into the city. The 1st thing they did was remove all the money from our banks—$60,000,-000—to pay "debts" we owed.

Sounds like the American cowboy Jesse James, Black Herman muses.

Yes, and they call *us* robbers . . . It was a miracle that they wrote anything. The *Sun*. It's only because someone within the New York *Sun* wanted to intimidate the Wallflower Order, he is the man we are after, according to Ti Toubon. You see this was to be a mystery war and I would imagine that after the Americans withdraw, it will be completely deleted from the American "History Books." They've always wanted to drive out the ancient enemy; the anti-Christ as some of them call it.

1st they intimidate the intellectuals by condemning work arising out of their own experience as being 1-dimensional, enraged, non-objective, preoccupied with hate and not universal, universal being a word co-opted by the Catholic Church when the Atonists took over Rome, as a way of measuring every 1 by their ideals.

Yes, Black Herman ponders, the usual. A man downtown is trying to imitate me. A man named Houdini (Ehrich Weiss) is attempting to do what I do . . . this man should know that he can't do what I do.

What *is* your specialty, Herman?

Lying buried underground for 8 days, Benoit. I have performed it all over the world. But please continue your narration.

Benoit Battraville drinks from the cup of rum . . . Artists who were found in possession of The Work were beaten whipped and subjected to a torture, a French invention called "blanchings"; they sent out squads of Marines to interrupt the ceremonies and destroy the wood sculpture and drums.

What did you do?

We merely practiced Catholicism up front and VooDoo underground. Similar to your New Orleans expression "doing the Calinda against the Dude."

Black Herman lifts a glass of white rum to his lips and returns the glass to the table.

The joke became "The Haitian people are 95% Catholic and 100% VooDoo." The Belgians and French were always bewildered when we laughed as they tried to interpret St. Jacques as Ogoun, the Warrior! the Gangster! the Fire!

Herman and LaBas chuckle.

The Americans were worse. We knew that we would suffer under the Marines because they were Southern Marines. Southerners being descendants of convicts from Europe, we knew they would not have the sophistication of, say, New Yorkers who had read Freud. The manner of torture they extended to their Black victims. The burning, the hanging. Burning was the traditional way used by early Europe of ridding people of the plague of the pagan religions.

How did this come about? LaBas asks.

We do not work the way you do. You improvise here a great deal; we believe in the old mysteries. I occasionally practice the Petro Loa. Not much but I raise the altitude a little. Kick up a fuss. You see, Charlemagne was arrested by the Marines for aiding the Cacos, peasants who had revolted against them in 1915, and he was forced to do hard labor in a convict's uniform in the street.

The Marines raped our women, they took a member of the

Assembly and kicked him in the seat of his pants in the presence of the people. They used what you call "Crackers" to administer our educational system. Our Superintendent of Public Instruction was a school teacher from Louisiana; they used our official limousines so that our own President had to borrow a car from the Occupation in order to make a trip into the interior.

PaPa LaBas and Black Herman listen, indignant.

Their slothful wives and children occupied villas with many servants while our men were used as cheap labor to build plazas resembling a picnic in Sheboygan.

Herman and LaBas laugh —

Deluxe Ice Cream, Coffee, 1 cent Pies, Cakes, Tobacco, Hot Dogs and Highways. Highways leading to nowhere. Highways leading to somewhere. Highways the Occupation used to speed upon in their automobiles, killing dogs pigs and cattle belonging to the poor people. What *is* the American fetish about highways?

They want to get somewhere, LaBas offers.

Because something is after them, Black Herman adds.

But what is after them?

They are after themselves. They call it destiny. Progress. We call it Haints. Haints of their victims rising from the soil of Africa, South America, Asia.

Well at any rate I am getting away from our story. Charlemagne escaped, and soon the cry was "Let all Haitians rise and drive the American Marines into the sea just as our ancestors did the French." He rallied the Cacos to his banner of Ogoun War Loa. I joined him. We are the 1st to fight a guerrilla war against modern armed forces. It was 1918, a few short years ago. It became a sport of the American Marines to shoot the Cacos on sight, but we countered by moving in small detachments during the night and ambushing many a Marine patrol. Soon the conch horns and the drums informed the people all over the country that we had returned to our ancient religion just as our ancestors the Egyptians the Nubians the Ethiopians did in times of trouble. The Marines became nervous. They didn't expect this.

Strange, there was nothing about this in the press? Black Herman questions. Even if it was a mystery war it seems that an explosion such as this would reach the ears of the people here.

We received help from the N.A.A.C.P., James Weldon Johnson

and his articles in the *Nation* magazine. There was no phone campaign among the rich telephone owners. No receptions in swanky Park Ave. parlors. No ads in newspapers or massive demonstrations. We weren't only a political cause but a cause that went to the very heart of Western Civilization. You see, there are many types of Atonists. Politically they can be "Left," "Right," "Middle," but they are all together on the sacredness of Western Civilization and its mission. They merely disagree on the ways of sustaining it. If a radio show began touting the achievements of Western Civilization over civilizations of others there would barely be a letter to the station from anyone, anarchist or Calvin Coolidge Republican . . .

We made a sacred journey to have Ogoun possess us to know our course. By this time I was close to Charlemagne and we went to Arcahaie where in the hills lived 1 Ti Bouton who "conversed with the streams and could produce rain in the dry season and make lightning strike" as someone said. He was so powerful he could make the *Titanic* sink a second time.

Ti Bouton did not like the secretary Charlemagne brought along, a mulatto who was trained in France and possessed by the White man's loas. He had made some remarks dismissing our ancient faith as "crazy" or "sick" and backward "mumbo jumbo."

That sounds familiar, PaPa LaBas mulls.

The mulatto was taking black out of blanc. Minstrelsy is not confined to your theaters.

What happened at the meeting with Ti Bouton?

Ti Bouton told us not to go to Port au Prince . . . Charlemagne did not agree with him because the weather appeared to be favorable and the invasion had been prepared. Ti Bouton told us that we would need a Great White Host in order to force the American Marines, who were rampaging the countryside machine-gunning 1000s of people, to withdraw.

Charlemagne dismissed this. He was a VooDooist but refused to practice the old ways. Ti Bouton told him that a Great White Host had to be captured. "A Star" of the Western occult, as they say in your movies. Their talk ended in a quarrel.

At dawn the next day we entered the Caco Trail of the Bel Air Gulch for our invasion of the city. We fought all night. There were casualties on both sides. But we were routed because the Marines had been tipped off by the mulatto secretary. The people who joined in our massacre warfare against the Marines were killed. Charlemagne was killed by a Southern Marine disguised as a Black woman who penetrated our line and shot him as he stood over a campfire. I went back to Ti Bouton. He told me that I must come here and find this White Host whom he said had been dispatched here on a mission for the Wallflower Order. A Knights Templar.

What is the Templar's job? PaPa LaBas asks.

It's something in connection with the Jes Grew phenomenon, the epidemic. He is supposed to work within the Negro to refine it. For this he needs a Talking Android; a Human Vaccine who will make Jes Grew seem harmful to the J.G.C.s; make certain that they don't pick up on it.

Do you know this man's name?

No, Black Herman, we just know that he's here in the city. You see, our loas adapt to change. We have a new loa with very special appetites. This 1 possesses a technological bent.

You mean you are going to sacrifice him?

No, LaBas, we are going to present him before the loa and the loa will do with him what it desires. We want you to help us in this.

We will be glad to, PaPa LaBas offers. Anything that I can do to help you in your effort to find this man . . .

We think that he will be working to acquire the Text that Jes Grew needs to thrive, if that's what it's looking for; they're not sure. They have several plans we know, finding the Text and destroying it, creating a Human Vaccine—a J.G.C.'s J. G. Repellent is another.

I will begin to look about. To get on the case.

Fine! Thanks to you and Black Herman we may be able to continue with this . . .

A tall Python man refreshes their drink after Benoit Battraville presses a button. Benoit Battraville rises and puts a record on a Victrola he has in the room. A recording made by Sweet Poppa Stovepipe: "Black Mud."

One thing, Benoit?

Yes . . .

The music begins to waft across the room.

Why if Charlemagne was repulsed by the practice of the Petro Way weren't you?

He was of the elite, I am a Blacksmith. Besides Petro is my

Order. We must always revive the ancient ways if they are to remain effective. Ti Bouton told us these things in a language he spoke: Le Guinee, named after the continent which sank 1000s of years ago. The continent the Greeks called Atlantis which some claim is buried beneath our island, the home of the loas.

The 3 listen. Black Herman's attention is drawn by a little wooden Erzulie ship which hung from the ceiling.

It's beautifully done work, the legerdemain Black Herman admires.

Yes, I have to keep an eye on her. She's in her Petro Moon and if I am not careful she will walk all over this town. I have had my technicians feed her . . .

That's a good idea, Black Herman says, otherwise she will "touch" somebody. This Templars thing incidentally. What are they?

It all began in 1118 A.D. when a man named Hugues de Payens organized it with the aid of 8 knights . . .

● ○

They talk all night. Benoit Battraville explains the Templars' mission and their employers, the Wallflower Order; they discuss techniques and therapy associated with The Work. Similarities and differences between South American, North American and African rites.

Black Herman and PaPa LaBas leave early in the morning as dawn comes over New York. Just as LaBas is walking down the ramp with Black Herman, he turns to Benoit Battraville standing in *The Black Plume*'s stateroom doorway.

You are very erudite in not only your own history but the history of the world and in a language we understand. What is the reason for this?

You actually have been talking to a seminar all night. Agwe, God of the Sea in his many manifestations, took over when I found it difficult to explain things. In fact this is his ship. He presides over our Navy.

LaBas smiles. That Old Work was some Work.

As he and Black Herman approach Black Herman's auto, Herman turns to PaPa LaBas.

Of course there was the man alternating with the spirit . . .

didn't you see him jerk from time to time. Jerk his head. Next time you go to a so-called Holiness storefront watch the soloist who is backed up by the choir of rattling tambourines; see if he or she doesn't jerk her head at a crucial moment "when the Spirit hits her."

It's all over the place, isn't it. I should have known. Different methods. Different signs, but all taking you where you want to go.

The men climb into the car and head from the pier. Then, into Manhattan.

PaPa LaBas thinks to himself as he rides alongside the silent Black Herman, *Perhaps I have been insular, as Berbelang said, limiting myself to a Mumbo Jumbo Kathedral, not allowing myself to witness the popular manifestations of The Work.*

43 Hinckle Von Vampton is frustrated by Jes Grew. The egregiousness of its invasiveness. Its total catch-on abilities. *The 2 candidates had shunned him as if . . . as if . . . they'd caught on. Was the Jes Grew an intelligence which, similar to the Wallflower Order, owned an administrative arm. capable of wising people up? Would his attempt at restoring the glory of the Knights Templar be spoiled? Yes, they had received a tentative acquittal but spectators were watching to see if they'd come through; whether they still had what it took. Jes Grew was on the Rise. If it captured New York its total control on the Radio would be complete. Warren Harding had said Let's End Wiggle and Wobble. But Jes Grew was wiggling wobbling rambling and shambling ringing and chaining. Up. Down. Any which-a-way. Couples were marathon dancing until they fainted in 1 another's arms. The Teutonics were holding meetings again at a resort called Berchtesgaden. Had they found out that he had failed? No 1 could be found to become his Talking Android, his pet zombie he could use any way he wanted to undermine Jes Grew. Tell it, it was promising but flawed. Tell it that it had a long way to go. Recently in Russia Claude McKay when approached by a liberal to address the revolution on behalf of the*

Black worker said, "I have no mandate from the Black worker to speak for him."

Individuality. It couldn't be herded, rounded-up; it was like crystals of winter each different from one another but in a storm going down together. What would happen if they dispersed, showing up when you least expected them; what would happen if you couldn't predict their minds? The Holy War in Haiti was going badly. They had broken into the humfos and destroyed the govis, brushed out the veves, killed the houngans in cold blood but as soon as they destroyed 1 humfos another 1 would rise. And what made it so confusing was that the new humfo only resembled the preceding 1 in essential ways so that not detecting a pattern they could have no plan of attack. Everyone, since the newspaper headline, had become an expert on Haiti. The men dressing in white linen suits; the women wearing the most outlandish geegaws and long colorful skirts. The colors blinded Hinckle. He preferred grey and dark colors. They would have to outlaw color this time around. Better make a note of this. There was no 1 and the time was running out. He had said 6 months and there is only a couple of weeks remaining.

He picks up the Aunt Jemima pancake mix box. He studies the picture. *Hey . . . maybe the Talking Android could be a 19th-century Mammy Juddy on the plantation who would once more serve me, the slavemaster, by scolding his daughters for behaving like tomboys and prevent Jes Grew from continuing its rise. No, that's too obvious. No, it seemed that the only 1 would be Woodrow Wilson . . . ! Of course he's too black . . . hey but wait a minute.* He examines the skin-lightener ads in a Race newspaper he had bought for leads on Talking Android candidates.

44   Hubert "Safecracker" Gould? Come in here!

The Peter-Lorre-eyed bunched-up man, about 5′1″ enters the room.

Yes Hinckle?

Listen, I got a great plan; by the way, where have you been all day?

I was in Harlem watching the little colored waifs play in the school yard. Some of them dropped their notes which I immediately swept into my briefcase and they would bawl but then I appeased the little chocolate dollops by awarding them peppermint candy. I am sure that some publisher will be eager to accept such a manuscript; some of it is quite good. I'll dash off an introduction and with the royalties why . . . why . . . I'll be able to buy a summer home in the Berkeley hills of that rising community on the West Coast where everyone goes about saying things like: Well can you prove this? I mean don't you think we need evidence for this? Who's your source?

Good for you, Hubert. I think I've solved the problem of the Talking Android, someone to . . . well, you know the assignment.

When did you recruit him? Today while I was gone?

He's been here all along.

What do you mean? I don't understand?

W.W.!!

Why he's too dark, Hinckle; they'll never accept him. I know, I've been to Harlem 3 maybe 4 times and I read the magazines.

Look at this . . . Hinckle says shoving the Race newspaper in front of his face.

Hubert "Safecracker" Gould's eyes expand.

Why Hinckle! Of course! You're a damned genius.

45 But I don't want to put that mess on my face. That stuff burns your face. There ain't nothing in the contract got to do with putting that cream on my face . . . procuring them old nasty animals is enough for me to be doing.

Well, I thought you wanted an editor-in-chief position with the *Benign Monster*, but I guess we overestimated his abilities, Hubert; come on let's go . . .

Wait . . . wait a minute, Woodrow Wilson calls to the men who are about to leave his suite located at the rear of Spiraling Agony. Bring it back here a minute.

Hinckle smiles at Hubert and returns to where W.W. sits at his desk. W.W. dips his fingers into the cream from the jar Hubert holds.

Bring that mirror over here.

Hubert takes an oval-shaped mirror with a scallop-decorated frame from the wall and hands it to Wilson. W.W. applies some of the lightener to his face and looks into the mirror; Hinckle and Hubert, stand behind him, beaming.

It don't look too bad; a little more and I'll be a light brown and then . . .

LAWD! LAWD! LAWD! WE COMES UP HERE TO FETCH THE PRODIGAL SON AND HERE WE IS GOT D WHORE OF BABYLON! LAWD IT'S WORSE THAN I THOUGHT!

The 3, Hubert, Hinckle and W.W., turn to see a huge man dressed in a black Stetson, Wild Bill Hickok flowing tie and black clergyman outfit and cowboy boots.

PA!!!

The 3 deacons accompanying Rev. Jefferson kneel as Rev. Jefferson stretches his hands toward the heavens.

Lawd we axes you to pray over this boy . . . mmmmmmmmmmmm
An' deliver this child away from these naked womens . . . mmmm
And sweet back mens. And save his soul from torment . . . mm

What is the meaning of this? Busting into my estate unannounced like this? Who are these men, W.W.? Hinckle asks, turning to his columnist.

W.W. is sobbing softly. It's my paw and his deacons, Publisher Hinckle Von Vampton.

Well it's a pleasure to meet you, Hinckle says, slithering over to where the quartet stand, menacing and strong in the doorway.

O no you don't. You wants to make 1 of them things out of me as well; I'm not going to stand for it.

Rev. Jefferson slugs Hinckle Von Vampton with a fist that has toted many a grain sack and tamed many a horse. Hinckle kind of floats to the rug, out cold. Hubert "Safecracker" Gould tries to flee through the door but is grabbed quickly by the 3 other deacons who've accompanied their pastor from Rĕ'-mōte Mississippi.

That's right men. Bust him up. It ain't no use to planting potatoes when it's hog-killing time.

In the other room, sure enough, Hubert "Safecracker" Gould can be heard squealing and knocking over furniture trying to escape their grip.

Pa . . . I was just trying to get out there.

Don't be using none of the city talk at me. We've been driving for 1 week. I couldn't believe it. You told me you were working for a magazine and I was proud and went around telling everybody about it then 1 of the sisters brought me a copy and I knew, son, that you had left the teachings of d church and well son, I'm here going to take you back to Rē'-mōte and try to heal yo' soul, you up here posing with all types of trash. Come here.

No, pa! Don't do that!

I said come here boy! Raising your voice at me! Rev. Jefferson walks toward his son with an open 12-foot cotton sack and doesn't stop until he gets him all the way. One squirming shoe shows and he pushes that in too.

Rev. Jefferson brushes his hands. Puts the wiggling, protesting sack over his shoulder steps over Hinckle Von Vampton and starts out to join his men to begin the journey back to Mississippi. The Rev. Jefferson, his deacons go outside and climb into their T Model Fords which at that time had such a reliable engine you could plow with it.

Once inside their cars, Rev. Jefferson and one of the deacons ride in the front of their car; the sack is on the backseat.

Rev.?

Yes, Deacon Jones.

Rev., what are you going to tell the folks back at the church when they find out that you resorted to beating on these men?

I got it all worked out, deacon.

How's that?

John 2:14.

I don't understand, Rev.

Christ and the money lenders. New Yorkers ain't the only 1s possess a science.

The deacon scratches his head as the 3 T Model Fords rumble on out of Spiraling Agony's path toward the highway.

●　　○

Hinckle Von Vampton comes to. He looks about W.W. Jefferson's suite. That preacher had a pretty solid punch to be a man of the cloth. Hinckle climbs to his feet and staggers out to the front of the mansion. The place is a mess. Chicken feathers are all over the floor. Brogan prints. Half-chewed chunks of tobacco. How had 1 man put it? "Quintessential Americans."

Well that's what these Southern preachers are; man, could they bop you one! What was that? The sound of moaning coming from the front yard. Hinckle walks out to see Hubert "Safecracker" Gould lying face down in the mud, groaning. He goes into the kitchen and returns with a pitcher of water. He walks over to where Gould lies and turns him over. His face is covered with the black mud. *Why of course*, Hinckle thinks, *why not?* Hinckle is desperate and would resort to any means in order to come through with the flying colors. He pours cold water on Hubert's face, and Hubert wakens from his unconsciousness. Hinckle helps Hubert to his feet and then goes into the house to make a phone call to a woman he knows.

46   An Android in mint-green long johns which cover everything but his face rolls into the room and salutes the Hierophant 1.

Yes?

Trouble, sir. Everything has been confirmed. He just entered the Lincoln bedroom, locked the door and removed a clandestine Victrola from under the bed . . . he then . . . he then . . . the thing muttered in its vocal monotone, flashing its eyes.

Well, go on.

He put on a record entitled "The Whole World Is Jazz Crazy" and began to tap his "pedal extremities" as Fats Waller would say.

Fats Waller? Who is this Fats Waller?

He's a piano player, sir. He wrote "Soothin' Syrup Stomp," "Stompin' the Bug," "Hog Maw Stomp," "The Rusty Pail" and one the boys down in central control enjoy called "Abercrombie had a zombie."

How did you become so familiar with this Jazz? The Hierophant gives the assemblage of wires and aluminum metal a steely questioning look.

You told us to keep an eye on Jes Grew, sir.

O, yes . . . true.

The Android turns about and leaves the room.

He thought it was antiseptic up here. He'd have to watch that Android in case the Germ was about. Warren Harding. Him too? Of course there had been rumors during the campaign, the book brought to Washington by guarded express car, written by 1 William Eastbrook and based upon interviews with Harding's neighbors of Marion Ohio who said that they had never treated his father as a White man. The books had been secretly destroyed in a bonfire.

Even the plates were destroyed. Another book, *Warren Harding, President of the United States*, worth $200,000 per copy, is available only from the "Rare Book Room of the New York Public Library."* 250,000 copies of a book which asserted Harding's Negro ancestry had previously been ordered destroyed by Woodrow Wilson. (It seems that the Haitian minister to Paris requested an audience with Woodrow Wilson to complain to this lying, hypocritical champion of "self-determination" the pain the American occupation was inflicting upon the Haitian people. The envoy was rudely dismissed by Wilson's Secretary of State Robert Lansing. Wilson later lay ill, helpless, exhibiting the symptoms of VooDoo vengeance, for example, lassitude, the inability to concentrate more than 10 minutes at a time.)† When Republicans approached Harding with these rumors and asked him to deny them he said, "How should I know. One of my ancestors might have jumped the fence."‡ What kind of answer was that? They had received reports from Hinckle Von Vampton that he had attended a Rent Party where he mingled with J.G.C.s and now this.

● ○

The author Mark Sullivan paints a picture I would imagine to be prolific with shadows, a waning witch-moon covered with shiny oil, 1 dark figure darting through a deserted street. The subject is the mysterious Harry Daugherty of whom the biographer wrote, "one of his eyes was imperfect, and the other, at the beginning of an acquaintance, seemed to circle round the man rather than focus on him, as if he was getting his impression, not from a physical man, but from some psychic aura about him, not visible to an ordinary eye." Harry Daugherty is not only Harding's

---

* *The Five Negro Presidents U.S.A.*—J. A. Rogers.
† *The Harding Era*—Robert K. Murray.
‡ *The Five Negro Presidents U.S.A.*—J. A. Rogers.

poker partner, the man who was to put up with the Presidents' swearing and drinking, but he is also the man "who pushed into the water" this reluctant candidate who would have preferred to remain in the Senate. You guessed it. Harry Daugherty is an agent of the Wallflower Order.

They thought that Harding would be perfect for the job of Jes Grew stopper. Hadn't he earned his 1st dollar cutting corn? Didn't he assist local farmers in painting their barns and thrashing? As a printer hadn't he learned the art of "sticking type, feeding press, making forms, and washing rollers?" Hadn't this man maintained William McKinley's flagpole on his lawn as a good luck symbol? Didn't he sprinkle his conversation with such wholesome expressions as "pleased as punch?" Wasn't his favorite reading matter "the funnies?" And his contribution to building the Ohio railroad; what about that?

Wasn't this a sedate businessman, newspaper editor and family man, a devoted husband of Florence, a dashing husband who campaigned often, dressed in white trousers, blue coat and saw-tooth hat? Here was a man whose opinions were those of Muncie, Indiana and now he had been exposed as Black.

They can't use the lone psychopath emerging suddenly as the President's party enters the train station. They used that with Garfield. No, they must use something different this time. Poison. It all adds up to guilty. He attended a Rent Party, exposed the Holy War in Haiti and now this. And when he was quoted as saying, "The Negro should be the Negro and not an imitation White man," what did he mean by that? Was that some kind of code he was giving to Blacks? You know, how they talk sometime you don't know what they're saying and as soon as you find out they done gone on to something else.

The Hierophant phones Harry Daugherty to tell him of his decision.

47 . . . Jes Smith, a friend, attempts to warn Harding but "commits suicide"* in Harry Daugherty's apartment. As soon as Warren Harding boards a train for what has become known to historians as "Harding's mysterious journey West," they begin

* *Our Times*, vol. 6, *The Twenties*—Mark Sullivan.

injecting the poison. By the time he reaches San Francisco by way
of Alaska on the morning of July 29 he is described by reporters
as "gray and worn."

They finish the job at the Palace Hotel in San Francisco.
Harding had the last word though. It is contained in a message he
was to deliver before the Hollywood Chapter of the Knights
Templar, entitled "The Ideals of a Christian Fraternity."* (*In this
way, he points his finger at his killers. Few historians have under-
stood this clue.*—I.R.)

48 That evening PaPa LaBas sits in the office of Mumbo Jumbo Kathedral. He has closed the place until further notice. He is thinking of the deaths of his assistants Charlotte, Berbelang; and of Abdul Hamid. Was there a common thread which united them? If he could only find the Text. Abdul must have had it. He must have really been on to something. The Text must be somewhere in New York because wasn't Jes Grew headed this way? Jes Grew would smell it out. He studies once again the epigram on cotton.

T Malice enters the room.

I went to see Earline over at Black Herman's.

How is she?

She's her old self. She took Berbelang's death hard they say but got over it. The sisters will take care of her for a few weeks. Think I'll go take in a show.

LaBas rolls a pencil in his fingers.

Where are you going? To a talkie?

No, thought I would go to the Cotton Club. There's a terrific comedy team called the Warp and Woof formerly of the Diastole and Systole who imitate 3rd-rate literary critics with a passion. They are hilarious. Then there's the Dancing Bales; that tap dance group taps so that the floorboards begin to creak.

Excited LaBas looks at T Malice. Say that again.

The Dancing Bales they dance so . . .

Come on let's go.

But where?

No time to explain. LaBas flies down the stairs to the car, T Malice gasping for breath as he tries to keep up with the old man.

49 Those who have been interviewed by Hinckle Von Vampton for Talking Android don't have very much longer to wait. The 3 black Buicks bearing Haitian license plates pull up to the intersection of what is now 8th Ave. and 125th St. The men climb into the 3 cars and are driven to the pier near the blind pig where recently a series of amorous adventures culminated in a 1 night stand which nearly lost an innocent trolley car operator his happy home. They board *The Black Plume* and wait in the stateroom until Benoit Battraville (so bad that he isn't mentioned in the index of one of the few books which cite him) enters the room.

Several aides have brought Dictaphones.

The men start to rise but Benoit Battraville signals them to keep their seats. He sits down and begins smoking a cigar; the men are served some white rum.

Gentlemen, thank you for your cooperation. Our request may sound a bit eccentric to you but my friend Nathan Brown tells me that you will cooperate. When Nathan Brown visited our Island last summer we got in contact with him to inform him of a strange plan the Wallflower Order had devised for putting an end to what has become known here as the Jes Grew epidemic. They were to dispatch a man here to groom a Talking Android who would work within the Negro to purge it . . . I enlisted the cooperation of Nathan to tell all of you to be on the lookout for such a man. He is a candidate for a plan we have. He has failed in his plan so I don't see how he would object to aiding the completion of ours.

The men laugh.

I am in a buoyant mood. My Ghede is getting the best of me tonight because I am happy to say we have success. PaPa LaBas called me a short time ago to tell me he had evidence to link a gentleman named Hinckle Von Vampton to the plot and he will arrest him and his assistants tonight at a gala affair at Irvington-on-Hudson. He will then deliver the gentlemen to our little ship and then we shall return to our Island. There is 1 other man who is associated with this pair, too, but our elder statesman Houngan Ti Bouton wants to handle this 1 himself. So if you would just cooperate, all of the men who were approached by Hinckle Von Vampton are welcome to remain in here and the others may depart. I thank you for your cooperation.

About 9 men finish their drinks and leave. Those remaining wait for further instructions from Benoit Battraville.

Now, as 1 of your theoreticians has already said, no 1 knows how a new loa is formed. But we know that when 1 comes about it must be fed, similar to the way you feed your Ragtime and Jazz by supporting the artists and making it easier for those who are possessed by those forms. Buying records and patronizing those places which are not in the hands of Atonists. You know that if you don't do this, Ragtime and Jazz will turn upon you or unfed they will perish. Similarly we have a Radio Loa who just came about during this war. It loves to hear the static concerning its victims' crimes before it "eats" them. I know this is a strange request but if you will just 1 by 1 approach the Dictaphone, tell just how Hinckle Von Vampton propositioned you, the circumstances and the proposals he made to you, we will record this and then feed it to our loa. This particular loa has a Yellow Back to symbolize its electric circuitry. We are always careful not to come too close to it. It's a very mean high-powered loa.

There is no further persuasion needed for these sensible hard-working artists. As the others drink rum and eat mangoes Major Young approaches the recording.

I walked into the cabaret 1 night. I was in the company of a mixed gathering and no sooner had I sat at my table than Hubert "Safecracker" Gould approached me and said that he wanted to introduce me to Hinckle Von Vampton. I joined this man who was wearing a black patch over his eye . . . a . . .

Excellent! Excellent! Benoit Battraville said as 1 of his attendants began to play it back. Soon the voice came on again

I walked into the cabaret one night . . . The voice comes across loud and clear. Major Young tells his story. He is followed by Nathan Brown. It goes on until the 10 or so men who had been approached by Hinckle Von Vampton have completed their narratives. It is close to 9:00 P.M. when they finish. They start to leave the ship, each of them being given an honorary houngan license. Nathan Brown pauses at the door leading from the stateroom.

Benoit?

Yes, Nathan.

You said you were going to teach me how to catch it.

Catch what, Nathan?

Jes Grew.

O . . . I think you ought to ask PaPa LaBas or Black Herman. You see the Americans do not know the names of the long and tedious list of deities and rites as we know them. Shorthand is what they know so well. They know this process for they have synthesized the HooDoo of VooDoo. Its blee blop essence; they've isolated the unknown factor which gives the loas their rise. Ragtime. Jazz. Blues. The new thang. That talk you drum from your lips. Your style. What you have here is an experimental art form that all of us believe bears watching. So don't ask me how to catch Jes Grew. Ask Louis Armstrong, Bessie Smith, your poets, your painters, your musicians, ask them how to catch it. Ask those people who be shaking their tambourines impervious of the ridicule they receive from Black and White Atonists, Europe the ghost rattling its chains down the deserted halls of their brains. Ask those little colored urchins who "make up" those new dance steps and the loa of the Black cook who wrote the last lines of the "Ballad of Jesse James." Ask the man who, deprived of an electronic guitar, picked up a washboard and started to play it. The Rhyming Fool who sits in Rĕ′-mōte Mississippi and talks "crazy" for hours. The dazzling parodying punning mischievous pre-Joycean style-play of your Cakewalking your Calinda your Minstrelsy give-and-take of the ultra-absurd. Ask the people who put wax paper over combs and breathe through them. In other words, Nathan, I am saying Open-Up-To-Right-Here and then you will have something coming from your experience that the whole world will admire and need. But your musicians are dying your novelists are exiled for telling the truth your poets are pawning their coats for 10 dollars your people are talking of the New Negro movement but they can't discuss more than 2 writers or a single painter or when they talk about Scott Joplin the Apostle of Ragtime I see shame in their eyes. Look, Nathan, our nation did not heed the prophecies of its artists and it paid dearly. We will never make that mistake again.

Nathan walks toward Benoit and embraces him. Nathan turns and walks toward the cabin door.

Nathan?

He turns around.

Now I know why they rub you J.G.C.s on their heads up here for good luck. You are walking fetishes. You are indeed beautiful.

Nathan waves goodbye to his friend and walks out the door. He's got that strange sensation at the nape of his neck. He has finally Caught-On.

> After the stock market crash, some New York editors suggested that hearings be held; what had really caused the Depression? They were held in Washington. In retrospect, they make the finest comic reading. The leading industrialists and bankers testified. *They hadn't the foggiest notion what had gone bad.* (My italics—I.R.)
>
> Carey McWilliams, from *Hard Times* (1970) by
> Studs Terkel

50 Hierophant 1 of the Wallflower Order has been in the dumps since Jes Grew came within 60 miles of New York. Things look hopeless. It has been an interesting 2,000 years but this is the end of the road. 2,000 years of probing classifying attempting to make an "orderly" world so that when company came they would know the household's nature and would be careful about dropping ashes on the rug. 2,000 years of patrolling the plants. He would miss the daily species count. The Ethiopian Leopard was just about due, would be no more and would become a job order for the taxidermist. Several other species he wanted to rub out including the Hawaiian Hoary Bat the Morro Bay Kangaroo the Vahontan Cutthroat Trout the California Clapper Rail. Regretfully he would have to take a rain check. He wouldn't live to see their extermination. Jes Grew was rising to shrieks of Hit me! Hit me!

The Hierophant is about to lift the famous cup containing the not-so-famous poison to his lips when the telephone rings. The red button on the Jes Grew board is lighting up. What is this? What is happening? 30% fewer cases in Ithaca, Schenectady cured, Syracuse rallying, Troy calm, normal. Glory, could it be, Lord? Lord Lord Lord, could it be? The Maiden snatched from the Dragon's jaws and all that jazz. Who could it be on the phone?

Looks like you made it, says the voice on the other end.

It is the only man in that bloody mid-Atlantic mess with some sense, Walter Mellon, "the Sphinx," a cool tycoon who knows the score. He is a practical man. A man who could be trusted. A Pragmatist! A man who isn't devoted to graphs and theory like a tweedy economics professor but someone who speaks freely of "jawboning," "bulls" and "bears." From his "throne-like swivel chair" Walter Mellon the Sphinx conducts the Order of the Wallflower in America. He is aloof and correct. He dresses in black, grey and constantly puffs on an indigo colored cigarette.

Mr. Walter Mellon, thank you, we've come through once again. May I make a suggestion?

Of course. Your counsel is very valuable to us, Mr. Mellon.

This is the way I look at it. Jes Grew tied up the tubes causing Dr. Lee De Forest to cop a plea at the press conference.

That is correct, Mr. Walter Mellon.

At the rate of radio sales, 600,000,000 dollars' worth will be sold by 1929, correct?

That is true, Mr. Walter Mellon.

Suppose people don't have the money to buy radios. It will be an interesting precaution against this Jes Grew thing, isn't that so?

I don't get what you're driving at, Mr. Mellon.

The liquidity of Jes Grew has resulted in a hyperinflated situation, all you hear is more, more, increase growth . . . Suppose we shut down a few temples . . . I mean banks, take money out of circulation, how would people be able to support the appendages of Jes Grew, the cabarets the jook joints and the speaks. Suppose we put a tax on the dance floors and get out of circulation J.G.C.s like musicians, dancers, its doers, its irrepressible fancy. Suppose we take musicians out of circulation, arrest them on trumped-up drug charges and give them unusually long and severe prison sentences. Suppose we subsidize the 100s of symphony orchestras across the country, have government-sponsored

Waltz-boosting campaigns, disperse the art from the Art Detention Center so that if the *Mu'tafikah* strike again all of the pillage won't be in 1 place.

But wouldn't these steps result in a depression?

Maybe, but it will put an end to Jes Grew's resiliency and if a panic occurs it will be a controlled panic. It will be our Panic.

Being a holy man, these matters confuse me. You know what is best. If you think it will work, by all means activate your plan.

Good! I am glad you see it that way.

The phone rings again and Hinckle's pet zombie Lester answers.

It's the Teutonics, sir.

What do they want?

They say they didn't want to say I told you so about the Knights Templar but with the Templars failure to come through on phase 2 of the campaign you will of course consider another 1 of their candidates for a go at the Grail? Bearing the ancient grudge, arising from the time they were driven by their rivals from the seaport town of Acre, they are eager to show these "daisies" up.

Who is the candidate?

They say they have a housepainter in the balcony.

O.K. Bring him downstairs to front row center. Give him a crack at it. What will be the rouse this time, territorial claims, national honor, for Him, a maiden, or that and more?

A grab bag with a few novelties tossed in. He's an original.

51   The gathering is held in a villa located at Irvington-on-Hudson, so named Villa Lewaro, an anagram upon the Hostess' name, by famed tenor Enrico Caruso. The purchasing price was $250,000 for this place which rests upon a hill overlooking a lake filled with swans and ducks swimming among water lilies.

The hill's slope rolls down into a mile of lawn. Inside the home, in 1 room, can be heard someone playing an étude by Chopin upon a 24-karat-gold-decorated white piano. The furniture is Hepplewhite and upon the walls hang paintings by Renaissance masters. The whole scene is dominated by a $60,000 pipe organ whose pipes are as tall as the 1s atop the Bethlehem Steel Co. in Lackawanna New York. Mingling among the guests, maids carry trays supporting succulent tidbits in blankets, antipasto, gherkins stuffed with nutmeats, marinated oysters in pastry, braised celery and shrimp puffs, cucumbers filled with crab meat. Champagne flows.

Princes of Europe rub elbows with Harlem poets, tycoons from Tin Pan Alley have brought their stables, playwrights, painters, publishers, producers, sports figures, Negro delineators, middle-aged Byron-Shelley-quoting Negro professors thrilled by their newly found Negroness and who remember when this particular revelation occurred, the time the day and what they were doing. Rudolph Valentino is asking a Black poet the pronunciation of the last word of the title of a film he is doing which allegorizes war death famine and pestilence. Race leaders, doctors, dentists and other professionals are also in attendance. Taking his threat seriously, many are wearing Cab Calloway for President buttons.

The majordomo announces the entrance of a woman Countee

Cullen called "the Queen of Ubangi"; she is short, stocky and wears white gloves which reach her elbows and an evening gown and white fur cape. On one side of her is Hinckle Von Vampton and on the other . . . the Talking Android!!

The people, strolling upon Thug-sewn Persian rugs, politely applaud Vampton and his Find as they majestically escort the woman down the winding marble staircase. This is a signal that the cultural program is about to begin and people take their seats in the library where a stand has been set up near the man who is still playing Chopin.

While they await the entrance, a man at the side of the room taunts the elegant tails-wearing red-cravated patent-leather-shoe-wearing musician.

Hey man, tickle out a few hot licks!

I beg your pardon but I only deal with the Classics. Chopin, Liszt, and their imitators are my forte.

Well excuuuuuuuuuuuuuuuuuuusssssssssss eeeeeeeee me! the man mimics the pianist, arching his nose in imitation.

The glistening party enters the room. Hinckle, the Hostess and the Talking Android face the people now in the straight-back chairs that have been assembled in the living room.

Ladies and gentlemen, we have the pleasure of introducing tonight Mr. Hinckle Von Vampton, editor of a very thrilling delightful and inspiring magazine, the *Bombay Master* . . .

Hinckle whispers into the woman's ear. She continues in a sing-song voice.

. . . O, I stand corrected. The *Benign Monster* magazine, you know, which was recently banned in Boston and has a colored man writing for it. Mr. Von Vampton has brought with him a man he considers 1 of the most exciting young poets to come on the scene, a man who is the dominant figure in Negro letters today, a man who like no 1 else captures the complexity of Negro Thought . . . Mr. Hubert "Safecracker" Gould!!!

The Hostess and Von Vampton take their seats as Hubert "Safecracker" Gould, white gloves, blackface, black tuxedo, walks to the back of the stand and begins to read his epic "Harlem Tom Toms."

HARLEM TOM TOMS

FOR BJF

I

O Harlem, great Negro sea of unrest
Allow me to dip my feet into thy Black
Waters where chippies swim like sad-
      Eyed fish
Engulf me, Harlem. Submerge me in thy watery
Cabaret until one hand surfaces only
      Yass! Yass!
O Harlem, if you are a sea, why . . . why
Dat makes Lenox Ave. one of your many
Swift currents, grappling me as I
Beckon to big Black bucks—lifeguards
On de sho. Up on de sho O Harlem
Where jazz is a bather writhing in de
Sand and claw-snapping crabs do dey
Duty. Where dippermouthed trumpets
Summon de tides
Root-t-toot! Root-t-toot! Root-t-toot!
And de tom toms play in sea shells
Da-bloom, Da-bloom, Da-bloom-a-loom

II

Yonder. What is dat yonder?
What is dat I see ova dare?
Could dat be some sort of white
Liner invading thy sea O Harlem?
Polluting thy waves, dirtying thy crests
O Harlem?
Let us torpedo de mother, O Harlem
Let us get rid of de bitch! (*expressions of shock from the audience*)
Befo she collides with us
De steamship of de White whore
Dreadful mistress who has ruined

Many a sea
Chumping some of dem. Streaming
Dem making dem into
Rivulets
O Harlem, let me drag you for
Her drowned victims
Capsizing in thy many streets
A demon-headed marlin Harlem
I is. Yass yass I is. I is
A zoot-suited shark avoiding
De narks, harpoon sharp
I tear into thy whale of a mouth
Like a catfish my whiskers bristle
As I drink from
De dark caves at thy bottom
Your octopi wrap thine
Many tentacles about my heart
O Harlem, and do you know what?
Dere's more. Plenty more O
Harlem inspiration of my pen
I be a minnow, a
Measly, minnow in
Comparison to thy . . .

But before he can continue the guests are interrupted by an argument emanating from the vestibule. The Hostess' countenance smiling through the recital becomes a frown as she rushes out to see her servants arguing with PaPa LaBas, Black Herman, T Malice and 6 tall Python men accompanying them.

Why . . . why get out of here you men you gate-crashers I don't want no conjure mens' detectives in this house you ain't society you ain't money you ain't no artist you don't have no degree.

Move out of the way lady, Black Herman says.

When some of the male guests come to the Hostess' assistance PaPa LaBas reveals his pearl-handled .22 and the woman faints dead away. LaBas and Herman walk into the room where the poetry reading is taking place and before the startled guests Black Herman announces:

Hinckle Von Vampton and Hubert "Safecracker" Gould? Come quietly.

Some other people rise from their chairs.

What is the meaning of this intrusion? or something on that order, they ask.

Especially pushy, Hank Rollings the Guianese art critic, an authority on Vermeer, especially resents this embarrassment of Hinckle Von Vampton; why, the man looked as if he had connections and might be able to get him a show; after all, there were so few Blacks who were as ready as he was.

Yes . . . LaBas, Herman, explain your actions.

This is the meaning, LaBas replies, walking over to Hubert "Safecracker" Gould and grazing a quick finger across his face, leaving a white streak. He then displays the black paint on his finger to the audience.

The people are shocked. The room buzzes.

We have come to arrest this man and his sponsor Hinckle Von Vampton.

Von Vampton begins to ease away from the room but is stopped by Buddy Jackson and some of his men.

That's not enough of an explanation, says the Guianese art critic whose reviews were phony, completely devoid of feeling; some kind of dry uninteresting geometry, intellectual calisthenics for stale Atonists, his way of convincing them that he was "human too." We won't yield these gentlemen until you explain rationally and soberly what they are guilty of. This is no kangaroo courtroom, this is a free country.

Hinckle and Gould nod their heads in agreement. Yes . . . that's correct, you will have to explain what charges you have against us before we will go anywhere, Hinckle says, emboldened by the Guianese's support.

Black Herman looks to PaPa LaBas.

Well if you must know, it all began 1000s of years ago in Egypt, according to a high up member in the Haitian aristocracy.

52 A certain young prince who was allergic to thrones attended a university in Nysa, a town in Arabia Felix (now Yemen). It was a land of dates coffee goats sheep wheat barley corn and live-stock. Across the Red Sea were Ethiopia and the Sudan where the young man would commute bringing his knowledge of agriculture and comparing notes with the agriculturalists of these lands. There were agricultural celebrations; dancing and singing, and in Egypt this rhythm was known as the Black Mud Sound. At this time in history those who influenced the growth of crops and coaxed the cocks into procreation were seen as sorcerers. The theater accompanying these rites, these agriculturalists' rites, was a theater of fecundation generation and proliferation, a theater that Victorian Sir James Frazer of *The Golden Bough* calls "lewd and profligate." The processes of blooming were acted out by men and women dancers who imitated the process of fertilization.

They would play upon instruments, reeded stringed and percussive, as they acted out the process; open their valves, and allow nature to pour through its libation. Osiris was so adept at the mysteries of agriculture that people began to circulate stories that his mother was the sky Nut and the earth his father Geb.

As Osiris danced he would experiment, but the dances were not esoteric, they in fact were quite basic and they caught-on. In the Sudan and Ethiopia he became known as "the man who did dances that caught-on," infected other people. Well, Osiris lived many years studying under the elders at Nysa until he returned to Egypt. (Some say he was driven out of Ethiopia, where his dances were banned.) In Egypt a dark cloud lay over the land. Cannibalism was still practiced.

Osiris was regarded by his brother Set as a dilletante, a recipient of a far-out education and one who would not know how to deal firmly with the enemies of the Egyptian people. That was Set, the stick crook and flail man. Dealing firmly with enemies, holding them by the hair and chopping off their heads. Set wanted to use the death of their father as an excuse for invading foreign countries. Set hated agriculture and nature which he saw as soiled dirty grimy etc. He was arrogant jealous egotistical and when Osiris issued a ban on men eating men, introducing the techniques he learned from the long-bearded Black men in the university at Nysa, Set began to plot his brother's downfall. He was also jealous that Osiris was to marry their sister Isis. Fine as she could be. Firm breasts, eloquence, all of those qualities that are later to show up in her spiritual descendant Erzulie (love of mirrors, plumes, combs, an elaborate toilet) whom we in the United States call the girl with the red dress on. (Bessie Smith and Josephine Baker are 2 aspects of Erzulie.) People hated Set. He went down as the 1st man to shut nature out of himself. He called it discipline. He is also the deity of the modern clerk, always tabulating, and perhaps invented taxes.

The eating of barley wheat and corn spread through Egypt like a prairie fire and the people began to do the Black Mud sound, to do alchemical theater (theater of the "Black country"), and that got Set even more annoyed. The people would plant during the day and at night would celebrate dancing singing shaking sistrums and carrying on so that Set couldn't get sleep and was

tired when he went out on the field and drilled marched and
gave commands to others. 1 day Osiris performed a miracle. He
danced so well that the vines began to imitate a particular slow
sinuous movement and from that day to this we have the creeping
vine. Osiris was called the Bull by the Egyptians who loved him
and greeted him as he toured Egypt with his musicians and their
sets of decoration having to do with procreation.

U.S. Bombing Tonnage in Three Wars

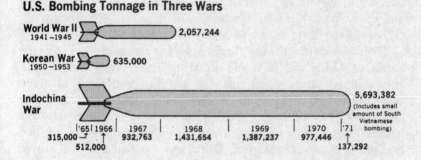

Set couldn't stand it. He would stand off to the side mad, balling
his fists and spouting invective. He considered the music "loud"
and "boisterous." Sometimes the dances were performed by
pigmies Osiris imported from the South because they were able
to execute the "dance of the Gods." 1 night Set went downstairs
and told everybody to "cut out that racket." He was greeted
only by catcalls and boos and when a young woman tried to
persuade him to dance with her he hurried from the room to the
general amusement of the court. And when later a guard came
upon him trying out these dances himself in secret, the gossip
leaked all over Egypt and he became the laughing stock of the
country. Set can't dance became the cry. Even Hully Gullying
children on the street would point out Set as the man who can't
shake it 'til he breaks it. The freak from Matovani. That did it.
Set would show them. Happy all the time. Enjoying themselves
when there was hard work to be done, countries to invade, popu-
lations to subjugate. Egypt was prospering under Osiris and there
was peace.

People were eating good, the crops were abundant, things were
going smoothly and Osiris and Isis were happily married. Their

sister Nephthys and her husband, their brother Set, didn't make out so well. He spent most of his time "out with the boys"; legislators, an unpopular group of poets who went about Egypt telling Egyptians that they could do better that they weren't ready and that they ought to try to make something out of themselves. Make ready for what? 1 man asked at one of their whistle stops. Ready for progress? Invading foreign countries and killing? The people didn't go for it and sarcastically called them The First Poets because in Egypt at the time of Osiris every man was an artist and every artist a priest; it wasn't until later that Art became attached to the State to do with it what it pleased.

Then somehing strange happened. People began to do the dance of Osiris and it would interrupt their tilling of the soil. It would hit them at all times of the day and some of them would wander through the streets talking out of their heads and making strange signs. Set circulated a rumor that this was because Osiris didn't really know the alchemical arts and had brought a curse upon Egypt. Osiris was worried and the people were grumbling. Well, there was a certain artist down near the harbor who painted arks. He was a man who had once made-out with Osiris' mother and had a big reputation for his decorative work. He called on Osiris 1 day and argued his theory that the outbreaks occurred because the mysteries had no text to turn to. No litany to feed the spirits that were seizing the people, and that if Osiris would execute these dance steps for Thoth he would illustrate them and then Osirian priests could determine what god or spirit possessed them as well as learn how to make these gods and spirits depart.

And so possessed, Osiris did his basic dances for many days until Thoth had them all down. A Book of Litanies to which people in places like Abydos in Upper Egypt could add their own variations.

Guides were initiated into the Book of Thoth, the 1st anthology written by the 1st choreographer.

● ○

Soon after, peace once again restored, Osiris became bored. Sailors had come to him with tales of much suffering and cannibalism in many parts of the world. Osiris announced that he was going to leave his wife Isis in charge of the affairs of Egypt which was a little thing because at that time as 1 historian wrote "The Egyptians had little difficulty in being good." Set saw this as his chance. He yearned for the old days when he went out to tell the people to "Move that chariot to the side of the road, O.K. where's your license," you know, stuff like that. On the day Osiris left there was a big celebration down at the port with guides from all over Egypt doing the dances of the gods. With tons and tons of cereal, Osiris Thoth and a crew and a fleet of 34 papyri boats set sail. It was midsummer, the 10th day of July, that he left.

Osiris toured the world with his International Nile Root Orchestra, dancing agronomy and going from country to country with his band; and a choir directed by a young comer named Dionysus whom you don't hear very much about in his Egyptian setting because the Egyptian writing is "royalty centered." With Thoth he taught people to permit nature to speak and dance through them, for so many 1000s of eyes looked through Osiris that he became known as "the many-eyed."

Just as fast as Osiris would teach these dances the people would mimic him and add their variations to fit their country and their clime. People began to welcome Osiris the Bull, the Seedman, and he became a familiar sight walking down the ramp or rather trucking down the ramp, his pet eagle "Jackie" perched on his shoulder, his faithful Birdman Thoth at his side, taking it all down. And people of all the many ports of the world where he traveled would say "Hey Seedman, what's going down?"

It was on his 2nd trip to South America that the rumors reached him. Because Osiris was teaching people how to make wine and if they didn't grow grapes, beer, Set was going about Egypt telling everybody that Osiris was a fraud and that he was traveling the world "drunk" and "fornicating," disgracing the name of the Fatherland. Set issued a challenge which travelers brought to Osiris. He was saying that if Osiris was so smart and a Human Seed and all, a Germ, would he perform the feat of the Germ. Could he be planted in the Nile and then spring from the waters. Surely if he had learned the arts of the sagacious bearded Black men in Arabia Felix at the University of Nysa he could perform this act. He said if he would do this that he, Set, would go somewhere and sit down and never complain again if people danced and sang. He didn't want to go down in history as a "party pooper." The devil was even hitting on Isis because he had eyes for her but she would just look upon her brother with disgust, this man who was going around putting the bad breath on Osiris. Osiris at this time was in Teotihuacán in South America where people of all races and from all over the world had arrived to watch the space ships their astronomers predicted would land. They landed after Osiris made a side trip to Olmeca where he remained long enough to pose for a portrait which was done in terracotta. He attended a 2-week festival as guest of an Inca king. It was here that he practiced Set's challenge for days at a time. It was easy. Osiris had developed such a fondness and attachment for Nature that people couldn't tell them apart.

He had never performed this trick but he knew that Nature wouldn't let him down for long. When Osiris and his band returned to Egypt the people turned out to greet him, dancing and being possessed as the guides led them through. They laughed as Isis blushed because they knew that that night he would give her his "rod of authority."

Set and his followers watched from the windows. That isn't a bad piece of tail, Set said commenting upon the attributes of his sister in the presence of Nephthys whom he treated like a dog, and called her a bitch a tomato a heifer a cow and all other words related to the farming he hated so.

That night Osiris and Isis made love and the result of this Union was the child Horus.

The next day was the day of the test. The people gathered at the mouth of the Nile as the legislators placed Osiris in the coffer and drove nails through it. Molten lead was used to keep it airtight. Osiris winked at the people before the lid was closed. The coffer was sunk into the water on October 24th.

That night the legislators came to the Nile and raised Osiris. They lifted the lid and saw Osiris lying there smiling in a deep death-like slumber, a trick he had learned "down home" among the heavies in the Sudan and Ethiopia.

They mutilated him and made believe that he was torn into 14 parts by fish, and from that day forward fish have been considered evil in Egypt. On October 31st the people came and saw the mutilated corpse, parts of which had been washed up on the shore, and the open coffer lying not far away.

Set stood there in triumph. There goes your Seedman eaten by fish, let's cut out all this farming jazz and go back to eating each other. Come here you, Set said in his John Wayne voice, swaggering toward a luscious woman, a succulent dish standing in the crowd.

Thoth knew this to be a lie. He had seen Osiris perform this act during their sojourn in South America. Among the Navaho Indians in North America, at Aztec festivals, around West African peoples who were known to repel an invader by "playing whistles and beating on drums," the news had circulated through many tribes that Osiris could perform this trick.

Thoth spoke up, demanding an autopsy, an investigation of Osiris' death. Set had Thoth arrested for his proposal. Thoth was taken into custody but escaped through the help of some of the guards who were still loyal to the memory of Osiris. Before going into exile, he ran to Isis and left his sacred Book in her hands; and then he went away. Some say he went into exile in the hills where he wrote magical books under a pseudonym which survived until the "civilized" Romans burned the library at Alexandria.

Isis began to walk about Egypt, screaming lamentations for her husband. At the moment of his triumph, Set began to hear unsettling stories. Osiris had been seen in the land. He had been seen wherever Isis had left a backbone, or a toe or an arm belonging to her dead husband. The people were beginning to call Osiris the Bull the Human-Seed as well, and wherever they found a Bull with a scarab under his tongue, an eagle on his back and a square on his forehead they began to celebrate Osiris' "living Spirit." When he heard of this, old Set ordered the murder of the Bulls and being a particularly mean cuss, ordered that they be tortured 1st. (This led to the sport that the American writer Ernest Hemingway took such delight in.) But wherever the Black Bull God Apis appeared and was murdered another Bull would take his place. Well this was driving Set up the walls. This was October 31st, the night that people went about wearing masks, being whatever they felt like in honor of the man whom Nature spoke through. Set sent out warrants for the Osirian guides who had learned The Work and they fled. Some of them fled to Down Home where they matched their knowledge with the necromancers in Ifé, Nigeria. Dionysus traveled to Greece where the Dance "spread like wildfire" although Homer doesn't mention it. He nevertheless helped himself to the stories Dionysus brought concerning Osiris, the man who traveled through the world and returned home to a wife under siege by conspirators. Dionysus kept the faith of his school chum and home boy. (Dionysus can be read as "God from Nysa.") When the King of Thebes forbade the feeding of Dionysus, the angry loa influenced the young people to revolt. When Proteus, King of Tiryns, closed a temple dedicated to Dionysus known as "the man of the black goatskin" a contemporary writer described the ensuing choreomania:

> They rushed out of doors and in frenzied dance raged over the countryside, singing weird songs, tearing their garments, unable to stop dancing.

Dionysus taught the Greeks the Osirian Art which lasted until the Atonists in the late 4th century B.C. convinced the Emperor Constantine to co-sign for the Cross. Dionysus taught the Greek guides to identify the Nature that spoke through mankind. The Work. Listen to Hippocrates:

> If they imitate a goat, or grind their teeth, or if their right side be convulsed, they say that the mother of the gods is the cause, but if they speak in a sharper and more intense tone they resemble this state to a horse and say Poseidon [Neptune] is the cause.

NOTICE

RICHARD, CHUCK AND JOHNNY WISH TO REMIND CALIFORNIA'S ROCK FANS THAT THE STAGE IS VIRTUALLY INDESTRUCTIBLE. ONE MAY ATTEND WITH NO FEAR OF MORTAL INJURY, SHOULD HE OR SHE FEEL THE CALL TO COME FORTH AND DECLARE HIS OR HER SOUL TO THE GLORY OF ROCK 'N' ROLL.

The Greeks established temples to these Egyptian-derived mysteries where people would go out of their heads so that the gods could take them over. (About the 10th century the Atonist priests will call this diabolical possession or corrupt the Greek word *daimon* so as to have evil connotations. Freud, the later Atonist [according to 1 biographer, a big fan of Moses, Cromwell and other militarists], is to term this "hysteria.")

The Greek and Roman masses were crazy about the Egyptian mysteries and celebrated them in the Temples of Osiris and Isis, much to the chagrin of the satirist Lucian, who in *Dialogues of the Gods* derided the animal figures associated with the royal couple; but the religions were too popular for criticism to affect anything and the people danced and sang and were touched by the Spirits under the careful watching of trained priests of Dionysus the choir master. They, the Greeks, would never have thought about calling these Hosts schizophrenics or catatonics, which were after all their own words. Paranoia and the like were clinical Atonist words invented by people who having lost the knowledge of what they were doing just kinda threw these terms out there. These rites lasted on up to A.D. 378 when the Atonists made havoc upon the temples of their opponents' "pagan" systems. Prior to their sacking, jealous politicians had burned the temples in 58, 50 and 48 B.C. Formerly the people could go to the temple and get away from it all through the guidance of a priest; now they were tortured and any Osirian behavior was seen as an escape from reality and such. All of the gods who were rivals of the 1 they called Jehovah (the cover-up for the Flaming Disc God) were driven underground and the many were reduced to 1; even Muhammad, 1 of Jehovah's allies in the priesthood, is depicted in a church carving as the devil.

The 4th century A.D. was a crucial period for both Atonism and the mystery Dionysus had brought from Egypt. Atonist scholars up to their old yellow journalism of the *Daily Heliopolitan* decided to depict Osiris as Pluto, a castrated god of the underworld (remember Taurus?) but they kept on Isis as Virgin Mary. In fact in many African locales the passion for Isis was transferred to the Atonists' Mary. This occurred in Africa and southern Europe. Mary was the mother of the Atonist compromise Jesus Christ. They made him do everything that Osiris does, sow like a farmer, be a fisherman among men but he is still a *bokor*, a sorcerer, an early Faust. Lazarus was a zombie! He was a sorcerer, a Maharishi yoga type who went around the countryside performing tricks. The quality of which the great man Julian the Apostate Emperor (called Apostate because he wanted in the 4th century, to revive the religions Dionysus brought to Greece) was to comment

. . . Yet Jesus, who won over the least worthy of you, has been known by name for but little more than three hundred years: and during his lifetime he accomplished nothing worth hearing of, unless anyone thinks that to heal crooked and blind men and to exorcise those who were possessed by evil demons in the villages of Bethsaida and Bethany can be classed as a mighty achievement.*

Julian knew the difference between a houngan and *bokor*, having surrounded himself with the solidest post-Osirian priests of his day. And Julian fed the loas publicly, to the ridicule and scorn of his countrymen who had been converted to Christianity. On February 4, A.D. 362, he proclaimed religious freedom in the empire and ordered the pagan temples restored. But the Atonists were too powerful for Julian. He was assassinated on a Persian battlefield 12:00 midnight June 26, 363. He failed in his gallant attempt to reverse the Atonist challenge. He foresaw the Bad News it was going to bring to the world. John Milton, Atonist apologist extraordinary himself, saw the coming of the minor geek and sorcerer Jesus Christ as a way of ending the cult of Osiris and Isis forever.

The brutish gods of *Nile* as fast,
Isis and *Horus*, and the dog *Anubis* hast.

Nor is *Osiris* seen
In *Memphian* grove, or Green
    Trampling th' unshowr'd Grass with lowings loud:
Nor can he be at rest
Within his sacred chest,
    Naught but profoundest Hell can be his shroud;
In vain with Timbrel'd Anthems dark
The sable-stoled Sorcerers bear his worshipt ark.

This from his Hymn in "On the Morning of Christs Nativity," which is nothing but a simple necktie party out to get Osiris' goat. And those "Timbrel'd Anthems dark" is the music that old Jethro played, the music of the worshipers of those festivals where they had a ball. Boogieing. Expressing they selves. John Milton

* Works of Julian the Apostate.

couldn't stand that. Another Atonist; that's why English professors like him, he's like their amulet, keeping niggers out of their departments and stamping out Jes Grew before it invades their careers. It is interesting that he worked for Cromwell, a man who banned theater from England and was also a hero of Sigmund Freud. Well the mud-slingers kept up the attack on Osiris, a writer Bilious Styronicus even rewriting Osirian history in a book called the *Confessions of the Black Bull God Osiris* in which he justified Set's murder of Osiris on the grounds that Osiris made "illicit" love to Isis who, he wrote, was Set's wife. He was awarded the Atonists' contemporary equivalent of the Pulitzer Prize for this whopper. Others went about calling Osiris, Moloch, which translated means "nigger cow."

Well the Atonist Church becomes stronger as the years pass but a strange thing happens. The rites associated with Osiris and other pagan gods continue underground. The only remedies the Church knew was to "beat the living shit out of them." Throwing those possessed by demons into dungeons, burning it out of them. They killed millions of people this way but it didn't put an end to the dance epidemics, heresies, witchcraft, infidels, and remnants of "pagan" religions. Well, if the Church had continued dealing with the foe in this manner, beating people up, raiding their apartments at 2:00 A.M., burning them at the stake, it would have wiped out a good portion of Europe's population. The rest of the population was being depleted by physical plagues. Much later came another Atonist compromise, Sigmund Freud, who refined the rhetoric of the Church and eased the methods of dealing with the problem. Freud saved many lives which would have ordinarily been dealt with by the Church in an inhumane manner. But when Freud came to America and saw what was going down over here it was too much for even this man. Freud fainted.

●　　○

After the exile of the Osirians, Dionysus, Thoth and other members of that fabled entourage, Set had problems. Every time he'd go out on tour his convoy was stoned. He had outlawed Dancing. Everything that Osiris stood for he attempted to banish so that he would cut this figure out of his life forever. Next he banished Music. And then as his mind deteriorated he banned Fucking.

And later even Life itself. He began to groove behind a real death cult that grew up about him. His legislators and their wives resembled a Billy Graham audience at Oakland Coliseum. The people began to grumble. There was talk of revolution. Talk that Horus had grown up in Koptos where Isis had gone into exile and was prepared to march on the old man. When the child was younger Set had dispatched an arch poisoner, but he failed because Isis was in possession of the Sacred Book and had developed some pretty strong *garde.*

Set decided that he would fasten his hold on the populace by performing a miracle the way Osiris used to. He had 1 of his *bokors* who practiced the art of the Petro Rites with the Left Hand to "come on up and give the folks a show." Well, being insufficiently trained the *boker* didn't know what he was doing; he only knew Dirty Work and raised the temperature of Egypt to over 50,000 degrees* resulting in something resembling an A-bomb explosion. Set and his followers fled to Heliopolis City of the Sun and decided to rule Egypt from there.

Set grew worse. The people began to return to their old ways, dancing and performing the rites as they remembered them, but without the Text and someone to ·tell them what to do—Osiris' assistants now dispersed in West Africa, southern Europe, and elsewhere—it resulted in degeneration. Set began to develop a weird relationship with the Sun. If you can understand Los Angeles you can almost get the picture; imagine 2 or 3 Los Angeleses and you got Heliopolis. The legislators lay around in the Sun all day and developed a strange Body Building scene on the beach. Set decided that he would introduce a religion based upon his relationship to the Sun, and since he was a god then the Sun too would be a god. Of course this was nothing new because the Egyptians had worshiped the "heat, light, orbs, and rays," had worshiped the Sun in a pantheistic manner. With Set, the Sun's flaming disc eclipsed the rest of its parts.

He made the legislators serve as his writers, as Thoth had for

* The temperature of the Loa Legba alone is 30,000 degrees.

Osiris. Maybe this would do it, he thought. And so the legislators went through the old texts and started rewriting things and doctoring them to make Set look good and Osiris look bad. By establishing his own religion based upon Aton (the Sun's flaming disc) he felt he would overcome the nature religion of Osiris. He would be the reverse of Osiris who was associated with fertilization and spring; he would become Aton the "burner of growing things," the Egyptian Jehovah who causes famine pestilence and earthquakes. Before he died he was in such a state that he believed that the Sun was dependent on him and thus he would walk around in circles all day thinking that when he walked the Sun made its course about the planet.

He really flipped. And he was to die watching the Bull God Apis rise all over the land. The Temples of Osiris and Isis were constructed in southern Europe, Nubia and the Sudan. It was becoming a world-wide religion. It was successful everywhere the remnant of the Osirian priesthood was; they knew what it was capable of and knew how to draw it out or make it depart. But in places where The Work wasn't known it would spring up unexpectedly and cause disastrous results or be mistaken for entertainment or be practiced with the Left Hand. Try as they may to popularize Atonism, the Egyptians weren't going for it. It became nothing but a club of old grumblers located in Heliopolis.

That was until Amenhotep 4 (about 1500 b.c.). He was a frail tall and weakling interior-decorator type who became an Atonist and changed his name to Akhnaton (devoted to Aton) while he spent sometime in Heliopolis hanging out on the beach the Atonists made popular, now a decadent, Joe Atlas scene.

When the fool moved the capital to Tel el Amarna they knew they had another Set on their hands and the Amon sect, the ones in charge of maintaining the Osirian mysteries, had the sucker offed. To make an uneasy pun they quit this 2nd Set.

●   ○

Fortunately Tutankhamen came to power and the people were allowed to do their stuff, working out this way on the wall in the hall every which-a-way. That was until Thermuthis, the stubborn, self-indulgent daughter of a weak Pharaoh. 1 day while bathing she discovered a child in a basket and against the advice of Baria, an old HooDoo woman, brought the child into the palace. No 1 could tell her anything. Thermuthis had had her "been to": her expatriate fling in Europe. Hadn't she hung out in the cafés and listened to Greek, the language of "civilization"? Hadn't she learned how to be vague? To flim flam? She looked down on her own people whom she joined her friends in mocking as they went about "practicing that superstitious mess." The Osirian cult had lost its prestige and now did its stuff "way out on the outskirts of town." There were rumors of dancing and "getting happy" and singing out here in the roadside temples. At Thermuthis' request the Pharaoh would have them raided once in a while. But since the Osirians were giving the guard some "ice"—emeralds, diamonds, lapis lazuli—as soon as a priest, houngan and houngonikon or mambo or an elder and his sisters were arrested he was soon back on the street in circulation. Thermuthis and some of her Greek friends went down to these places one night and were appalled at the frankness of these rituals; the Pussies and Dicks on the walls as decoration, the low-down gut-bucket music. They were snobs. (The opening night crowd of charlatans at a racist N.Y. museum.) All day they sat around discussing such things as "If I stand in the water today am I the same person who stood there yesterday etc. etc." you know. Jiving the citizens of Egypt.

Her adopted son Moses (1350–1250 B.C.) had different ideas. He sneaked off to the Domain of Osiris every time he had a chance. Manetho the 3rd-century B.C. Egyptian historian contends that he even became an Osirian initiate and changed his name to Osarsiph.*

The people, down at these places which bore the aroma of plants growing wild in the fields, called him Pharaoh. The Egyptian scribe Manetho also refers to him as a Pharaoh, most likely the successor of Thermuthis' father. These orchestras of brass, sistrums and drums would play a music that was influenced by the stars. They played under the stars to 1000s of what they remembered of the Osirian Mysteries. Moses, the young Pharaoh-to-be, would sit in and join in with his brothers. The fingers of these men who worked the crops brought the electricity of the earth to their strings, these men who drank from the cold Blue Nile, whose lips had touched the

* *Isis Unveiled,* vol. I, p. 555.—H. P. Blavatsky.

waters of this magic river, brought this Nile sound to their instruments. Well 1 night they were sitting around and Moses asked them what was the heaviest sound they had ever heard. All the men agreed that it was old Jethro the Midianite who could still play the sounds of the spirits and had a legendary instrument that sounded like an orchestra and knew all the "old songs." It was rumored that he was a descendant of an actual follower of Osiris who had gone into exile after Set's purge. They said that he could play so well that lions assembled on the grounds of his farm and went to sleep, that the crops would weave their leaves toward the huts and climb into the bedroom window. That Nature had blessed him with daughters so that there would be more like him. Moses felt that he would have to study under this man. He would have to somehow gain this man's confidence and perhaps he would teach him everything he knew.

The next day Moses set out to see Jethro. When he came upon the town in whose suburbs Jethro dwelled he went into the local Spirits Temple and made inquiries about Jethro. The Spirit Tasters told him all about Jethro and that he could see his daughters tending to Jethro's cattle if he went outside of town. They told him where and how far to go. Moses revealed himself as a Pharaoh-to-be and hired the men to stage an episode for him. They would go and pretend to rustle Jethro's cattle and Moses would come riding out of the hills and divert them. (Moses really liked melodrama.) Well this was done and Moses came out of the hills and repelled the rustlers whom he had paid to perform such a stunt at the Temple of Spirits. The women took their rescuer home and introduced him to their father Jethro. Jethro was happy and persuaded Moses to remain at his home and "drink and eat as much as you want and make-out with my daughters."

Why not? Moses thought. They weren't bad and he could just write down everything that Jethro said and when he returned to Egypt he would turn the place out. That night Jethro took out this instrument that must have had about 25 strings. He then put some kind of early styled harmonica in his mouth. And with his feet he beat on some kind of tinny thing. Then he started twanging on that many-stringed monstrosity and zipping his fingers up and down that thing and making that thing cry so that several times Moses leaped in the air and said, Damn! If he could learn that he could be the Hierophant of the surviving Osirian Order. Moses asked Jethro would he mind if he wrote all of this down. Jethro was grateful to this man. He almost considered him a son and told him that this would be fine.

Well the next few months Moses would help the women tend the cows, using them any way he desired, and at night Jethro would play and Moses would write it all down. Soon they were doing duos as Moses slowly learned Jethro's art. Well when Moses had learned all of Jethro's songs and had made Jethro create upon these strange instruments he played, Moses packed his papyri instruments and was bidding Jethro goodbye. He said he would play his songs in the temples and while he was playing them he would always have a kind place in his heart for Jethro.

Just as Jethro was bidding Moses goodbye Jethro told him "It's too bad you're leaving because that's not enough. You must know the words to the songs and that's a family secret." Moses paused. "Family secret?" "Yes unless you know the words the music becomes ½ right, not all right." Moses told Jethro and his daughters that he was going to set out but the moon looked ominous. Perhaps he could remain with them for a few more days. That evening Moses asked Jethro to teach him the words. Jethro told him that they were family secrets. He would only pass them on to a son-in-law.

● ○

Well, the next day Moses told Jethro that he was in love with Zipporah and wanted to marry her. Jethro, trusting, was overjoyed because he had developed a great fondness for Moses. Moses married Zipporah and as her dowry Jethro taught Moses the family words. Well, Moses and his wife Zipporah were about to leave because he wanted as quickly as possible to return to Egypt to "show off my lovely Black bride to my stepmother, the Pharaoh and my high-yellow sisters and brothers."

1 day when you return, Jethro said, you can take a trip to Koptos where there is in existence the Sacred Book said to have been written by Thoth himself.

What? Moses asked.

I said 1 of these days Isis will show you the real Book of Thoth—the original sound. The 1 located in her temple at Koptos, guarded by the deathless snake. It has to be gotten during the right moon or it will be the Book in its evil phase.

Moses sighed, *Now he tells me!* He told his father-in-law that Zipporah didn't look too well and that he would remain around a few more days before they set out on such an arduous journey. Zipporah pleaded that she felt all right but Moses insisted. Jethro was pleased that Moses was so concerned for his daughter Zipporah and rebuked her for sassing her husband. Moses after a few weeks told Jethro, his wife and her sisters that he felt like going on a camping trip to get some air and that he would return soon.

Moses went into the woods and traveled to the mountains. He wanted to contemplate. He went atop Mount Horeb and fasted and meditated for days. On the night of the 12th day he was so weak, having lost many pounds, he thought he was going to die. It was then that a vision came to him. It seemed, the Specter, to be a man dressed in old-style Egyptian clothes 1000s of years before even Manetho had recorded the 30 Dynasties. He told Moses that he knew his problem. He knew that Moses wanted to find out how to circumvent the death'less snake who guards the temple at Koptos: Isis and Osiris' Temple. The Specter said he knew that Isis would succumb to a certain line because it was "that time of the month." He said that he would tell Moses what to do, but first Moses had to promise that he would restore the cult of Aton to Egypt.

Moses laughed. Man, the way people are into animal and vegetation rites and calling everything that moves a spirit, I would be the buffoon of Egypt restoring something as arid as that. The present mysteries, although frowned upon by the aristocracy, including my mother, are extremely popular with the masses. Why there would be revolution. The Specter began to fade-out when Moses reconsidered, *I must play this Book! I must find it!* He had developed a real thing about it.

Wait. Wait. Of course I will do what you say. How do I go about getting this Book?

You have to talk trash and feed her.

What is that? Moses said recognizing this as ancient dialect that would have to be revealed to him.

Set told him what he meant by these things and after Moses had gotten it all down he returned to Jethro's ranch looking like a new man. The next day Jethro was sitting on the porch, chewing on some herbs and swinging in a hammock he had made for himself. Some of the old red-eyed Black men from the hills were gathered about the master playing their stringed and percussion instruments, cowbells, mouth harps, calliopes.

Moses seemed like he was trying to tiptoe away when Jethro stopped him because by now Jethro knew that he was being used.

Where are you going, son? Koptos?

The men ceased playing their instruments. It became so quiet you could hear the crickets for it was the crepuscule.

Aren't you taking Zipporah with you, said this man, his face a dark wood, his grey hair blue in the early twilight.

I'll . . . I'll er return for her before I go to Egypt, Moses said.

The men returned to playing their instruments. Jethro stopped them. He rose and addressed his son-in-law.

If you get it out of her it will be useless to you; only a few things about converting rods to snakes; simple *bokor* tricks, the rest will be so awful that you will wish you had never known The Work. Son, she's in that Aspect of herself with this Moon and you won't be able to receive the better side of her Book . . .

Look, leave me alone. Silly old man out here in the backwoods. How dare you talk to me that way; I'm a Pharaoh, or soon will be 1.

Moses jumped on his horse as tears came to Jethro's eyes. As he was about to ride away Moses rode to Jethro's porch where all the men were assembled and he dropped "a couple of bucks" on old Jethro.

Here's the copyright fee for the junk you taught me, he said sarcastically.

Jethro took the dollars and flung them at Moses who rode off into the night.

He wouldn't listen and now he will be merely a 2-bit sorcerer practicing the Left Hand.

It wasn't your fault, Jethro, you warned him, a friend consoled.

The old men resumed the playing of the instruments.

52   Moses arrived in Koptos a few weeks later. There were statues all over the town devoted to the ancient theme of Isis and her child Horus who according to some versions returned and overthrew his father's murderer, Set. It is also said that Horus was the result of a coupling of Isis with the deceased Osiris. People were wearing emblems of the Mother and Child and their pictures were etched on coins. Moses was directed by a traveler to the Temple of Osiris and Isis. He walked until he came upon the temple outside town. He entered between 2 of its 6 columns. In the main room was a smoking pit, a retainer of sacrificial refuse; a statue of Osiris and Isis, holding the child Horus; and friezes depicting Sea Fights, the mysteries: Thoth, Nephthys, Horus, Anubis, Osiris the Eater of the Dead armed with two knives, Osiris Khenti, Amenti, Lord of Abydos and others. There were the animal-shapes: crocodiles serpents birds and rams. The colors of the rooms were green blue and yellow. Grains were scattered about the floor. The room was littered with tom toms pipes and drums. The air of funk was being dispersed by burning incense. It had been quite an afternoon. Several pigmy kings of about 4' 10" had danced all afternoon intermittently, leaping into the air. Moses went into the kitchen and munched on some cereal that had been left in some ritual bowls. He drank some wine; he went past the dining room and into the bedroom of mysteries which was covered with pictures of male and female genitalia. Fatigued from traveling, Moses lay down on the bed and went immediately to sleep. At about 2 A.M. he awoke to someone running her hands through his hair and kissing him. It was Isis in the Petro aspect of herself. She was dressed in a scarlet see-through gauzy gown and covered with the odor of a strange perfume. He had never smelt anything so intoxicating to the brain. Her hair was giant black-bird feathers, her eyes blazing.

He would have to be careful. There were stories of mangled bodies carried through the air in the cruel beaks of giant birds. Men "bleeding like hogs," wandering about the temple senseless at dawn. There were tales of her victims condemned to traveling the world. Headless, pitiful men who brought the plague to the cities.

I will give you what you want if you give me what I want.

She was so fine that if she dived down the abyss Moses would have plunged in after her. Moses was sweating as she removed her gown and began to make love with him. Moving her thighs about his legs, running her hands across his penis.

Well, Moses thought, as he responded to her caresses, I only hope the bird handles me gently.

Suddenly she leaped to her feet, her prominent firm black breasts swinging, her hands on her hips.

What have you brought for me?

Moses removed from his satchel everything Set instructed him to bring: brightly colored scarfs and liquors, jewelry and delicate chickens for her to eat. She handled the scarfs and tasted the liquor. Moses, when he saw her delighted expression, thought that he had passed the test but she hurled the things to the ground with 1 gesture.

That isn't enough, she said, returning to the bed and lying next to him. You must talk to me. Baby, please talk to me.

Set knew his sister all right and Moses began to talk to her the way the Osirians talked to her in their rites. He told her how much he loved her and that he would die for her. Cut his throat swim in a river of thrashing crocodiles fight lions for her pussy. He said that he would cuss the day he was born if he couldn't have it and that he would walk all over Egypt crying like a baby. He said that he would gouge out his eyes and dust off the feet of all the dock workers in Egypt, jump off a cliff and lock himself in a cave for the rest of his life. And every time Moses would say another lie Isis would moan and sigh and whimper and purr like a kitten as Moses' hand moved down and touched her Seal. He fished her temple good. She showed him all her rooms. And led him into the depths of her deathless snake where he fought that part of her until it was limp on the ground. He got good into her Book tongued her every passage thumbing her leaf and rubbing his hands all over her binding.

When he was through he had gotten it all down. All down. Had it down pat. He left the goddess in slumber as he rose, collected his gear together and then set out for Egypt.

Well, Moses announced to the populace that he would give a concert with music and songs better than the Black Mud Sound, which was dying rapidly and played only by a few old fools in the hills. He said that this would be a dignified concert and that everyone would have to leave them old nasty-assed animal fetishes and "rattlers" and all these other "flesh-pipes" back home and that there would be no savage dancing. Don't be bringing none of that silly shit to my gig, Moses said. I'm the 1. For once music wouldn't just be used as a background to dancing but he would be a soloist and no 1 in the audience would be allowed to play a whistle or beat a drum or rattle a tambourine. The Osirians were furious. They knew this to be an Atonist trick and decided to disrupt the concert.

Well, the night of the concert the people were herded into the concert grounds. (Non-attendance was equated with treason.)

Moses began to play Jethro's songs but they weren't coming across like the way they had at the old man's fireplace. They sounded flat, weak, deprived of the lowdown rhythms that Jethro had brought to them. An applause sign was placed up and Moses received applause. A man who didn't go along was taken outside and beaten with flails and crooks. From a box seat, Thermuthis and her expatriate friends applauded loudest of all; 1 Greek said he would return to Greece and announce that Moses sounded even better than Osiris must have sounded himself. Moses then played the songs of Jethro with the words but his voice sounded feigned, his mimic of Jethro's dialect phony, and at this point some grain was thrown up on the stage and people were imitating snakes by HIIIIII-SSSSSSSSSSIIIIIINNNNNGGGGGGGG. That corner of the park was beaten until blood streamed down the aisles.

Well, during the intermission Moses went back stage and his Atonist supporters, ass kissers who traveled with him everywhere he went since his return to Egypt, were drinking beer and told Moses how good he was and began to pat him on the back. Moses knew something was wrong. He was told by 1 of the ushers that fights were breaking out in the stadium and that they would have to call for the Army if the violence got out of control.

Don't worry, Moses said, I will next do the songs and dances I learned from The Work, the sacred Book, and that way the people will rejoice and love me and young girls will follow me everywhere.

Well, Moses went on stage and began gyrating his hips and singing the words of the Book of Thoth, and a strange thing happened. The ears of the people began to bleed. Some of them charged the stage and tried to get at Moses but the Atonist thugs beat them back. 1 Osirian priest could no longer take it. He and several others knew what Moses had learned and knew how it was using him.

Moses couldn't understand. Why hadn't the rites and the words and the dances congealed? Why hadn't the contagion broken out? Why weren't people talking in strange tongues and having happy convulsions?

Moses examined his guitar. Something was wrong. But then the Osirians rose from the rows they occupied and began blowing

their whistles and the beautiful sounds filled the air. They didn't know The Work that Moses knew, but in his hands it wasn't doing him any good anyway. The people began to relax. Removed instruments of their own they had smuggled into the park and began playing them along with the Osirians who were marching toward the bandstand playing the instruments. The people began to dance. Moses couldn't stand it.

Arrest those men, he said as the men came closer to where he stood and began to mount the steps. 1 Osirian—a Black Osirian, a crocodile wrestler known by his friends as "The Hunter"— lunged for Moses but the Atonist thugs surrounded him, stabbing him and making him bleed and then stomping him while he was down until he lay on the floor dead. Seeing this, the whole audience charged the bandstand and Moses was whisked away by some Atonists. People began stoning the royal chariots as they raced for refuge in the Palace. Looting and the killing of Atonists went on all night.

The people surrounded the Palace. Some of them leaped over the barricades set up by the Pharaoh's militia. They hurled missiles at the residence; inside, Moses' mother Thermuthis sobbed softly. She cried the way they did in Greece, civilized, dignified, not the piercing wailing from the viscera associated with the mourning Isis who walked all over Egypt sharing her pathos with her people after her husband's murder. (Thermuthis cried the way 1 of my relatives from Alabama described as "crying proper."—I.R.) The Greek friends were trying to reach the boats as quickly as they could—2 of these loafers, brothers, thought of supporting themselves by selling an idea of a frieze dealing with the murder of "The Hunter" at the hands of the Atonist thugs.

Moses thought that he could calm the multitude by going out to the balcony and "reasoning" with the people (his mother's sophist friends had gotten to his head too), warning them that he would not truck any rowdiness and that horrible punishments were in store for those who persisted in this unruliness.

Ladies and gentlemen of Egypt. I will unleash the Holocaust upon you this time if you persist in this action. We must have sanity and logic during these times of change and upheaval.

A rock busted the cat's lip.

In anger Moses flung his rod to the ground where it immediately transformed into a snake.

The people laughed. They called him mountebank and sorcerer, fakir in a pejorative sense of the Petro Asson, and other names associated with cheap charlatans who would raise the dead for 15 dollars and change.

The crowd began pushing into the Palace. Moses then ran back into the apartment where his mother was sobbing softly, touching her soft smooth flabby face with a handkerchief.

He berated her: For heaven's sake will you cut that out. I'm trying to concentrate.

Then the idea hit him. Moses ran into his apartment and removed a leaf from the Book Isis had given him. He returned to the balcony where below the crowds had taken trees and were now using them to pound on the Palace gate. Moses uttered The Work aloud. 1st there was silence. Then the people turned toward the Nile and they saw a huge mushroom cloud arise.

A few minutes later, screaming of the most terrible kind came from that direction. The crowd dispersed, trampling 1 another as they rushed for the shelter of their homes. This was a turning point in the Book's history.

The practice of the Left Hand had now arisen to the level of that of the Right Hand. As the distinguished musicologist Fats Waller was to comment later: "Formerly the right hand was given all the work and the left hand shifted for itself, thumping out a plain octave or common chord foundation; now it's more evenly divided and the left hand has to know its stuff."

Moses' explosion made even Set's magicians look small. The next day fish and other river creatures dead and dying washed up on the shores of the Nile.

The VooDoo tradition instructs that Moses learned the secrets of VooDoo from Jethro and taught them to his followers. H. P. Blavatsky concurs: "The fraternity of Free Masons was founded in Egypt and Moses communicated the secret teaching to Israelites, Jesus to the Apostles and thence it found its way to the Knights Templar." But this doesn't explain why he received the Petro Asson instead of the Rada. My theory is that it was due to the fact that he had approached Isis at Koptos during the wrong time of the Moon and stirred her malevolent aspects thus learning this side of the Book. Others say that shortly afterward Moses and his Atonist followers went into exile.*

When Jethro heard of the incidents occurring in the North, the nuclear attack and the outraged mob, he told Zipporah. She took it well. She was glad that Jethro hadn't, in a fit of rage, sent the white leprosy to Thermuthis, Moses' mother. Jethro was a good man and once you begin the Petro work it's hard to quit.

Many years later when Moses returned home 1 day from "communicating with his God" he found his children dancing before the despised Bull God Apis, the animal which carries the living spirit of Osiris. Moses heard the "heathen sounds"† (timbrel'd anthems dark, boogie, jazz, down-home music, funk, gutbucket) he hadn't heard since the old days in Egypt. Moses grabbed the awful Book from his sons and daughters who were enjoying themselves, dancing their tails off. Moses wanted to get rid of the Book, having sworn off it, but was afraid to burn it. He feared The Work's power. So instead he hid it in a tabernacle where it was lost and became known as 1 of the "lost Books of Moses."

●　　○

Centuries went by until 1118 when the Knights Templar built their headquarters on the site of Solomon's Temple. The organization was an imitation of Hasan-ibn-al-Sabbah's Assassins which had similar offices: Grand Masters, Grand Priors, Priors, Knights, Esquires, Lay Brothers, and the Templars even adopted the Muslim colors so as to distinguish themselves from their rivals the Teutonics and the Hospitalers. They were a bunch of filthy ruffians, thugs and excommunicated "holy sinners" who wore their clothes until they rotted off their backs; maybe not so bad when you consider that this was a time when the King of France only changed his clothes 3 times a year. They were bully boys who justified their existence by harassing "sacriligers adulterers and others in the name of the Cross." (As usual they left themselves to be the judges of who was guilty of these vaguely defined crimes.) Their stock rose and when they saved the 2nd Crusade from annihilation they were in a position to write their own ticket. Hinckle

---

* *Introduction to African Civilizations*—John G. Jackson, with introduction by John Henrik Clarke.
† Book of Moses: 8, 9, and 10th—Henri Gamache.

Von Vampton was the Templar librarian. One night while stacking books in the basement of the library he came upon a secret passageway which led down some concrete steps into an ancient room. It was here he came upon the Book of Thoth, the sacred Work Isis had given to Moses. The Work of the Black Birdman, an assistant to Osiris. (If anyone thinks this is "mystifying the past" kindly check out your local bird book and you will find the sacred Ibis' Ornithological name to be *Threskiornis aethiopicus*.)

He showed the Book to Hugues de Payens, their leader, who was feeling heady because it was shortly after his trip to the Church Council of Troyes where he had won for the Templars immunity from excommunication. They began to translate the hieroglyphics but the Book was not going to be their whore any more and gave them the worst of itself. It was saving all of its love and Rada for when it united with its dance and music. What they derived from the Book were strange ceremonies which were called the "Rule of the Temple" . . . a rule scholars claim has been lost. They practiced these Petro rites in secret and this is when their fortunes reversed. The great Black Sultan of Egypt and Syria named Saladin also known as Salāh-al-Dīn-Yūsuf ibn-Ayyūb with an army of 70,000 men drove them from the "Holy Land" in 1187. Hinckle Von Vampton fled with the sacred Book.

This was only the beginning of their downfall. In alliance with kings of Europe they attempted to regain Jerusalem in 1244 but this time they were massacred by Mongols by 1248; and in 1250 the Arabs once more defeated them. In 1303 they lost their function completely because by this time there was no "Holy Land" to protect, all of it having again come under control of the Muslims.

Philip 4 of France, a king the Templars had saved from a Paris mob, despised the Templars. Some say he was inept and jealous because they wouldn't admit him to the Order: he wasn't strong enough to pass the qualifications. They were also money-lenders and when he hit on them for a loan they refused. Finally he approached their then leader Jacques de Molay with a plan. They would launch another Crusade in alliance with their rivals the Hospitalers and this time it would be directed by the Prince of France. Philip thought this a clever way of disposing of their wealth. When Jacques de Molay refused the offer, Philip got his pope, Clement, a "sick man," to bring them to trial. In 1307 Pope Clement ordered the kings of Europe to arrest all Templars within their territories. Philip arrested de Molay on the charge of practicing strange rites of a blasphemous nature which involved worship of the Black god Baphomet. The Templars were merely exercising their rites according to the way the Book had deceived them. 37 Knights Templar were immediately burned at the stake in Paris and 50,000 were rounded up throughout Europe and slain. The 2 leaders were executed and died with curses on their lips concerning the king and pope. Hinckle got away. The Templars went underground. A corrupt form of their rites continued as Masonry, which you will notice also traces its origin to the Temple of Solomon.* Wherever Hinckle traveled in Europe he was hidden by sympathizers from generation to generation. This went on for 100s of years until he came to America in the 1890s and all of the symptoms of Jes Grew were here so they began to rise as they sensed a potential coming together with the Text. Years passed. The Wallflower Order, a secret society of enforcers established when the Atonists triumphed in the West, was hot on his trail; scouts were thinning out all over America looking for the Templar librarian. The Wallflower Order was closing in on Hinckle because, since the Book of Thoth was lying fallow, wherever Hinckle traveled J. G. would rear its head. That was when Hinckle Von Vampton got the bright idea. He selected 14 J.G.C.s and paid them a monthly salary just to send the Text around to each other in a chain, each time changing the covering so that the authorities wouldn't get suspicious. The conditions were that they not cultivate friendship with 1 another.

So it went around in circles, this private express. Hinckle Von Vampton got a job with the New York *Sun* and it was then that he sent out the feeler to the Wallflower Order in the shape of that headline exposing their Holy War in Haiti after their mouthpieces in America had been informed that the story would not be played up. Of course the Wallflower Order investigated to find out who had the goods on them and it turned out to be Hinckle. 1st they ransacked his apartment because they wanted the Book more than they wanted his corpse. They felt that by burning the Book they would sterilize the Jes Grew forever. He made a deal

* *Concise History of Freemasonry*—Calvin I. Kephart.

with them to the effect that his Order would have to be in charge of the Crusade against Jes Grew in order for him to return the Book, if indeed this is what Jes Grew craved. Well 1 of the 14 people on the list, we don't know who, gave the book to Abdul. The Text became stationary as Abdul began to translate The Work and this is when Jes Grew brought it on up and started to move toward Manhattan.

With its Text Jes Grew would become Rada instead of the Petro of Moses and the Templars. Well, when Hinckle wrote letters to the 14 asking them to return the Text (they accepted the money thinking that he was just another eccentric millionaire, the kind who leaves all his money to his cat) he learned through his columnist W. W. Jefferson that Abdul was in possession of a Book whose description matched the one he had sent out. He approached Abdul for the Book and when Abdul resisted he murdered him. Abdul left behind an epigram on American-Egyptian Cotton

> Stringy lumpy; Bales dancing
> underneath this center lies
> the Bird.

We deciphered this to mean that the Book was buried beneath the center of the Cotton Club, the nightclub where Abdul had been arrested for loitering and for attacking the flappers. The night he was arrested he apparently had just finished hiding the sacred Book there. He translated the Book before he died and a copy of his translation was in the hands of a publisher who rejected the Book but the original treasure was safe underneath the Cotton Club. When we dug up the box containing the Book we found the Templars' seal on the top and we traced it to Hinckle Von Vampton as the scout the Wallflower Order of the Atonist Path had assigned to create a Talking Android; the 2nd phase of the Wallflower plan, that of creating a "spokesman" who would furtively work to prepare the New Negro to resist Jes Grew and not catch it. It was the seal on the box of the Book that connected us with Hinckle Von Vampton and if you will just look he is wearing it right now.

The guests turn to Hinckle, who manages a weak smile, his face red, clutching the pendant he wears about his neck: 2

knights riding a horse, a symbol of the Templars' poverty vow.
When we heard that tonight he was scheduled to introduce
"the only Negro poet with any sense," it all became clear and
we rushed right over.

> Studies of the magic and ritual of Africa have . . .
> established with some certainty that all systems for the
> disturbance of consciousness practised by the African
> Negro are derived from ancient Egypt.
> *Witchcraft* (1965)—Pennethorne Hughes

> Is such an etymology to be trusted? One of the fragments
> of myth still to be found in Haiti makes Guede the first
> dead man to be saved by Legba, who called his soul up
> from beneath the waters. If the baton wielded today by
> the Guedes is the counterpart of Osiris' severed penis,
> which fathered Horus upon Isis, the matter may have
> something in it . . .
> *The Invisibles: Voodoo Gods in Haiti*—Francis Huxley

53 A hush falls over the gathering. The Hostess, having
been given smelling salts, comes around but when she sees LaBas,
Herman and T Malice and the 6 Python men standing next to
them she faints again and has to be taken by 7 men into the
Louis 14th "Sun King" bedroom upstairs.

Hinckle Von Vampton and Hubert "Safecracker" Gould are
sweating profusely. The Guianese art critic Hank Rollings finally
speaks up.

I don't believe a word of it. You made the whole thing up.
If Hinckle Von Vampton was paying the men to keep the manu-
script moving who would have been so foolish as to give it to
Abdul?

Yes, Von Vampton speaks up forcefully, explain that 1 will
you . . .

And besides, Hank Rollings continues, according to your story
Hinckle Von Vampton and Gould would be a 1000 years old.

Hinckle and Hubert "Safecracker" Gould smile nervously.

They are, Black Herman says. Hinckle and his cohort Gould, an original member of the 9 Knights, learned to cheat death. They never revealed this even to their leader; it's an Arab formula they learned.

Why, who would believe such nonsense; it's the silliest, most fatuous thing I ever heard!

Listen folks. I'm the easiest guy in town to get along with, Hinckle says, turning to the guests. I just brought "Safecracker" Gould up here in blackface because I wanted to introduce the new Coon musical he is writing. The name of which will be *Harlem Tom Toms*. Those of you who are media people understand the benefits of promotion, don't you? An ancient manuscript being sent around in circles. Absurd . . . who would have given it to Abdul in the 1st place.

I did.

The crowd turns to . . . to . . . Buddy Jackson!!

Jackson makes his way to the front of the crowd.

I was known on your list as Willie B. Johnson. I never met you but each month I received your checks which I gave to widow women and children who had no shoes. You see I am the Grand Master of the Boyer Grand Lodge ⚹1 inaugurated March 18, 1845, by the Prince Hall Grand Lodge or African Lodge ⚹1 chartered in 1776 by the Duke of Cumberland, Grand Master of the Grand Lodge of England. I am a representative of the United Brothers of Friendship, Sisters of the Mysterious 10, Daughters of the Prairie of the Benevolent Protective Herd of Buffaloes of the World, United Order of the Fisherman of Galilee of the Eastern and Western Hemispheres; I am a delegate from the Eastern Star, Grand Fountain Order of True Reformers and a troubleshooter for the locals: Crystal Fount, Rose of Sharon, Lily of the Valley, Good Intent, Ark of Safety, Neversink, Hand in Hand, Gassaway, Rising Star of the East and Mount Pisgah . . . at your service, Buddy says bowing, removing his checked-cloth cap and cigar.

Smiling, Black Herman, PaPa LaBas and Buddy Jackson exchange the ancient Black handshake, the vulva embracing the phallus.

But you're nothing but a cheap hoodlum, a brown-skinned

society matron covered with foxskins shouted arnchy from the rear.

Shut up you, Black Herman reprimands the woman, now embarrassed and shaking all over.

Permit me to introduce my Deputy Grand Warden, Junior Grand Warden, Grand Treasurer and Grand Secretary. Several men step forward, 2 of them the 1s who had abandoned their wigs in front of the Plantation Club the night Schlitz the "Sarge of Yorktown" got his.

But how did you become interested in the case, Buddy? LaBas asks.

The Caucasian lodges downtown didn't want anything to do with us. They refused to recognize our lodges even though we had been chartered by Prince Hall who in turn was chartered by England. We didn't want to be around them anyway; at least most of us didn't. When our New York lodge requested a state charter they refused on grounds that we were "illegitimate." They kept pulling this "exclusive territorial jurisdiction" business on us which means that there can only be 1 lodge in a state—their lodge. If this were true most of their lodges would be illegitimate and as a matter of fact according to Masonic scholars they are. They had 1 of their people, General Albert Pike, term us "inferior brutes" in a tract he authored entitled "Morals and Dogma" and in Appendix 1 of the 1899 proceedings of the Grand Lodge of Illinois we were called "ignorant, uneducated, immoral and untruthful." We broke away from their National Compact, a document of questionable repute, and we changed our name from General Boyer Lodge named for a Haitian General to the United Grand Lodge of Free and Accepted Masons. We still wondered why they kept up their assault even when we made it plain that we didn't want anything to do with them. We decided to run their Caucasian lodge members out of Harlem. The members included everyone from Schlitz the "Sarge of Yorktown" to the Police Commissioner.

We felt that if we could run our own lodges, which involved bookkeeping, rules and regulations, that we could run our own businesses. But still the vicious campaign against us continued unmitigated. So you know what we did?

What, PaPa LaBas asks, keeping the pistol on Hinckle and "Safecracker" Gould, the grease paint now commingled with the sweat of Gould's perspiring face.

We had some of our light-skinned brothers. You know, some of those invisible legions which extend all the way to the highest offices in the land. The loyal Blacks who are passing for White; soldiers of our 5th column that George Schuyler writes about— Prince Hall, the founder of the African Lodge #1, resembled a White man himself . . . well anyway we had the fair mulatto brothers infiltrate their Caucasian lodges and then we found out why they didn't want us around and didn't want us fooling with Masonry and naming our lodges Temple of Solomon so and so.

We found out about this Knights Templar, a Grand Master who had entered the country in 1890, and how he shunned them when they invited him to be with them because he looked down upon their knowledge of The Work. We learned what we always suspected, that the Masonic mysteries were of a Blacker origin than we thought and that this man had in his possession a Black sacred Book and how they were worried that we would find out and wouldn't learn that the reason they wanted us out of the mysteries was because they were our mysteries! Get to that. They were accusing us of trespassing upon our own property. We didn't care actually. We had invented our own texts and slang which are subject to the ridicule of their scholars who nevertheless always seem to want to hang out around us and come to our meetings and poke into our ceremonies. The Charter of the Daughters of the Eastern Star as you know is written in our mystery language which they call slang or dialect. 1 of the brothers told us 1 night that even the Catholic Mass was based upon a Black Egyptian celebration. Well, when they kind of suspected that we knew what was going on, they sent in the Sarge of Yorktown and his boys to do their Dirty Work. To get rid of me and my officers. It may have looked like a gang war but in reality it was a struggle between who were in the Know. The White man will never admit his real references. He will steal everything you have and still call you those names. He will drag out standards and talk about propriety. You can imagine my surprise when the Book came to me with Hinckle's instructions. I decided to play along, sending it around for 14 times and accepting his fee, but on the 15th round I learned that Abdul knew the Egyptian writing and I gave it to him.

Much of the party by now is sitting on the steps leading to the upper bedrooms. Some have returned to another room where they are dancing. Others listen intently.

I am still skeptical, the Guianese art critic says. It could still be a trick. If you have the Book let us see it.

The others join in a chorus, requesting that LaBas show them the Book he found beneath the center of the Cotton Club's dance floor.

Why certainly, PaPa LaBas answers. Herman, while I watch these 2 culprits will you please go and get . . .

His gangly assistant T Malice rushes into the room—

54 PaPa LaBas! Black Herman! Jes Grew is dissolved! It's all on the radio.

What! PaPa LaBas turns to Black Herman.

Aha! exclaims the Guianese art critic. That proves that your premise is not based upon sound empirical fact, he says, arching even the British accent. In times of social turbulence men like you always abandon reason and fall back upon Mumbo Jumbo. For if this Jes Grew delusion of yours was seeking its Work as you so crudely put it, and you were in possession of The Work then why has it fallen flat on its face? Answer that one!

Yes, answer that one, Hinckle and Hubert echo the Guianese art critic.

Now surrounded by supporters, the Guianese art critic Hank Rolling continues.

You don't have to answer nothing, LaBas. Herman. Me and my men will help you carry these culprits to the lock-up if you want.

No, we will prove to these people that the Book is real. Otherwise they won't take us seriously. Herman replies, rejecting Buddy Jackson's offer.

The Guianese stands with some of the other guests. He has his arms folded and is tapping his foot. That scornful, triumphant smile again.

Go get the Book, T!

T Malice goes out to the car and returns with a huge gleaming box covered with snakes and scorpions shaped of sparkling gems.

The ladies intake their breath at such a gorgeous display. On the top can be seen the Knights Templar seal; 2 Knights riding Beaseauh, the Templars' piebald horse. T Malice places the box down in the center of the floor and removes the 1st box, an iron box, and the 2nd box, which is bronze and shines so that they have to turn the ceiling lights down. And within this box is a sycamore box and under the sycamore, ebony, and under this ivory, then silver and finally gold and then . . . empty!!

The desecraters Hinckle and Gould exchange smiles.

We will deliver these men anyway, PaPa LaBas says as he and Black Herman begin to push Hinckle Von Hampton and Gould toward the door.

This is illegal, you can't remove these men on the basis of such flimsy evidence, the Guianese protests, attempting to place his body between Gould, Vampton and their captors.

Buddy Jackson removes a blackjack from his back pocket and slugs the art critic, who sinks to the floor.

Just as LaBas and Herman and their assistants, the 6 unidentified men, and T Malice reach the door, it opens and in walk some proletariat Black women and their little children. The little children point to Hubert "Safecracker" Gould, author of a children's anthology, 1-time carpetbagger, now "radical education expert" and former charter member of the Knights Templar known by this esteemed body as "the Caucasian blackamoor."

That's him, that's the man, mommy, a pigtailed little girl cries, pointing out Hubert "Safecracker" Gould. He took our homework and hung around the school playground, taking down everything we said on a recorder.

The mamas rush across the room and commence bamming Hubert "Safecracker" Gould all about the arms and legs with their umbrellas.

No! Wait, sisters! Black Herman cautions, let us have him before you jump on him, we'll take care of the child molester, be assured.

Someone may call upon your children to give accounts of his deeds, but for now we'll take care of him.

Black Herman, one of the mothers warns, wagging her finger in his face, you'd better do something with this man or else it's going to be me and you.

Gratified that they will receive justice, the women leave the house.

●　　○

Black Herman and LaBas leave with their captives but just before exiting the "Queen of Ubangi's home" LaBas turns and gazes once again at this gathering which illuminated the florescence of the 20s like sapphire does, a stone sometimes confused with lapis lazuli, turquoise, and hyacinth but good as protection against spirits which would do us harm; the stone that steadies our nerves and wards off the Evil Eye.

Guarded by 3 men in each car, LaBas' Locomobile and Herman's President Straight 8, the party heads for Manhattan.

You'll never make this stick. Biff Musclewhite is in Europe but he will return and he will release us from you so-called, would-be detectives, Vampton threatens, smiles confidently.

LaBas doesn't pay heed to the prisoner he is carrying. When T Malice reaches 125th St. in Harlem the Locomobile turns right then downtown and another right toward a deserted pier.

Hey where are you going? The Tombs is downtown!

Well, as you said. LaBas answered, we're jacklegged detectives and don't have a license from New York authorities, but we have jurisdiction in Haiti though. We are delivering you to Other Authorities.

But . . . I don't understand?

You'll understand.

They reach the street of the deserted pier. It is midnight, blood on the moon.

What's the meaning of this? Hinckle says as he is shoved out of the car. Black Herman and the others are removing Hubert "Safecracker" Gould from the President Straight 8. By this time he has been so harassed he is rumpled like a Harpo Marx caricature.

The men push the prisoners up the ramp of *The Black Plume* and into the stateroom. Benoit Battraville enters.

He feigns surprise. What have I done to deserve such a visit by such distinguished guests?

I'll sue . . . I have connections. Why this ship is docked here illegally . . . you'd better let us go, I know plenty of people on high, Hinckle says.

Just a minute Hinckle, Benoit replies. We are going to take you on a little excursion.

Black Herman and LaBas, having delivered their promises, turn to leave.

There are some little children; Hubert "Safecracker" Gould solicited some manuscripts of theirs. If you want them to give evidence they will be glad to testify, LaBas offers.

Very good, Herman and LaBas. Thank you for your cooperation but I don't think that we will need them.

LaBas pauses. You know Jes Grew is waning. What do you think happened, Benoit?

I know but I can't say. I don't think that we Haitians should intervene in your internal affairs. You will find out, figure it out for yourself, all that we can do is provide you with a base, being closer to Africa than yourselves.

The 3 men shake hands.

Well goodbye, Herman, LaBas, I wish you much success and luck. Remember to serve your own loas.

1 thing, LaBas asks. You said there was 1 more co-conspirator in town. How are you going to deal with him?

Ti Bouton is going to take care of him personally. A rare command performance by the master.

Hearing the protests of Hubert Gould and Hinckle, the 2 men leave the ship.

Why I'll . . . I'll take this all the way to the Supreme Court, Hinckle protests.

Yeah, me too, Hinckle, the Knight agrees with his Grand Master.

LaBas and Herman walk toward their cars.

I guess I won't be seeing you for a year or so, LaBas.

Where are you on your way to?

Some Indian priests want me to recover a jewel missing from the great Buddha's forehead. A Seek-Out job which should keep me busy for the next few months.

Call when you return.

Will do, Black Herman says, climbing into his car and driving away.

LaBas and T Malice head toward the Mumbo Jumbo Kathedral. What do you suppose went wrong?

I don't know, T, we should have opened the trunk which contained the Book but we were so excited we didn't. Foolish.

When they reach Mumbo Jumbo Kathedral and start to enter they are accosted by a beggar, a white-haired, ragged beggar. The little Black man looks as if he hadn't bathed in months, his clothes are in tatters, the buttons on his shabby overcoat missing. He looks as if he bore the pain of the ages in his eyes.

Gentlemen, please help a fellow down on his luck. Please!

Poor fellow, LaBas says reaching in his pocket for a quarter. What happened to you?

I am 29 but I don't look it. I said the words that night when we turned the Plantation Club upside down. I said the words and she vanished into thin air hehehehhehehehehehehehehheeh. Into thin air, do you hear? She just went away. Flew away like a delicate, beautiful white bird. A WHITE BIRD, DO YOU HEAR? the man cries, clutching LaBas by the lapels.

Please my friend. Here is a quarter. Go buy yourself some warm soup.

O thank you sir, the man says hobbling off in the direction of a restaurant.

Looks like hard times, T Malice says to LaBas as they watch Doctor Peter Pick rush to the luncheonette to spend his handout.

When they walk up the stairs of Mumbo Jumbo Kathedral, LaBas removes his key and begins to open the door. The door opens. Surprise.

Earline! They both embrace her. It is like a family reunited.

I was a sick girl, but I feel great now.

Well at least there's something to be joyous about, Earline.

You heard about Jes Grew, huh pop?

Yes, Earline, I heard.

LaBas and T Malice walk into the deserted room of the Kathedral.

O pop, here's a letter that arrived today. The mail is so slow. It's from Abdul Sufi Hamid, mailed the afternoon of the day his last message came.

Let me see, LaBas says, rushing out and tearing open the envelope.

Dear LaBas;

It was a pleasure meeting you the other night. You and that Herman fellow proove that even anachronisms have their charm! I called you so that you could have a look at the manuscript I translated into the language of "the Brother on the Street"

A copy sent to a publisher was lost in the mails. All I received was a rejection slip indicating that it had been returned. O well, maybe it will turn up someday. Does n't really matter. They say they can no longer find a market for this work. Is n't that incredible!! A Sacred Black work, if it came along today would go unpublished!

They seem only interested in our experience's seamy side. But this is necessary now. Works of reform. Works, which will assist these backward, untogether niggers in getting

themselves together. We must change these niggers!
Change niggers! Niggers, change! Change! Change!
Niggers! Make them baaaaaaad niggers!

Hopefully, one day all of us shall be able
to express a variety of opinions, styles, and
values, LoBus, but for now we need a strong
man, some one to "whip these coons into line."
Let the freedom of culture come later. I
know this sounds contradictory but I don't
have God's mind yet!

I really wanted you and Herman to
see this Book, the Book of Truth, but now
you won't have a chance... for I have
burned it!! it has gone up in smoke!!.

When i translated it I didn't give
it too much thought, but now that I
have had a chance to read it over
a few times,

3

I have decided that black people could never have been involved in such a lewd, nasty, decadent thing as is depicted here. This material is obviously a fabrication by the infernal fiend himself!! So, into the fire she goes!! It is our duty to smite the evil serpent of carnality.

I am going to sell the beautiful, precious box, the Book of Thoth arrived in, from the proceeds I will build a great Mosque in whose reading room, only clean and decent books shall be kept A fence is coming to my office this afternoon to inspect it —

I left behind a code dealing with
Egyptian - American Cotton so that if anything
happened to me someone could locate the
Book of Thoth, this serves no purpose now
so I will destroy the note as soon as I
get a chance. I will remove the
box from the Cotton Club where it's
stored and return it to the office
for the fence to see.

As - Salaam Alaikum!
Abdul Sufi Hamid

Censorship until the very last. He took it upon himself to decide what writing should be viewed by Black people, the people he claimed he loved. I can't understand. Apparently after Abdul burned the Book, Jes Grew sensed the ashes of its writings, its litany and just withered up and died. Better luck next time.

What do you think was eating him, pop?

Earline, who has been standing in the door taking it all in, lowers her head, sorry that LaBas perhaps won't live to see the thing he ached to see.

I think I understand. He set himself up as a roadblock checking all of the data that passed through the senses of 1000000s. A Patrolman of the mind handing out tickets to any idea or thought that sped or made U turns. This was just too much traffic for

1 man to handle. It drove him into a crisis. He couldn't stop the influences coming in on 1 people. Multitudinous, individual—like the 1000 1000000000 stars of a galaxy. The energy was just too much for him and he must have known that in the end he would receive the rebellious wrath of those ancient people who will not allow someone to tamper with their Sacred Head. A Head is like a temple in our tradition.

Is this the end of Jes Grew?

Jes Grew has no end and no beginning. It even precedes that little ball that exploded 1000000000s of years ago and led to what we are now. Jes Grew may even have caused the ball to explode. We will miss it for a while but it will come back, and when it returns we will see that it never left. You see, life will never end; there is really no end to life, if anything goes it will be death. Jes Grew is life. They comfortably share a single horse like 2 knights. They will try to depress Jes Grew but it will only spring back and prosper. We will make our own future Text. A future generation of young artists will accomplish this. If the Daughters of the Eastern Star can do it, so can they. What do you say we all go down to the restaurant and have a sandwich?

That's a good idea, pop, Earline says.

She puts on her black felt hat which she wears cocked over her right eye. It's a handsome contrast to the ribbed grey knit dress and the black belt around her waist. Large black beads rest on her chest.

The trio walk down the stairs and into the street. They walk a couple of blocks until they come to the restaurant. Inside LaBas orders 3 hamburgers. A radio in the restaurant's rear room, used as a living room by the family who owns the store, is on.

S.R.: A GRATEFUL NATION POURS TELEGRAMS INTO THE PRESIDENT'S OFFICE. ACCORDING TO THE WHITE HOUSE POLL THEY ARE RUNNING 20-1 IN THEIR ENDORSEMENT OF HIS STRINGENT METHODS IN DEALING WITH THE JES GREW CRISIS. PEOPLE MAY BE STARVING, PRESIDENT HEEBER SAID, SALES MAY BE DOWN, CABARETS AND SPEAKS CLOSED, BUT DANCING IS FINISHED. THERE ARE HARD DIFFICULT DAYS AHEAD. WE MAY HAVE TO GO THROUGH A PERIOD OF ANXIETY. BUT IF WE PERISH, NO 1 CAN SAY WE DIDN'T PERISH WITH DIGNITY.

. . . AFTER A WEEK OF RECREATION IN EUROPE, BIFF
MUSCLEWHITE, CURATOR OF THE CENTER OF ART
DETENTION, SAILS FOR HOME ON THE INVINCIBLE SHIP
THE <u>TITANIC</u>; HE IS DISMISSING RUMORS THAT HE WILL
SEEK THE GOVERNORSHIP . . . HAITIAN WITHDRAWALS
DUE SOON . . . A LIST FOUND IN THE POCKET OF THOR
WINTERGREEN, A WHITE <u>MU'TAFIKAH</u> WHO COMMITTED
SUICIDE IN THE TOMBS, LEADS TO THE ARREST OF THE
<u>MU'TAFIKAH</u>, THE NOTORIOUS ART-NAPPERS . . .

Earline and T Malice have finished eating. The waitress hands
LaBas the check.

75 cents for 3 hamburgers?

Don't look at me, the waitress says. The wholesalers say they
have to pay more for beef, the farmers say that the price on feed
has gone up, the wheat farmers want more money, the tomato
farmers have struck in support of the wheat farmers, people ain't
cutting the mustard the way they used to. At this rate we'll all be
out on the street selling apples before long.

LaBas reaches into his pocket and puts the money on the counter,
the 3 people prepare to leave the premises.

What a beautiful doll! Earline cries, seeing the Black god Baphomet dressed in the sheik outfit, the turban with the ruby shining
from its center. O isn't that cute, she says to LaBas and T Malice,
pointing out the little doll on a shelf behind the waitress. Where
did you get that? Earline asks.

O my mama works for some crazy White man on Long Island.
She was "carrying" some stuff the other night and she brought this
trunk home the White man kept in his room. Well, we got it
open and we found the little colored doll. Looks nice there, don't
he?

He's adorable, Earline says.

Well, whats say we leave? PaPa LaBas asks.

Pop, can I have the car tonight, you know I'm returning to
Lincoln University Monday for the fall semester and this young
fox . . . well she . . .

Sure take it.

T climbs into the car. Earline stands next to LaBas outside the
restaurant.

Pop?

Yes?

I must have really been silly with my carrying-on, my nervous breakdown.

I don't think it was a nervous breakdown, I have my theory. Nervous breakdown sounds so Protestant, we think that you were possessed. Our cures worked, didn't they? All you have to know is how to do The Work.

Yes, I want to learn more, pop. I'm thinking about going to New Orleans and Haiti, Brazil and all over the South studying our ancient cultures, our HooDoo cultures. Maybe by and by some future artists 30 to 40 years from now will benefit from my research. Who knows. Pop, I believe in Jes Grew now.

You do?

Yes, she answers as they walk past a fashion store whose inventory of Haitian clothes and jewelry has been drastically reduced in price; down the streets of boarded-up cabarets, past closed-down speaks and out-of-business record companies. The street is nearly deserted, gone now is the zest of the days when people were waiting for Jes Grew to invade and join its jazzed-up scouts already on the scene.

Pop, you know I neglected to replenish the altar's 21st tray for many days.

That might have had something to do with you being touched that way.

True.

You should have explained to me what that particular rite was all about, pop, maybe I would have respected it. How are young people to know these things unless you older 1s tell us what you've been through? Sometimes I think we are ashamed of our experience no matter how loudly we proclaim its beauty. Each generation is condemned to repeating the errors made by the former. It's a cycle.

I didn't think you wanted to listen to my talk.

Pop, I have 2 tickets to a play at the Lafayette Theatre. Would you like to go? The curtain is in a ½ hour.

Love to, if you don't mind going with an old man.

O pop, don't give me that, pop, you're only as old as you feel.

The couple heads toward the theater a few blocks away. Soon they see the title of the new play, a play about the future.

Mumbo Jumbo Holiday

PaPa LaBas remembers that Black Herman had praised it but the Atonist critics had criticized it as a lot of Bull. Well at any rate, it seemed to be packing them in.

Epilogue

In the year 1909 ". . . it began as a flair-up. Localized in a few places, the South, the West and the Northeast. It knew neither class, race nor consciousness." An Atonist, whose cover was editorial writer for the *Musical Courier*, wrote in 1899:

> Society has decreed that ragtime and cakewalking are the thing, and one reads with amazement and disgust of historical and aristocratic names joining in this sex dance, a milder edition of African orgies.

Cakewalking and ragtime are symptoms of that X factor. The stumper of *Psychic Epidemologists*. It was 11 years before Hinckle Von Vampton's message, to those in the know, that Sigmund Freud was dispatched to America for the purpose of diagnosing this phenomenon. (Sigmund Freud as you will recall is the man who grew up in a town dominated by the 200-foot steeple belonging to a church named for the Virgin Mary. It affected him. He began to trace Man's "neurosis" to situations arising from this elemental relationship. The Mother and Son! [How many times do you hear of Electra?]

Freud, whose real talent lies in the coinage of new terms for processes as old as the Ark. He is as gifted as an American soap canvasser at this. This is why perhaps he was better known here than in his own Vienna.

Freud drinks from a Dixie Cup as the party sails into New York harbor. He stands in awe before Niagara Falls. He then pushes into the hinterland of the American soul and here in this astral Bear country he sees the festering packing Germ.

Freud faints. What he saw must have been unsettling to this man accustomed to the gay Waltzing circles of Austria, the respectable clean-cut family, the protocol, the formalities of "civilization." Smelling salts are administered to their teacher by followers who've not seen such an outburst since their teacher waxed all "paranoid" when someone awarded him a medal upon which was etched the Sphinx being questioned by the traveler. Or on another occasion when Carl Jung confronted him with the fable of the fossilized corpses of peat moss.

What did this man see? What did this clear-headed, rational, "prudish" and "chaste" man see? "The Black Tide of Mud," he was to call it. "We must make a dogma . . . an unshakable bulwark against the Black Tide of Mud," uttered this man who as a child returned from church and imitated the minister and repeated his sermons in a "self-righteous manner."

A tall, bespectacled man summons a news conference.

Q. What did the Doctor mean by "The Black Tide of Mud?"
A. He meant occultism.
Q. Why, then, did he employ the language of the Churchman: "Dogma"?
A. It was merely a figure of speech.
Q. But according to his theories, don't figures of speech have latent significance?

. . . Please, Dr. Jung pleads. No more questions. I must return to the Doctor.

1 reporter insists on 1 more question.

Q. Before you leave, Doctor, can you give us Dr. Freud's impressions of America?
A. He considers it "a big mistake."

Freud, who disliked prophecy, was in no position to make a diagnosis. He admitted once that he could not discover "this 'oceanic' feeling in myself." Lacking harmony with the world, he was unable to see what it was.

Later Jung travels to Buffalo New York and at a dinner table discovers what Freud saw. Europeans living in America have undergone a transformation. Jung calls this process "going Black."* This chilly Swiss keeps it to himself however.

Strange. It seems that the most insightful pictures of America are done by Europeans or Blacks. Myrdal, Tocqueville, Jung, Trollope, Hernton, Clarence Major, Al Young, or Blacks who know both Europe and America: Wright, Baldwin, Chester Himes, John A. Williams, William Gardner Smith, Cecil Brown. I

* "The Complications of American Psychology," first published (1930) as "Your Negroid and Indian Behavior"—Carl G. Jung.

once leafed through a photo book about the West. I was struck by how the Whites figured in the center of the photos and drawings while Blacks were centrifugally distant. The center was usually violent: gunfighting lynching murdering torturing. The Blacks were usually, if it were an interior, standing in the doorway. Digging the center.

The clock on the wall strikes 10:00 P.M. The lecture should have concluded an hour before. But when PaPa LaBas gets started he doesn't stop. He's a Ghede. Garrulous gluttonous satirical sardonic but unafraid to march up to the President's Palace and demand tribute.

What did Freud mean by The Black Tide of Mud? Why were there later to be assassinations of cultural heroes? In 1914 Scott Joplin, who, after announcing that ragtime will "hypnotize this Nation," is taken to Ward Island where they fritter away his powers with shock therapy. Scott Joplin has healed many with his ability to summon this X factor, the Thing that Freud saw, the indefinable quality that James Weldon Johnson called "Jes Grew."

"It belonged to nobody," Johnson said. "Its words were unprintable but its tune irresistible." Jes Grew, the Something or Other that led Charlie Parker to scale the Everests of the Chord. Riff fly skid dip soar and gave his Alto Godspeed. Jes Grew that touched John Coltrane's Tenor; that tinged the voice of Otis Redding and compelled Black Herman to write a dictionary to Dreams that Freud would have envied. Jes Grew was the manic in the artist who would rather do glossolalia than be "neat clean or lucid." Jes Grew, the despised enemy of the Atonist Path, those Left-Handed practitioners of the Petro Loa, those too taut to spring from sharp edges, wiggle jiggle go all the way down and come up shaking. Jes Grew is the lost liturgy seeking its litany. Its words, chants held in bondage by the mysterious Order "which saved the 2nd Crusade from annihilation by Islamic hordes." Those disgraced Knights. Jes Grew needed its words to tell its carriers what it was up to. Jes Grew was an influence which sought its text, and whenever it thought it knew the location of its words and Labanotations it headed in that direction. There had been a sporadic episode in the 1890s and it was driven back into its Cell. Jes Grew was jumpy now because it was 1920 and something was going on. A Stirring. If it could not find its Text then it would be mistaken for entertainment. Its basic dances were said to have been recorded by the secretary to the first Seedy Fellow himself.

Jes Grew was going around in circles until the 1920s when it impregnated America's "hysteria." I was there, a private eye practicing in my Neo-HooDoo therapy center named by my critics Mumbo

Jumbo Kathedral because I awarded the Asson to myself. Licensed myself. I was a jacklegged detective of the metaphysical who was on the case; and in 1920 there was a crucial case. In 1920 Jes Grew swept through this country and whether they liked it or not Americans were confronted with the choices of whether to Eagle Rock or Buzzard Swoop, whether to join the contagion or quarantine it, whether to go with Jes Grew or remain loyal to the Atonist Path protected by the Wallflower Order, its administrative backbone, composed of grumblers and sourpusses to whom no 1 ever asked:

"May I Have This 1?"

Papa LaBas notices that some of the students are leaving the hall. It is nearly 10:30 P.M.

I will end now . . . Are there any questions?

A woman, whose hair has been sprayed and sculpted into a huge soft black ball of cotton raises her hand.

Yes?

PaPa LaBas, how did you live to become 100 years old?

Serving my *Ka*, daughter. Even a healthy body is useless unless the spirit is provided for with its own unique vitamins. There is a prescription for every soul here. The process has been developed from our ancient artificers until now.

You mean, the woman continues, that there are signs which determine our spiritual heritage?

Yes. In a superficial way it operates in a manner similar to the way natal astrology works: the notion that what happens in the heavens has an influence upon our lives on earth. Of course what is known as "natal astrology" has been corrupted by the Atonist scholars who've over 1000s of years brought their traditional prejudices to the art. We do not use the systems employed by the Egyptians Aztecs or Babylonians. Taurus for example is described as—in his main qualities—reliable patient slow honest trustworthy. Sounds to me like the deft hand of the Atonist Path who've had it in for Taurus for 1000s of years; unable to resist any opportunity to emasculate this figure—and get this, his colors are pastels—they've created a weak Bull. Saks 5th Avenue window dressing. Wonder does he play football and appear on talk shows?

Early tabloid editors as they were, they doctored the ancient texts at Heliopolis. Who worked about a horseshoe-like table in this early center of Yellow Journalism where they made their heroes look radiant, glowing; umbraging the heroes of others in this City Room of Hypocrisy.

Compare this description of Taurus with that of a Black loa, by the Haitian houngans who've maintained The Work largely uncorrupted. The Loa Agovi Minorie boasts when mounting a woman that his phallus is so hard that the brilliance of his organ's bulb resembles that of a mirror.

Houngans in Haiti as well as Priests of Africa and South America are able to identify any Spirit or God that possesses a person, an art the Greeks knew, taught to them by an aide to the Human Germ who went into exile after the Master was assassinated by the arch Atonist in Egypt.

The Greeks established temples to the Egyptian's Osiris and Isis where people were allowed to go out of their minds so that spirits could enter their heads; all under the watchful eyes of trained priests who knew the knowledge that Dionysus brought from Egypt. It is in this dictionary, which was committed to memory by the Human Germ's aides when they fled to the Sudan and Nubia and brought to the Americas when the slaves came, that you will find something to fit your head. 1000s of loas some of whose qualities are modified when conjoined with certain rites just as those of the 12 Houses of Astrology are when matched with the planets. The rites, principally Rada and Petro, are not inherently good or evil; it depends upon how they are used. The houngan practices the Rada rites with the Right Hand. Cheap, evil *bokors* practice the rites with the Left Hand. The Left Hand Work, Dirty Work has been frowned upon from the time of the ancient Egyptians until North America.

So wherever the untampered word exists the Atonists move in. They know that Jes Grew needs its words and steps, or else it becomes merely a flair-up. Without substance it never fully catches on. When the people defeat their religious arm they move in their secular troops, men good at confusing people by making up new words that would be palatable to the masses who confuse quackery with profundity. Exorcism becomes Psychoanalysis, Hex becomes Death Wish, Possession becomes Hysteria. This explains why Holy Wars have been launched against Haiti under the cover of "bringing stability to the Caribbean." 1 such war lasted longer than Vietnam. But you don't hear much about it because the action was against niggers. From 1914 to 1934 Southern Marines "because they knew how to handle niggers" destroyed the government and ruined the economy in their attempt to kill Jes Grew's effluvia by fumigating its miasmatic source. The Blues is a Jes Grew, as James Weldon Johnson surmised. Jazz was a Jes Grew which followed the Jes Grew of Ragtime. Slang is Jes Grew too.

The Black professor interrupts PaPa LaBas.

This is all we have time for, PaPa LaBas. Thank you very much for being with us tonight. PaPa LaBas is an eccentric old character from the 20s who thrills us with his tales about those golden times and his role in bringing about the holiday we are celebrating today.

The students smile at this old man accepting his inevitable envelope containing the honorarium. He loves to come to the university for his annual lecture on Jes Grew. All the students are wearing Jes Grew buttons of their own design.

· Papa LaBas sprightly walks through the door of the classroom wearing his opera hat, the smoked glasses, carrying the cane, that familiar 1920s outfit—The Handsome Stranger of the 1919 Poster, by R. di Maga—fatal, skeptical—

PaPa LaBas?

Someone is calling, a cracked old voice. He turns about. It is he. The old man who in his devotion to empirical method had washed out any prophecy for which his ancestors were famous. He had written derisively of it after the last flair-up when Jes Grew launched a trial balloon, sent out a feeler; he had sought to inoculate the populace by writing that it would have to imitate Crane and Twain before it would amount to anything. That it was a fad like Flagpole Sitting and Goldfish Swallowing. His imagery was about as contemporary as he was because the craft of Jes Grew put him into a tizzy. He didn't know what to make of it. In his last lucid interview he had regretted that he had opposed Hoffman Rubin Zimmerman the Beatles and the poet in the Balaam seat, Negro delineators in the tradition of Paul Whiteman, Dvorak, Fred Astaire, Sophie Tucker, Mae West, Dan Rice, George Gershwin. Singing the Blues. Getting hot. Contacting Jes Grew Carriers so that some of it would rub off. Using the word Man as a fugitive part of speech. He had denounced their warped syntax composition and grammar; but now he wished he had bent a little. It was too late. The imitators were on the decline and the members were taking over. Jes Grew was latching onto its blood. After all Liverpool ain't Memphis and the Monterey Jazz Festival no Bucket of Blood. Now the delineators were taking a backseat to the Jes Grew Carriers, those jockey-dressed amulets on the Southern Lawn of America's consciousness. Those who made Sutter's Gold prospectors jittery by their presence.

Those who would never be allowed at the Free Enterprise gaming wheels, blackjack tables and slots because of that Black gentleman there in the beret with the goatee and whiskers. He threw 7, 7 times. They called it HooDooing the dice. The Jes Grew factor.

The Carriers were learning too. As long as they were stagemen, like those clowns who were so adept in the art of rap they could recite the 1st 15 listings in the telephone book and still entice the masses. They were supplied with Town Hall, Carnegie, the Grand Ballroom of the Hilton Hotel, but when they went after the fetishes of the Atonist Path strange things happened. The mysteriously unfulfilled orders from the bookstores. The tapes turned up missing. The microphone in that innocent little box about 15 feet from where you're speaking. You know, what Atonists call "paranoid fantasies" began to occur.

It all came down to Kipling's vision. They all, Left, Right, etc., wanted to wear their pith helmets riding on their cultural elephants but Sabu no longer wished to be their guide.

But now this pitiful creature who said something about "Black Studies so much blackeyed peas" had to stand on the soapbox as the Religious Atonist had before. Lecturing on Freud and Marx and all the old names. He resembled the embarrassed gargoyle dismayed and condemned to watch his former worshipers pass him by as they went into the centers of Jes Grew. Pagan Mysteries.

Sometimes he would yammer on and on about his mother and dad in the garment district and how hard it was for them. Everyone should be sheltered, fed, there was no disagreement about the body. It was what to do about the head.

LaBas felt everybody should have their own head or the head of God which the Atonist's mundane "system" wouldn't admit. *Homo economicus*. The well-fed the will-less robot who yields his head to the Sun King. The sad old creature wanted the

Jes Grew Carriers to have his head. Cut out this Jes Grew that keeps a working man up to all hours of the night with its carryings on. The Ballyhoo of its Whoopie. Its Cab Calloway hidihidiho.

He wanted them to have *his* head. An Atonist head. While LaBas wanted them to have the heads their people had left for them or create new ones of their own. A library of stacks a 1000 miles long. Therefore he and PaPa LaBas disagreed about what to do with the head, not the body.

PaPa LaBas attempted to ignore this ideological tramp but wasn't able to; the man followed him out to the automobile parking lot.

LaBas, why do you mystify your past? These youngsters need something palpable. Not this bongo drumming called Jes Grew.

Bongo drumming requires very intricate technique. A rhythmic vocabulary larger than French English or Spanish, the 1-time vernacular languages.

Come now, the old man smiles. Come now, PaPa LaBas.

The man stands next to the driver's window as PaPa LaBas climbs into his automobile. The man puffs on his pipe. The man's face is bloated. Sanguine.

Each year the students would invite PaPa LaBas to the campus to discuss the Harlem Renaissance. After all, he had attended this "Negro Awakening." The Cabarets, the Speaks, and he knew the many painters, show people, film makers. He knew Park Ave. as well as those on Striver's Row. He went to the celebrations at Irvington-on-Hudson as well as to the Chitterling Switches. But the children seemed more interested in the fact that he was 100 years old than anything else.

PaPa LaBas begins the electric starter. One of the gas lamps was broken. The beautiful interior furnishings faded. The French telephone removed long ago.

The man is still standing there. The strange wounded expression. Do aging anteaters smile?

PaPa LaBas, you must come clean with those students. They must have a firm background in the Classics. Serious works, the achievements of mankind which began in Greece and then sort of wiggled all over the place like a chicken with its neck wrung. (He had once written in a private interview that he didn't know whether to dismiss Jes Grew or go with it. His language reflected this indecision.)

PaPa LaBas continues to ignore the man. He wants to get home, they are having greens and hog's head to celebrate the Holiday.

Will you please move over?

The car jolts forward. The 1914 Locomobile Town Coupe has by this time developed a mind of its own. The man crashes to the pavement of the parking lot like a sandbag. His glasses are sprawled on the ground in front of him. He doesn't appear to be hurt because he lifts himself from the pavement and begins a ponderous trot in pursuit of the car. He stops and clutches his chest as if in pain.

PaPa LaBas watches him in his rear-view mirror as the man, a sad figure, turns and slowly walks toward the campus. He would sleep there under an elm until the next morning when he would climb on the soapbox and harangue about Freud Marx Youth, etc. etc. The man himself a relic from another age like the 1 letter in the neon sign that is off the blink. The poor frumpy, frowzy, man. He wouldn't last long. Couldn't be more than 70–75. A mere youngster. PaPa LaBas steers the car over the bridge. He saw the lights of Manhattan. Chuckling to himself he thought of the lecture: the flights of fancy, the tangential excursions, a classroom that knew what he was talking about.

People in the 60s said they couldn't follow him. (In Santa Cruz the students walked out.) What's your point? they asked in Seattle whose central point, the Space Needle, is invisible from time to time. What are you driving at? they would say in Detroit in the 1950s. In the 40s he haunted the stacks of a ghost library. In the 30s he sought to recover his losses like everybody else. In the 20s they knew. And the 20s were back again. Better. Arna Bontemps was correct in his new introduction to *Black Thunder*. Time is a pendulum. Not a river. More akin to what goes around comes around. (*Locomobile rear moving toward neoned Manhattan skyline. Skyscrapers gleam like magic trees. Freeze frame.*)

Jan. 31st, 1971   3:00 P.M.
Berkeley, California

Partial Bibliography

1. Abraham, Hilda C., and Ernst L. Freud, eds. *The Letters of Sigmund Freud and Karl Abraham, 1907–1926*. New York: Basic Books, 1965.
2. *The Ancient Book of Formulas*. New York: Dorene Publishing, 1940.
3. Bassett, Margaret. *Profiles and Portraits of American Presidents and Their Wives*. New York: Grosset & Dunlap, 1969.
4. Bauer, W. W. *Contagious Diseases*. New York: Knopf, 1934.
5. Beradt, Charlotte. *The Third Reich of Dreams*. Chicago: Quadrangle Books, 1968.
6. Berger, Meyer. *The Story of the New York Times, 1851–1951*. New York: Simon & Schuster, 1951.
7. Blavatsky, H. P. *Isis Unveiled*. 2 vols. Point Loma, Cal.: Theosophical University Press, 1936.
8. Brill, Dr. A. A., ed. *The Basic Writings of Sigmund Freud*. New York: Modern Library, 1938.
9. Brome, Vincent. *Freud and His Early Circle*. New York: Morrow, 1968.
10. Brunn, H. O. *Story of the Original Dixieland Jazz Band*. Baton Rouge, La.: Louisiana State University Press, 1960.
11. Budge, E. A. Wallis. *Osiris: The Egyptian Religion of Resurrection*. New York: University Books, 1961.
12. Bulfinch's *Mythology*.
13. Burland, C. A. *The Exotic White Man*. New York: McGraw-Hill, 1969.
14. Cass, Donn A. *Negro Freemasonry and Segregation*. Chicago: Powner, an Ezra A. Cook Publication, 1957.
15. Castle, Irene. *Castles in the Air*. New York: Doubleday, 1957.
16. Castle, Mr. and Mrs. Vernon. *Modern Dancing*. New York: The World Syndicate Co., 1914.
17. Chang, Chung-yuan. *Creativity and Taoism: A Study of Chinese Philosophy, Art & Poetry*. New York: Julian Press, 1963.
18. Charters, Ann. *Nobody: The Story of Bert Williams*. New York: MacMillan, 1970.
19. Charters, Samuel. *The Poetry of the Blues*. New York: Avon Books, 1970.
20. ——— and Leonard Kunstadt. *Jazz: A History of the New York Scene*. New York: Doubleday, 1962.

21. Christman, Henry M., ed. *The American Journalism of Marx and Engels: A Selection from the New York Daily Tribune.* New York: New American Library, 1966.
22. Churchill, Allen. *Remember When.* New York: Western Publishers, Golden Press, 1967.
23. —— *The Year the World Went Mad.* New York: Crowell, 1960.
24. *The Classification of Cotton.* U. S. Department of Agriculture, Miscellaneous Publication #310, revised June 1956.
25. Como, William. *Raoul Gelabert's Anatomy for the Dancer.* New York: Dance Magazine, 1964.
26. Conrad, Jack R. *The Horn and The Sword: The History of the Bull as Symbol of Power and Fertility.* New York: Dutton, 1957.
27. Craige, John Houston. *Black Bagdad.* New York: Minton, Balch, 1933.
28. —— *Cannibal Cousins.* New York: Minton, Balch, 1934.
29. Crawford, Morris DeCamp. *The Heritage of Cotton: The Fibre of Two Worlds and Many Ages.* New York: Putnam, 1924.
30. Crowley, Aleister. *The Book of Thoth: An Interpretation of the Tarot.* Berkeley, Cal.: Shambala Publications, Kashmarin Press, 1969.
31. Daniken, Erich von. *Chariots of the Gods.* 1st American edition. New York: Putnam, 1970.
32. Daraul, Arkon. *Witches and Sorcerers.* New York: Citadel Press, 1966.
33. Deran, Maya. *Divine Horsemen: The Voodoo Gods of Haiti.* New York: Chelsea House Publishers, 1970.
34. Dixon, Robert, and John Godrich. *Recording the Blues.* New York: Stein & Day, 1970.
35. Dunham, Katherine. *Island Possessed.* New York: Doubleday, 1969.
36. Fortune, Dion. *Psychic Self Defense: Occult Pathology and Criminality.* London: Rider, 1930.
37. —— *Sane Occultism.* London: Rider, 1929; Aquarian Press, 1967.
38. Freud, Martin. *Sigmund Freud: Man and Father.* New York: Vanguard, 1958.
39. Freud, Sigmund. *New Introductory Lectures on Psycho-Analysis.* London: Hogarth Press, 1949.
40. —— *Therapy and Technique.* New York: Collier Books, 1963.
41. Gibbon, Edward. *The Decline and Fall of the Roman Empire.* 3 vols. New York: Modern Library.
42. Gilbert, Clinton Wallace. *Behind the Mirrors: The Psychology of Disintegration at Washington.* New York: Putnam, 1922.
43. Goethe, Johann Wolfgang von. *Faust: A Tragedy.* Translated by Bayard Taylor. New York: Modern Library, 1950.
44. Gold, Robert S. *A Jazz Lexicon.* New York: Knopf, 1964.
45. Gouve, Leon. *The Siege of Leningrad.* Stanford University Press.

46. Guillain, Georges, M.D. *J.-M. Charcot, 1825–1893: His Life—His Work*. New York: Harper, Paul B. Hoeber (Medical Book Dept.), 1959.

47. Handy, W. C. *Father of the Blues*. New York: Collier Books, 1970.

48. Hadlock, Richard. *Jazz Masters of the Twenties*. New York: MacMillan, 1965.

49. Hays, H. R. *In the Beginnings: Early Man and His Gods*. New York: Putnam, 1963.

50. Herman, Black. *Secrets of Magic-Mystery and Legerdemain*. 4 vols. in one. Dallas, Texas: Dorene Publishing Co., 1938.

51. Hoffman, Frederick J. *The Twenties: American Writing in the Postwar Decade*. New York: Viking, 1955.

52. Horrobin, David F. *The Human Organism: An Introduction to Physiology*. New York: Basic Books, 1966.

53. Howe, Ellic. *Astrology: A Recent History including the Untold Story of Its Role in World War II*. New York: Walker & Co., 1967.

54. Hurston, Zoran. *Voodoo Gods: An Inquiry into the Native Myths and Magic in Jamaica and Haiti*. London: Dent, 1939.

55. ——— *Mules and Men, Negro Folktales & Voodoo Practices in the South*. New York: Negro University Press, 1955; Harper & Row, 1970.

56. Huxley, Francis. *The Invisibles: Voodoo Gods in Haiti*. New York: McGraw-Hill, 1969.

57. Inquire Within (pseud.) *Trail of the Serpent*. London: Boswell, 1936.

58. Jackson, John G. *Introduction to African Civilization*. New York: University Books, 1970.

59. Julian the Apostate. *Works*. London: Heinemann, 1923.

60. Jung, C. G. *Psychology & Religion: West & East*. Collected Works, vol. 2. (Bollingen Series, vol. 20.) New York: Pantheon, 1958.

61. Katz, Bernard, ed. *The Social Implications of Early American Negro Music in the United States*. New York: Arno/New York Times, 1968.

62. Kephart, Calvin I. *Concise History of Freemasonry*. Fort Worth, Texas: Henry L. Geddie, Co., 1964.

63. Kirstein, Lincoln. *Dance: A Short History of Classic Theatrical Dancing*. New York: Putnam, 1935.

64. *The Koran*. Translated by N. J. Dawood. Maryland: Penguin Books, 1956.

65. Kramer, Samuel N., ed. *Mythologies of the Ancient World*. New York: Doubleday Anchor, 1961.

66. Lawler, Lillian. *The Dance in Ancient Greece*. Middletown, Conn.: Wesleyan University Press, 1964.

67. McIntosh, Christopher. *The Astrologers and Their Creed: An Historical Outline.* New York: Praeger, 1969.

68. Mackenzie, Norman, ed. *Secret Societies.* New York: Holt; London: Aldus Books, 1967.

69. McLean, Jr., Albert F. *American Vaudeville As Ritual.* Lexington, Ky.: University of Kentucky Press, 1965.

70. Montague, Ludwill Lee. *Haiti and the United States, 1714–1938.* New York: Russell, 1940, repr. 1966.

71. Moore, Carman. *Somebody's Angel Child: The Story of Bessie Smith.* New York: T. Y. Crowell, 1969.

72. Munsell, Albert H. *A Grammar of Color.* New York: Van Nostrand Reinhold, 1969.

73. Murray, Robert K. *The Harding Era: Warren G. Harding and His Administration.* Minneapolis, Minn.: University of Minnesota Press, 1969.

74. *The New York Times. How to Read and Understand Financial and Business News.* Prepared by Financial & Business News Staff. 9th rev. ed. New York: Doubleday, 1963.

75. Nicholson, Irene. *Mexican and Central American Mythology.* London: Paul Hamlyn, 1967.

76. Oliver, Paul. *Savannah Syncopators: African Retentions in the Blues.* New York: Stein & Day, 1970.

77. Olmsted, Frederick L. *The Cotton Kingdom.* New York: Modern Library, 1969.

78. Osman, Randolph E. *Art Centres of the World: New York.* London: Michael Joseph; New York: World, 1968.

79. Ottley, Roi, and William Weatherby, eds. *The Negro in New York: An Informal Social History 1626–1939.* New York: The New York Public Library, 1967.

80. Pollitzer, R., M.D. *Plague.* Geneva: World Health Organization, Palais des Nations, 1954.

81. Prescott, William H. *The World of Incas.* Geneva: Minerva A Pierre Waleffe Book, 1970.

82. Rigaud, Milo. *Secrets of Voodoo.* New York: Arco, 1969.

83. Russell, Francis. *The Shadow of Blooming Grove: The One Hundred Years of Warren Gamaliel Harding.* New York: McGraw-Hill, 1968.

84. Russell, Tony. *Blacks Whites and Blues.* New York: Stein & Day, 1970.

85. Sachs, Curt. *World History of the Dance.* New York: Norton, 1937; paper 1963.

86. Schortemeir, Frederick B. *Rededicating America: Life and Recent Speeches of W. G. Harding.* New York: Bobbs-Merrill, 1920.

87. Sparger, Celia. *Anatomy and Ballet: A Handbook for Teachers of Ballet.* London: Adams & Charles Black, 1949. 4th ed. New York: Hillary, 1965.

88. Speiser, Werner, et al. *The Art of China, Spirit and Society*. New York: Crown, 1960.

89. Stearns, Marshall and Jean. *Jazz Dance: The Story of American Vernacular Dance*. New York: MacMillan, 1968.

90. Stillman, Edmund, and William Pfaff. *The Politics of Hysteria: The Sources of Twentieth-Century Conflict*. New York: Harper & Row, 1964.

91. Sullivan, Mark. *Our Times: The United States, 1900–1925*, vol. 6, *The Twenties*. New York: Scribner's, 1935.

92. Summers, Montague. *The History of Witchcraft and Demonology*. New York: Barnes & Noble, 1926; University Books, 1956.

93. Tallant, Robert. *Voodoo in New Orleans*. New York: MacMillan, 1946.

94. Teevan, Richard, and Robert C. Birney, eds. *Color Vision: An Enduring Problem in Psychology*. Princeton, N.J.: Van Nostrand, 1961.

95. Veronesi, Giulia. *Style and Design, 1909–1925*. New York: Braziller, 1968.

96. Wilcox, R. Turner. *The Mode in Hats and Headdress*. Rev. ed. New York: Scribner's, 1959.

97. Williams, Martin. *Jelly Roll Morton*. New York: A. S. Barnes, a Perpetual Book, 1962.

98. Williams, Sheldon. *Voodoo and the Art of Haiti*. London: Morland Lee, n.d.

99. Winslow, Charles Edward Amory. *The Conquest of Epidemic Disease*. Princeton, N.J.: Princeton University Press, 1943.

100. —— *Man and Epidemics*. Princeton, N.J.: Princeton University Press, 1952.

101. Witmark, Isidore, and Isaac Goldberg. *From Ragtime to Swingtime: The Story of the House of Witmark*. New York: Furman, 1939.

102. Ziegler, Philip. *The Black Death*. New York: John Day, 1969.

103. Zinsser, Hans. *Rats, Lice and History*. Boston: Little, Brown, Atlantic Monthly Press, 1935.

104. Zweig, Stefan. *Mental Healers: Franz Anton Mesmer, Mary Baker Eddy, Sigmund Freud*. New York: Viking, 1932.

About the Author

Ishmael Reed is the author of over twenty-five books and plays, including *Yellow Back Radio Broke-Down, Flight to Canada, Conjugating Hindi, Why No Confederate Statues in Mexico, Why the Black Hole Sings the Blues, The Haunting of Lin-Manuel Miranda,* and the Audible originals *Malcolm and Me* and *The Fool Who Thought Too Much.* He is also a publisher, television producer, songwriter, radio and television commentator, lecturer, and has long been devoted to exploring an alternative Black aesthetic: the trickster tradition, or Neo-HooDooism. A regular contributor to *CounterPunch* and founder of the Before Columbus Foundation, Reed taught at the University of California–Berkeley for over thirty years. He has received the MacArthur Fellowship, the L.A. Times Robert Kirsch Lifetime Achievement Award, and the Lila Wallace–Reader's Digest Award. Reed has been nominated for a Pulitzer Prize and is the only person to be nominated for the National Book Award in two categories in the same year.